The Approval of Sheep

Karen Storey

Burton Mayers Books

Copyright © 2025 Karen Storey

Content compiled for publication by Richard Mayers of Burton Mayers Books. Cover by Martellia Book Design.

First published by Burton Mayers Books 2025.

All rights reserved.

No part of this publication may be reproduced or transmitted in any form or by any means, electronic or mechanical, including photocopy, recording, or an information storage and retrieval system, without permission in writing from the publisher.

The right of Karen Storey to be identified as the author of this work has been asserted by her in accordance with the Copyright, Designs and Patent Act 1988

A CIP catalogue record for this book is available from the British Library

All rights reserved.

ISBN-13: **9781917224130**

Typeset in Garamond

This is a work of fiction. Names, characters, places, and incidents either are the product of the author's imagination or are used fictitiously. Any resemblance to actual persons, living or dead, events, or locales is entirely coincidental.

www.BurtonMayersBooks.com

For the Rockcliffe Twins

Author's Note

To my fabulous American readers: Although I live in England, I was born and raised in the USA. I'm keenly aware there are differences in spelling between the Americans and the British. For this book, I chose to honour the British grammar as my story and characters are set in London and in Wales. This is just a little heads up that you'll see the letter 'u' added in certain words (as indeed in 'honour') and sometimes the letter 's' instead of 'z'.

Chapter One

Gordon sat at his sister's dining table and picked up his wine glass, the nerves in his stomach twisting as he gathered the courage to ask his question. His high-flying brother and his wealthy sister would most likely laugh. When they realised it wasn't a joke their reaction could turn to alarm.

He set the glass down. They would be right. The plan that had been forming in his mind since yesterday lunchtime was insane.

Staring at the tablecloth, he ran his finger along the embroidery covering the seventeenth century French walnut table beneath. With the room's recently restored oak panelled walls, his sister's dining room refurbishment probably cost more than what he paid in a year's rent.

'Why are you so quiet?' Charlotte said.

'I was just admiring this cloth. Mum hasn't stopped talking about your "impossibly grand" dining table beneath.'

'Oh this old thing?' Charlotte said. 'It's just something I picked up from Sotheby's.' She glanced across at her husband. 'Richard spotted it actually.'

Gordon nodded, then looked over at the open wine bottle plonked in the middle of the table. A slithering red drip, like a tiny mischievous spider, crept its way from the bottle's neck, then trailed through the white label, before making a break towards the pristine tablecloth. Gordon touched his finger to the bottle's base, catching the drop before it reached its target.

'When's Eleanor back from Paris?' Richard asked Mark.

'Tomorrow afternoon. They keep her busy at that firm.' Gordon's brother shook his head, yet his eyes shone with pride.

Charlotte turned towards Gordon. 'Tell me about work. Creaton still a cretin?'

'Edward Creaton is an excellent boss.'

'With all that unpaid overtime he makes you do?'

'I choose to do it. I love that hotel.'

Charlotte rolled her eyes. 'I'll never understand your obsession with that place.'

'I understand it,' said Mark. 'He wants to emulate Granddad.'

Gordon bit his lip, then smiled. 'Different hotel, though. Anyway, there's talk of redundancies, but—'

'Oh no!' The three others chorused.

'That's too bad,' Richard said. 'It's not your fault. You're not in charge of economic ups and downs….'

Gordon took a deep breath. Little did his family know that in his fantasies he sometimes pretended that instead of working for The Remblents Hotel Group, he was the U.K. government's chief finance minister. Chancellor of the Exchequer. He'd pull his shoulders back as he walked to the underground station, swinging his briefcase. Then stand a little taller while he waited for the train to arrive onto the platform.

Until the morning he realised if the chancellor lived and worked at eleven Downing Street, he wouldn't be taking the tube at eight am. The crushing of that particular fantasy left him with a strange grief while he went about his work routine. He was forced to think up a whole new daydream for the next morning's commute. For several weeks he became an incognito billionaire taking the underground trains for kicks.

'Gordon, are you listening to me?' Richard said. 'I can put you onto someone in my office who deals with employment law, make sure the redundancy is fair.'

'No, it's okay. I'm not losing my job. I've got a plan that makes sure of that.'

Richard raised his eyebrows.

Ask the question. Ask him now. Gordon turned to his brother-in-law. 'Do you know much about property law?'

Richard pursed his lips. 'I don't specialise in property law. It's corporate I deal with.'

'Okay, but you might still know the answer to this.'

'Go on.'

Gordon swallowed. 'Back in the early 1900s, a guy sells a piece of land. He gets a Right attached to it that says he still has permission to run sheep through the land. This Right gets passed down onto descendants.'

Richard's brows furrowed. 'What's your question?'

'Well, over the years, the land gets sold again and someone builds over the land. Does the Right still exist?'

'Probably. Restrictive covenants don't expire. Although wait. I'm not sure. There could be a statute of some sort.'

'There can't be. Why would the solicitors be worried about it if there was a statute?'

'Oh no, no.' Mark said. 'Don't do this, Gordie. Don't even think of buying some dirt cheap house with a dodgy Right attached.'

'I'm not buying anything.'

'Good.' Mark pressed his lips together then leaned towards his younger brother. 'Look, with these redundancies going on, if you need a little help,' Mark raised an eyebrow. That ridiculous mannerism he'd perfected as a teenager by holding one brow down until he'd trained the muscles of the other to lift separately.

'Trust me, I'll be fine,' said Gordon. 'I shouldn't say this, but when all the restructuring is out of the way, I may be up for a promotion.'

Mark's eyes softened with pity. 'Don't get your hopes up. At forty-two it's a bit late to make something of yourself.'

Gordon's eye twinged. He dipped his head and placed a finger over his eyelid to stop the twitching.

'What's wrong, Gordon?' Charlotte asked. She turned to Mark. 'Why did you have to say that?'

'What's he doing?' Mark asked. 'Oh the eye thing.'

'Stop it, Mark,' Charlotte said.

'What? Oh.' Mark's face reddened as he mumbled into his glass. 'I'm sorry Gordie. I didn't mean to upset you.

I'm just trying to help. Get you to see the writing on the wall with your job.'

Gordon sat up, his eye twitch easing to a small twinge. 'What you don't understand is I'm putting together a plan. One that can't fail.' His cheeks burned. Oh, it can. It can fail so spectacularly his career might never recover. 'I just need more information.'

'That's good news,' Charlotte said. She edged her chair back and stood. 'Is everyone ready for dinner?' She turned and walked towards the kitchen.

Gordon pushed his chair away from the table and strode after her into the spacious stainless-steel kitchen. The kitchen's stark modernity such a contrast to the classical dining room, he felt momentarily unsteady, as if passing into another dimension. Charlotte's back was to him as she stirred a pot on the wide range cooker.

'Do you need any help?' Gordon asked.

'Oh. Thanks. Can you get some plates out of the cupboard for me?' She stopped stirring then turned towards him. 'You know that Mark is only like this because he's jealous of you.'

Gordon turned and opened a cupboard above the steel counter. Rows of crystal champagne flutes sparkled back at him. 'Me?' he said. 'Mark's jealous of me?'

'Oh, come on. You were the one Granddad always chose to go with him to the hotel, and you were the one he showed off to his friends. Mark hated it.'

Gordon's heart swelled. 'Was I really the favourite?' He closed the champagne flute cupboard, then with his shirt cuff, quickly wiped his splodgy fingerprints from the shiny door. He opened the next cupboard. Rows of vintage porcelain teacups and saucers. How many people did his sister invite for tea?

'Oh, you know you were,' Charlotte said. 'Anyway, why isn't Stacey here tonight?'

The affection in his heart shrivelled to humiliation. He closed the teacup cupboard and opened the next door.

Wine and sherry glasses.

'It's the next cupboard,' Charlotte said. 'Did you and Stacey have an argument?'

'Not really.'

'What's not really?'

Gordon removed his fingers from the next cupboard door before turning slowly towards his sister. 'I proposed.'

Charlotte dropped the spoon into the pan. She turned to him open mouthed. 'Oh, Gordon. I'm sorry.'

His heart slowing, he forced a grin. 'Honestly, it was pretty funny when I thought about it afterwards.'

Charlotte stared at him

'I'd invited her out to this lovely restaurant. After we finished our main course I said to her, *There's a reason I asked you to meet me here tonight. I've been silly about something and I want to make it up to you.*'

'Why, what did you do?' Charlotte said.

He grimaced. 'That was Stacey's question. I told her it's what I hadn't done. Then I nodded at the waiter. He popped the champagne cork. I got up from the table, then knelt at the side of her chair.'

'You got down on one knee? At the restaurant?'

'Yeah.' He hung his head and sighed. 'I kind of wish I hadn't now.'

'Oh no.' Charlotte stepped forward.

He shook his head, then pressed his lips into a pretend smile. If he let Charlotte show him too much sisterly tenderness, his voice might crack.

'What happened next?' she asked, almost in a whisper.

'She just stared at me, then said,' Gordon attempted to imitate Stacey's voice, '*What are you doing down there?*'

Charlotte laughed, then immediately covered her mouth. 'Sorry, I guess it wasn't funny.'

'Oh, it was.' His throat tightened at the memory. 'And it gets better. I'd already bought the ring. It was in this little velvet box and I got it out of my pocket, then lifted the lid.'

Charlotte gazed at him wide eyed. 'And then?'

Gordon shrugged. 'She sort of gasped then left the restaurant.'

'No!'

'Yes. The waiter stood there with champagne foam dripping down the bottle. He finally put it down on the table and left.'

'What did you do?'

He grimaced. 'I got up, made myself smile as I looked around, then said, *Anyone want to propose tonight with a half price ring? I'll even throw in this bottle of champagne.*'

Charlotte laughed. 'You didn't! Oh sorry.' She covered her mouth again. 'I'm not supposed to be laughing.'

Gordon shrugged. 'Please do. They all did. A few people even applauded.'

'What?'

'Well, that's when I picked up the champagne bottle and plonked it on the next table. The old couple there were a bit stunned, but I hope they enjoyed it.' His eyes moistened at the memory and he blinked rapidly.

'Oh Gordon…'

He remembered the sympathetic cheers as he pulled some notes from his wallet, dropped them on the table and then strode towards the door. He had even waved at them all while his heart splintered into jagged pieces. Maybe in his next fantasy he should be a famous stand-up comedian.

Charlotte shook her head. 'I hate that it's happened like this for you, but I have to say, it might be for the best. Richard and I never thought Stacey was right for you.'

His cheeks tingled. 'You never said… although…' memories of stiff smiles between Stacey and his sister at the last family gathering rose to the surface.

Charlotte bent, opening the oven door. Wafts of garlic and onion whooshed up. Her famous Moroccan chicken. She closed the door, then stood, turning to gaze at him. 'Poor you,' she said with a sigh.

'No, don't do that. I know what you're thinking when you look at me. You don't have to feel sorry for me.'

Her cheeks reddened. 'You have no idea what I'm thinking when I look at you. You're my brother, that's what I see.'

'I haven't told Mark yet about Stacey and me.'

She sighed. 'I don't think he and Eleanor will be surprised.'

'He resents me. He was supposed to be the only son.'

Her cheeks flushed. She turned back towards the stove. 'Stop it,' she said. Then she turned towards him again. 'Have you ever thought about having therapy for that? It was a long time ago and you still think about it.'

Gordon ran a hand through his hair. 'No. I'm over it. Can't you see I've changed?'

'Really?' She bit her bottom lip. 'You're still going after women who are all showy on the outside, like you're trying to prove something to yourself.' She sighed. 'Plates are in the next cupboard. Take them through?'

He turned and opened the next sleek door, then grabbed four of the plates. It would be okay. Mark, Charlotte, they've done well for themselves, as was always expected. It wouldn't be long before Gordon surprised them both. He's not that hapless younger brother they assume. Hell, sometimes he's even an incognito billionaire, or the Chancellor of the Exchequer mistakenly finding himself taking an underground train.

Later that night, back at home, he trudged through his flat's narrow sitting room to look towards the dark windowsill. The photo of Granddad with a young Gordon. Taken during lunch at the lavish hotel where Granddad had treated him for his thirteenth birthday. That was the day he decided he was going to be just like Granddad, a famous hotelier.

As Gordon gazed at the photo, his ribs tightened. This may well be his last chance. He leant towards the windowsill and picked up the picture frame. The photo had faded from sunlight hitting it over the years, but Granddad's proud expression still shone through. Gordon placed the photo down again, then moved his fingers along the sill to touch a smooth leather pen pouch. Granddad's precious 1978 Mont Blanc fountain pen. It would be Gordon's good luck piece when he eventually attended his interview for promotion.

A little while later, he climbed into bed and pulled the duvet close. In the dark, anxiety over the looming redundancies descended. No. He wouldn't allow it to happen. He would succeed. Yes, the scheme in his head was crazy, but his colleague Tej said it. 'The next director will be whoever gets Creaton a baaa-gain for getting rid of that sheep covenant.'

Angst pushed heavily on his chest and he breathed in slowly. The Chancellor of the Exchequer surely had moments of doubt. How would he handle it?

Gordon breathed out.

He'd form a plan.

A big woolly plan.

Chapter Two

Gordon made his way through the opulence of the high-ceilinged hotel. The staff service lift stood behind the sleek mahogany reception area. This morning, keeping his chancellor persona in mind, he ignored the staff lift. Instead, he strode past reception and through the gleaming corridor flanked by marble pillars. Halfway up the grey and white columns, baskets overflowed with a daring burst of terracotta lilies and lavender roses. Gordon inhaled their scent as if to breathe in their boldness.

He reached the sweeping staircase leading up to the second floor. The unremarkable finance office crammed itself into a box-shaped area between the guests' airy conference rooms and the hotel directors' boardroom. This grand corridor diversion added an extra three and a half minutes to his journey. It was worth it.

Inside the finance office, his colleague Tej sat at his own desk chatting across to Bethany.

Gordon crashed into his seat and switched on his computer. As his emails loaded, one appeared from Edward Creaton. The subject:, 'Redundancy Meeting.'

His mouth dried.

'What's up?' Tej asked. 'It's like you've seen a ghost.'

Gordon stared at his screen, then swallowed. 'Email. From Edward.'

'Ah. Communications from the devil. Remember what I said about that scar above his nose. His parents had to remove the 666 from his forehead when he was born.'

Gordon's fingers shook slightly as he opened the request for a ten o'clock meeting.

'What's the worried look for?' Tej asked. 'Creaton likes you. You're his golden boy. You'll probably be up for that big new role. Rumour has it that in six months' time…'

Gordon stared at his computer screen. A redundancy meeting with Edward Creaton. Today. He wasn't ready. Pushing his chair away from his desk, he hung his head and gazed at his shoes. Perfectly polished. Granddad once said you could tell the measure of a man by whether or not he polished his shoes.

'You've got nothing to worry about,' Tej said. 'You're a business athlete.'

Gordon breathed out heavily. 'I don't even know what that means.'

'Neither do I.' Tej laughed. 'I saw it on someone's Linked In profile once and thought it sounded good. That I might use it one day. Tell you what. I'm giving it to you as a gift.'

Gordon opened the email. *The purpose of this meeting is to discuss the proposed redundancy…* The words on the screen blurred. He'd have to put his plan into action today.

'What's that look about?' Tej said pointing towards Gordon's shoes.

'I give my shoes a quick shine every night,' said Gordon.

'No, not the shoes.'

Gordon looked down at his feet. That's when he saw it. Two different coloured socks. One orange and one navy. The corner of his eye twitched and he squeezed both eyes shut as he remembered rushing into the dark bedroom this morning to grab some socks from the drawer. He'd shoved his feet into the beautifully polished brogues, before striding to his front door determined to master any office politics ahead.

He swallowed, then turned to Tej. 'I need your help with something. You know that joke you always tell about sheep being allowed to run through this hotel?'

'Yeah, what about it?'

'You said something yesterday at lunchtime. You said whoever could get rid of this covenant for the hotel would probably get that director position. Were you serious?'

'You're messing up my joke. I said whoever got a baaa-gain for paying off those descendants would get that promotion.'

'Tej. Is this covenant thing real?'

The corners of Tej's eyes creased as he laughed. He inched his chair closer to Gordon. 'Before you started working here, these insurance brokers came into our old office at the hotel in Mayfair. They tried to get Creaton to take out an insurance policy that was going to cost an extra thirty or forty thousand.'

'Go on.'

'This was five years ago, when the Remblents Group were buying this hotel. The solicitors found this crazy Right…' he paused. 'It lets this family in Wales run sheep through the building. The solicitor said we should purchase some sort of insurance policy against it being used.'

'I don't understand. What if the descendants just decided to use it anyway?'

Tej shrugged. 'Hey, I don't know all the details. I was just sitting outside Creaton's office being entertained by the commotion inside.' Tej chuckled and shook his head. 'I think he actually called the insurance brokers "greedy bastards." Accused them of trying to screw money out of us for a covenant no one in their right mind would ever use.'

Gordon turned back to his computer screen and typed 'covenant,' then 'sheep' into the search bar.

Tej snickered. 'You could hear Creaton's shouting all the way to the staff room. That's why Bethany has that cotton ball with google eyes and little black ears stuck to her computer as an inside joke about sheep…' He paused. 'Hey, are you listening to me?'

Gordon stopped typing. Over on Bethany's desk, the goggly-eyed fluffy ball stared back at him. 'What's the insurance report filed under?'

Tej laughed. 'Mate, why do you want it?'

'I'm not sure yet.'

'Bethany might know where the records are,' Tej said. 'She was there when it all happened.' He stood. 'Want a coffee? I'm heading to the café downstairs. I might need your help. There's this barista with a mad crush on me. Keeps asking me out. I'd say yes, but she's a bit full on. Come be my wing-man. You'll get a free croissant out of it.'

'Can't. I need to prepare for this meeting.' Gordon reopened the emails on his screen. His finger hovered over the accept key for the ten o'clock redundancy meeting, then stopped.

If the Right exists what would the insurance have protected them against? A payout to the descendants?

He rose, then strode towards Bethany's desk.

She glanced up from her screen. 'Hey, Gordon.'

He perched on the corner of her desk and gazed at the cotton ball made up as a sheep. 'Is it true about that covenant? You know, someone having the right to run sheep through this hotel?'

She smirked as she peered towards the closed door of Edward's office. 'I'm not supposed to talk about it. Neither is Tej. We had to sign this agreement to keep it confidential. I've told Tej before if Edward finds he's mouthing off about it, he's toast. Tej keeps saying the agreement only counts if he talks about it with people outside the hotel, but I'm not sure.'

'They made you sign a non-disclosure agreement?'

'HR called it a confidentiality agreement.'

Gordon swallowed. His fantasy of bursting into Edward's office with a speech of how he was the right person to approach the descendants had to rearrange itself in his head. How could he negotiate buying the Right at a bargain (every time he thought this, Tej's bleating face appeared) if he couldn't admit he knew about the covenant?

Frustration gripped him. For all he knew, the hotel could have sorted this problem out years ago, perhaps done a quiet deal with the descendants without Beth or Tej knowing.

'What's up with your socks?' Beth said.

Gordon stood, then shrugged. 'Don't tell anyone. I'm a secret clown. When I go home in the evenings, I do the whole thing.... Clown costume, make up.'

Beth laughed. 'You're so full of shit.'

'I wear crazy socks to remind myself of this other persona. That's why I wanted to find out if I could allow some sheep in here. Get them to be part of my circus act.'

'I think you mean lions.'

Gordon smacked his forehead. 'I always get that wrong.'

Beth chuckled and shook her head. 'Why do you really want to know about the sheep covenant?'

Gordon swallowed. 'I wanted to help Edward sort it. Get myself up for that promotion.'

Bethany smirked.

'It's not just a rumour like Tej says. Edward actually mentioned it a while back when I started doing those extra hours unpaid.'

Bethany's eyebrows pinched. 'Oh. Right.'

Gordon sighed. 'You think it's just a silly dream. With the redundancies, I don't blame you.' He strode back to his desk.

'The archives,' she said.

'What?'

'That's where the information about that meeting with the insurers will be kept.' She leant over her computer screen to stare at him from beneath heavy false lashes. 'But I never told you that. Got it? If you drop me in it, I'll shove a clown nose so far up your backside that whenever you sit you'll honk.'

This time he took the staff lift straight to the basement. He made his way to the archive room, crammed with rows of metal filing cabinets, and found the finance section. He found a cabinet marked I to R. He opened the first draw, his fingers searching through the 'I' section for a file labelled 'insurance.' Nothing.

His fingers kept moving. Someone could have easily shoved it into the wrong section. He searched past J, then K. Where the hell was the insurance document? Wait, the name of the insurers…. Marden, no Morden. Pelling Morden, that was it. His fingers crept through P. Heart palpitations built as he passed every file until he got to Q. He moved his thumb to R and froze.

Rejected Insurance Proposal. What? Who filed it under this obscure heading?

He lifted the file from its folder. Pelling Morden. Insurance advisories for purchase.

Gordon smiled, then whispered to himself. 'Found it!'

Slipping the file under his blazer, he took the lift back up and headed straight to the men's room.

He sat in a stall on a closed toilet seat reading through the broker's report. Back after the turn of the last century, a farmer by the name of Owen Priddy from Bryn Nefyn, Wales sold some London land to a company who had put up a small guesthouse. Part of the deal was to allow Priddy to run sheep along the back of the guesthouse on the days he needed to get them to market. A deal he needed to keep with some local sheep owners. The Right allowed him to run the sheep every Thursday.

The main door to the lavatory opened. A woman's giggle.

'Are you sure you want to do this?' A man's whisper.

'Come on,' she cooed. 'It's been my fantasy for weeks.'

The cubicle next to him opened then clicked shut. More female giggles.

'I should be back at my desk,' Tej said.

Tej. Oh no. Oh Jesus. Here? Gordon's stomach turned at the noises of this woman getting hot and heavy with his colleague a few inches away. He forced himself to read another paragraph.

'Just a quick play,' the woman said, 'I need to get back to the café in ten minutes anyway.'

Gordon stifled an exasperated sigh and read on, ignoring a groan on the other side of the metal wall. It appeared that, some years later, after the land got sold to the guesthouse owners, they in turn sold it to a company who built a hotel. The hotel was built directly over the sheep run land. Maybe Owen Priddy hadn't used it for years. Or perhaps he'd died. Who knows? But somehow, as this hotel changed hands over the years, they forgot about the covenant. Until the solicitors handling the recent purchase found it.

'Shall I do that again?' the woman said.

'Yeah, okay. No. Stop.' Tej panted. 'No, keep going.'

Balancing the open file on his knees, Gordon pressed his palms over his ears to read the next line. The current descendent and Right holder was a Mr Alan Priddy who lived in Bryn Nefyn, North Wales. The insurance was for ten million pounds compensation for the hotel in case any covenant descendant, present and future, insisted on using their Right and the hotel had to cease trading.

Cease trading? Shit. This was serious. Bolting from the closed toilet seat, Gordon slammed open his cubicle door.

'Hey! Who's there?' Tej called out.

Gordon strode through the corridor towards his boss' office. He checked his watch. It was nearly ten o'clock. He buttoned his blazer as he pushed open his boss's door.

'Ah, Gordon. Have a seat.' Edward said.

He pulled a chair towards the front of his boss' desk.

'Don't do that.'

Gordon stopped. 'Do what?'

'Could you put the chair back where it was and sit down?'

He pushed the chair against the wall, then sat, crossing his feet at the ankles.

'You've read the email?' Edward asked.

Gordon nodded.

'It's not a happy situation I'm afraid, but we have no choice,' Edward said. 'The hotel group doesn't need two assistant finance managers.'

Gordon nodded again slowly. 'So Tej and I are fighting each other for the remaining assistant manager role?' He bit his lip. While Tej was fumbling with a barista in the men's room, their jobs were in danger of going down the toilet.

'Tej is fine,' Edward said. 'He's been here long enough, he'll find a space somewhere even if both roles go.' He winced. 'Forget I said that to you. That's confidential.'

Gordon held his breath. Edward trusting him with a company secret was a good sign.

'I'm sorry,' Edward said. 'Your role is being made redundant.'

Gordon breathed out. 'Me? Wait… but there are other roles, right?'

'There are always roles for a man like you, Gordon.'

His heart beat faster. Perhaps this was his moment. He might not need to think about the covenant at all. It was just possible things were going his way at last. 'Tell me about the options.'

'Well, there are two vacancies in the department for input clerks,' Edward said. 'A demotion, I'm afraid, less money. But it's a job.'

The beating of Gordon's heart rushed to his ears. 'A demotion? But, you and I talked about me becoming a director?'

Edward's face pinched into a frown as he leant forward. The thin white scar between his brows disappeared into a line above his nose. 'No,' he said softly. 'Nothing I ever confirmed.' He leant back and stared at the framed photo on his desk of his four-year-old granddaughter.

The hair on the nape of Gordon's neck stiffened. This wasn't happening. When Gordon finally landed a job at this hotel just short of two years ago it was supposed to be the beginning. A two-year contract and then his next role would be for a higher position. This is what Edward had led him to believe.

His chest tightened. A directorship, that's what Edward had mentioned two months ago. Back in September when Gordon had sat in this same room listening to Edward's hopeful words which signalled to Gordon that fate had deemed it time. That destiny would soon take away the rickety set of wooden steps he'd been born with so it could hand him a silver ladder towards success. One that led towards the dream he had long promised his late Grandfather he would one day achieve.

'You're supposed to have a consultation with HR first, but between us, I'll let you have a look.' Edward slid some papers across the desk. 'These are the vacancies for the clerk's roles. Unless you want to take the redundancy? The figure from HR is on the top page. You've been here what, just under two years?' Edward shook his head. 'Technically, we don't have to give you anything, but…' he pressed his lips together, then sighed. 'We have a shared history you and I. You know, I shouldn't really do favours because of it, but I won't forget how good your grandfather was to me when I started as a young lad in this business. He was my mentor.'

'Mine too,' Gordon whispered.

Edward sat tall. 'I've asked HR to be charitable.' He stood and took the papers from the desk.

Gordon shuffled his feet beneath his chair.

Edward glanced towards Gordon's feet, his eyes narrowing.

Gordon's stomach twisted with nerves. Don't let him see your socks. What would the Chancellor of the Exchequer do in this situation? He'd probably stretch out his legs shrugging, 'So what? Look at my shoes. Polished so brightly the lights from the ceiling reflect off them.' Stretch your legs out. Show him, show him. Grin and say, *I read in the Financial Times that mismatched socks sharpen the thinking.*

His throat dry, he pushed his feet further beneath the

chair. He couldn't do it. Outrageously mismatched socks torpedoed the glittering land of the polished shoe.

Edward handed him the paperwork. Gordon stared at the top page, the words morphing into dizzying ink marks. He could just about make out the line that said one and a half week's pay. This was charitable? His fingers tensed, causing the edges of the pages to crumple.

'Did you want to ask me anything?' said Edward as he returned to his chair behind his desk.

This was his chance. His only chance. Gordon cleared his throat. 'I'd like to stay here. I think I have skills to offer you that will make you want to keep me.'

Edward leaned back and sighed. 'Look. Have you still got my private email address?'

Gordon nodded.

'I'm happy to give any prospective new employer of yours a personal reference.'

Gordon's mouth dried. 'But, I think I can do something for you.' Oh God. How could he broach this? His heart thudded out each second of silence in the room while his boss gazed at his granddaughter's photo.

Gordon nodded towards the picture frame. 'It's special, that bond, isn't it?'

Edward raised his eyes and looked at Gordon.

'Your granddaughter,' Gordon pointed towards the photo. 'What's her name? Oh wait, it's Amandine, isn't it? Your daughter married a Frenchman?'

Edward scribbled a note on the paperwork in front of him.

'The ladies in the office,' Gordon shrugged nervously. 'They talk about people's kids.'

Still scribbling, Edward nodded.

Gordon cleared his throat. 'Do you know what else they talk about?' He paused. 'That sheep covenant.'

Edward's pen stopped moving. He slowly raised his eyes to Gordon. 'What did you say?'

His heart pounded. Quick. Protect Tej and Beth. 'One

of the ladies who left here recently. I forget her name. She mentioned something about it.'

'Idle office gossip.' Edward said. 'Look, sorry Gordon, I've got another meeting in a few minutes.'

Think of something. Now. 'What I wanted to say is I know it's real. Alan Priddy is a family friend.' His heart beat faster from the lie.

Edward dropped the pen to his desk. 'And?'

'Alan Priddy wants to exercise his family's Right.'

After a long silence, low laughter rumbled from his boss.

Gordon looked up. Edward tilted his head back and laughed again. He then sat forward, grinning. 'Please don't tell me this friend of yours is planning to run his sheep through the hotel. Bloody hell, wait, I think I'd like to see him try that.'

'This isn't a joke, Edward. If the hotel gets declared not fit for purpose….'

His boss's eyes narrowed. 'Go on.'

'Well, that's what could happen, isn't it? The hotel could in theory be closed down? Which is why those brokers recommended you take out insurance for ten million pounds.' Gordon paused to add emphasis. 'You need my help. I know you didn't purchase the insurance.'

'Get out.'

Gordon stood. 'That wasn't a threat, Edward. It's an offer to help. You've always said you valued my hard work and attention to detail. I think I could really go above and beyond here and sort this out.' He stared at the floor, steadying his breath. Edward Creaton is the opposition ordering him out of the House of Commons. He breathed in to summon every fantasy version of himself as a hero. Not just the Chancellor of the Exchequer, but Gordon, the song writing rock star of his teens who didn't give a damn. Gordon, England's football captain from his twenties. *Don't you know who I am, heard of Tottenham Hotspur?* The actual chancellor would stand firm while waiting for the Speaker of the House to intervene. Gordon's breath quickened. There was no Speaker in this room. Just Gordon and Edward.

'Why are you still standing in my office?' Edward said. 'Tell Tej to get in here. I know he's behind this.'

'Tej has nothing to do with this.' *Too busy scoring free croissants,* he wanted to add. 'I found the file myself. In the archives. I wanted the insurance information so I could help you. Help protect the hotel. And I truly believe I still can. With or without the insurance.'

Edward glared at him.

'Edward, listen. What if I can convince the farmer to take a payoff to stay away? I can broker a good deal to buy the Right from him.'

Edward pursed his lips, turning to gaze towards the window. 'Tell me how you know this farmer?'

'My brother-in-law knows him.' He swallowed and focused his eyes on the wood grain of Creaton's desk. There was a scratch mark, and a small indentation. His sister would know a good French polisher but now was probably not the time to suggest it. Gordon gathered some more fabrication and breathed out. 'The farmer told my brother-in-law all about the covenant. They were talking about the fact I worked here and it came out.'

Edward raised his eyebrows.

'I can fix this,' Gordon said. 'Get them to agree to sell you the Right at a reasonable cost. But I want something in return.' His toes tingled with nerves before he stood taller. 'I want the promotion you've been talking to me about. The directorship.'

His boss sat back in his chair and sighed. 'With the redundancies, we can't create that role for at least six months.'

'I understand. You can give me one of those clerk roles temporarily.'

Edward nodded. 'How much do you think they'd sell that Right for?'

'I'm going to aim for about £10,000.'

'Is that it?'

'That's what I'll aim for. I'll speak to my brother-in-law. He's a solicitor. He'll give me some advice.' Gordon turned to leave, then stopped. 'Oh, and I'll need some time off to go up to Wales.'

'Understood.'

Gordon smiled and strode towards the door.

'Gordon,' Edward said.

'Yes?' He turned.

'I'll need proof. Written proof of Alan Priddy's threat. Not for me, you understand. But for the board.'

Chapter Three

Outside the car windows, green hills rose and fell. White dots of sheep, as if from a painter's brush, dappled the fields. Ahead, in the distance, sweeping hills appeared before Gordon in almost 2D, with bracken and heather forming jagged patterns across a jade mountain canvas. He lowered his window to breathe in the cool air, the sweetness of cypress and pine rushing into the car. A sense of calm filled his chest as he breathed out.

This was finally it. The point in his life when he would make real the promise to himself, and to his Granddad. He'd no longer be the unlucky younger brother in his family's eyes. No, he would take that 1978 Mont Blanc pen with him into The Remblents boardroom, then sit with his fellow board members at the long ebony table. When he pulled the precious resin pen from his pocket to sign his director's contract, his grandfather's pride would descend through to his fingers.

Stacey. Would he tell her? His throat tightened with the ache of missing her. He really had thought she was the one. He swallowed back the memory of his humiliation at the restaurant, and breathed in to numb the ache in his heart from the unanswered calls and texts.

Yes, he would tell her. In one final text. If she showed interest only because of a promotion, then his sister was right. She couldn't have been the woman for him.

He breathed out heavily.

As he drove on, he forced his mind into rehearsing the conversation with the Right descendent. He couldn't let on he worked at the hotel. The farmer could phone the hotel in a day or so with questions. Gordon couldn't risk the farmer speaking to one of his colleagues, or worse, to Edward. There's no way Edward could find out that the farmer wasn't a family friend. That the farmer hadn't instigated the threat to run the sheep. Gordon's heart thudded. Another lie. Just a small one. Yet all would lead to good outcomes for both parties. Getting this agreed would mean the hotel could never be threatened by this crazy Right at any point in future, and the current descendent would get a nice unexpected windfall. There should be a different word for lies that benefitted everyone.

Gordon breathed in the clear mountain air. He could tell Mr Priddy that he used to work for the insurance brokers, and that's how he knew about the covenant.

Raindrops splattered on the windscreen. He lifted the button to raise the car window, his fingers shaking with a tingle of doubt. No. This would work. Of course it would. A friendly chat with the farmer. An offer of money. A quick meeting with Edward. With barely any bother, a deal would be struck. Although, he still needed Alan Priddy to put a threat in writing. His stomach clenched from the loathing of pushing himself deeper into untruths.

He turned up a winding hill. Overgrown gorse tapped against the passenger windows as he rehearsed the speech to Alan Priddy in his head. 'Do you know you have a Right to run sheep through a London hotel? I know the company. I believe I can convince them into giving you a pay-out.'

The windscreen wipers screeched along the dry glass. 'Make up your mind, rain,' Gordon muttered. He switched off the wipers, then resumed rehearsing his speech to Mr Priddy. 'We have to make it convincing that you intend to actually run the sheep. I'll be the go between, but you must pretend it's your idea. Trust me, this will work.' His throat tightened again, as if to squeeze shut the lies he'd not yet uttered.

The road widened as it stretched out towards the hill's edge. He drove, climbing with the car further up, and then glanced through the passenger window towards the valleys below. His first time in Wales and he hadn't appreciated how stunning he would find its scenery. Hills the shades of emeralds and forest greens swept past, their beauty dizzying as he drove. He breathed in and forced himself to stare at the tarmac ahead, allowing the sat nav to guide him until it instructed him to take the next left.

Gordon swung the car into a tight turn, then pushed his foot on the accelerator as it rumbled up a gravel and dirt path. Whether the farmer actually needed the money wouldn't matter. If you got all six numbers on a lottery ticket, you wouldn't rip it up and throw it in the bin just because you were financially sound. He drove past a wall of oak trees, their branches still clinging to yellow-brown leaves. His sat nav ordered him to turn left again, leading him towards a leaden coloured stone cottage. Its crooked roof canopy looked as though the next gust of wind would send it crashing to the valleys below. Perhaps evidence this farmer could use some cash.

Gordon switched off the engine and pulled up the handbrake.

A skinny figure in a faded black T-shirt and jeans emerged from the doorway of the cottage. At first glance, the old fellow looked as though he was auditioning to be one of the sheep. His white hair was as fluffy and ragged as an unshorn lamb. His T-shirt had 'RON MAN' emblazoned across it. It took a moment for Gordon to realise it must have once said 'Iron Man,' a Black Sabbath song.

'Are you lost?' Ron Man called out.

'I'm looking for Alan Priddy.'

The man skipped down a path overgrown with weeds and, with a wide smile, stepped towards the car. His teeth were large, uneven, and nicotine-stained. He had a lined face, but it was taut enough to suggest he was younger than Gordon originally thought. Mid-sixties maybe.

'Are you Mr. Priddy?' Gordon asked.

'Aye. So what if I am?'

Gordon reached for the car handle. Which persona should he take on? Chancellor of the Exchequer might be too formal. Maybe the laid-back rock star. Ron Man looked the sort who might appreciate that. He stepped out, his feet hitting the mud and the gravel. 'Can I call you Alan?'

'If you want.'

Gordon stood, then casually outstretched his hand.

Ron man stared at it.

Gordon lowered his hand. 'I wanted to talk to you about the covenant.'

'Which one?'

'There's more than one?'

'I reckon the U.K. has millions of them, don't you?' the man said.

Gordon opened his mouth to answer, then stopped. 'I have no idea.'

'We can google it.'

Gordon exhaled sharply. 'Look, did you know you have a covenant that allows you to bring your sheep to the Remblents Hotel in London?'

Ron man gestured as if holding an invisible cup of tea, his pinky extended outward. 'You want to take one of the fluffy ladies out for scones and Earl Grey down in the big smoke?'

Jesus. The guy was nuts.

Ron Man stood grinning at him.

Gordon looked past the man and at the view beyond the cottage. Phantom grey mountains rose beyond clover topped hills. Fleece-like clouds hovered over the peaks. The nearest hill appeared lopsided; as if its jagged peak jumped, then just missed reaching towards heaven, landing to the right of the landscape instead.

The sound of footsteps fell behind Gordon. He turned. A man in worn jeans and a button-down shirt, older than Ron man, maybe in his late seventies, approached. His heavy boots crunched along the gravel as he neared.

'Can I help you, sir?' The older man asked.

'I wanted to have a word with Alan Priddy.' Gordon gestured towards Ron man.

'I'm Alan Priddy,' the older man said.

Gordon looked from Ron man to the second man, then back to Ron man. 'You told me you were Alan Priddy.'

'I did not. I said I was Mr Priddy, and you asked if you could call me Alan. I was being polite and not denying your request. Besides, I'm the nicer brother.'

'Rhys,' Alan said. 'That's enough.'

'I was just playing.'

'Is there something I can do for you?' Alan said to Gordon.

'He wants to talk to you about Hen Daid's sheep covenant,' said Rhys.

Alan pursed his lips. 'Why do you want to talk about that?' he asked Gordon.

'So you know about it?'

'Course we do,' Alan said.

'Taid used to laugh about it,' Rhys said. 'Joked how we should bring a sheep to London for lunch in that fancy hotel.'

'Taid?' Gordon asked.

'Grandfather,' Alan said. 'Taid is Welsh for Grandfather.'

'Okay, it's good you know about the covenant because I have an interesting proposition for you.'

'I doubt it,' Alan said.

'Please. I've come all the way from London.'

Alan sighed. 'I'm not sure you can tell me anything I don't already know.

'Give me five minutes,' Gordon said.

'You've come all the way from London for five minutes?'

'It's worth it.'

Alan gazed at a field of sheep on a hill beyond the cottage. 'Okay, I guess you better come in.' He turned and said to Rhys. 'We'll just use your place, if that's okay.'

'Sure.' Rhys grinned. He winked at Gordon. 'By the

way, our sheep only eat their scones with the jam on top. If your posh boy waiters put the jam on first and smother it with cream after, there'll be trouble.' He gave a high pitched laughed, almost like a whistle of air from a punctured tyre.

A tractor tyre, no doubt.

They sat in a square room cramped with sofas. The air was musty with the smell of stale nicotine mixed with the scent of something like burnt leaves. Gordon eyed the sofas, then counted. Six, one against three of the walls. A second row of sofas had been pushed in front of those. All shabby, saggy, stuffing escaping from split arm rests.

Gordon looked at Rhys. 'You fix sofas?'

'Nah. Wanted a second sofa in here a few years back.'

Gordon looked around. 'You've got half a dozen.'

'My friend Simon down at the Ty Coch Inn told folks I was after a sofa and asked if anyone had one going spare. Next day his mate Jac turned up with his trailer.' Rhys turned and patted the sofa behind him, brown and faded. 'Said he was getting rid of this one anyway.'

Gordon stared at him. Jesus, this guy was bonkers. 'And the others?'

'Day after that, Lewis and his wife turned up with that sofa behind the blue one. Next day Elis turned up with the green one. I couldn't say no every time someone turned up. It would be rude.'

'But why keep them?'

'Oh, he's never getting rid of these sofas,' Alan said. 'God knows I've tried convincing him.'

Rhys lifted his chin and stared at Gordon. 'It reminds me of how kind people can be. Every time I walk into this room, I smile.' He turned to Alan with a broad grin.

Alan ignored him and instead looked at Gordon. 'Why are you here?'

Gordon's cheeks burned as he breathed out. 'I used to work for an Insurance Broker. It was my job to get The

Remblents Group to insure against the covenant.'

'But why? It's worthless,' Alan said.

'It isn't. Do you know what it would do to that hotel if you exercised that Right?'

'And now you want to help them?'

'No, actually.' Gordon's heart thudded. 'I want to help you.'

'Why?'

Gordon swallowed. 'I always thought it was wrong that you didn't get paid for the Right.' The heat from his cheeks rose to the tips of his ears. This was going to take more than just agreeing a figure. If he could get Alan on board, he'd still need to give Edward proof that the Priddys had intended to run the sheep. 'Do you still have the original paperwork?'

'I have the deed that Hen daid left us.... Great Grandfather. I showed it to an actual lawyer in Port Merion. He reckoned it was still valid, but that hotel group, they didn't care about any of that.'

Gordon sat forward. 'You've spoken to the hotel group?'

Alan stretched out a leg into the limited floor space. 'About four years ago. We had some debts.' He winced. 'Anyway, I went down to London. Met with the directors in charge of that hotel. I offered to sell them the Right.'

'And?'

'They laughed at me. Told me I could keep it. I said, "you mean you'd be happy for me to bring an entire load of sheep through the hotel?" One director, this guy with a thin white scar between his eyebrows—'

'Edward Creaton.'

'That's the fellow. He looked at the others and he said, "What do you think? We could make a feature of that. Advertise that we're the only hotel in London with land still used as a sheep run." Then he turned to me and said, "No, we're all good here. You keep that Right."

'He was bluffing,' Gordon said.

'Didn't seem like a bluff. As I got up to leave, he laughed at me. I looked at them all. Those other directors, the pity in their eyes, I could see they felt sorry for me.' Alan's lips pressed together. 'I never want anyone feeling sorry for me.'

Gordon's heartbeat slowed. He understood that feeling. The one he got sometimes from his brother, Mark. He sat forward and hung his head. Edward hadn't mentioned the descendants had already approached the hotel. He looked at Alan. Of course this gentle farmer wouldn't have understood the hotel's sneaky opening tactic. 'Look, I know these directors. They won't want sheep running through their flagship hotel. They couldn't afford to risk it. You need to call their bluff.'

'How?'

'Send out a letter, or an email. Give them dates to expect you with the sheep.'

'No, no. You wait a minute. You honestly expect me to show up there with a load of sheep?'

Rhys laughed. 'There's no way he'd bring those sheep to London. What if they misbehave, Alan?'

'Enough, Rhys.'

'Back in nineteen-ninety-six,' Rhys said to Gordon. 'He entered our sheep in a local agricultural show. Them sheep were terrible. Didn't go into the pens the way they were supposed —'

'That's enough Rhys.'

'The villagers. They've never let Alan forget. They still shake their heads and talk about it whenever we go into town.'

Gordon looked at the older farmer. 'We won't actually need to bring any sheep to London,' he said in what he hoped was a reassuring tone.

'Let's prove our sheep can run through the hotel!' Rhys jumped up and pointed at Gordon. 'I say yes, we'll do it!'

'We will not,' Alan said. 'Sit down, Rhys.'

Rhys sat and glared at Alan.

Alan turned his head and stared at the doorway.

Gordon shifted in his seat, making the sofa frame whine beneath the cushions. He glanced towards the corridor. The yellowed paint on the sitting-room door frame had cracked. Patterns of dried mud fingerprints decorated the halfway mark. Somewhere in the house, a clock ticked out long seconds of silence. Gordon glanced around the room, searching for something to change the mood, get them on board. Except there was nothing in the room apart from shelves of dusty photo frames and six shabby sofas.

Finally, Gordon asked, 'You still got those debts?'

'No,' both men said.

Gordon's heart thudded. 'So, you don't want any money?'

'Don't need it,' said Alan. 'You're wasting your time, son.'

Gordon stood. 'Okay.' He let out a long sigh. It wouldn't help to pressure them. 'Let me know if you change your mind.' He turned and walked out of the room, through the open front door and back down the gravel path towards his car. What a stupid bloody waste of six hours' driving time. He grabbed the car door and huffed, his temples pounding from despair.

Quick footsteps crunched into the gravel behind him. 'Hey,' Rhys called out. 'Wait up.'

Gordon turned and sighed.

'He sold some of our taid's ….. grandfather's land. That's why some of the debts are gone.'

Gordon grimaced. 'Good. I'm glad you're all sorted.'

'Well, not exactly. Alan doesn't like to talk about it much. It upsets him.'

'There are more debts?' Gordon asked.

'I believe so. But worse, that land he sold is up for sale again. Alan's been worrying himself about what could happen. Nobody wants some big development cramming in around our sheep fields.'

Gordon exhaled heavily. There was no way these people were going to accept ten thousand pounds. Although, he might be able to get the hotel to part with a little more. 'What sort of amount are we looking at?'

'As much as we can for running the sheep through the hotel. You want us to run sheep through the hotel, right?'

'It would never get that far. The idea was to threaten it so you could get some money for the Right.'

Rhys shrugged. 'Do you think we'd get enough to buy a bit of the land back?'

'Depends. How much would you need?'

'For hill ground? Not a lot. Going rate is about one thousand pounds an acre.'

'What if I were to get him ten acres back?'

'Don't know. But I reckon I might be able to convince him.'

Gordon leaned against the car door, staring out at the fluffy dots of sheep grazing on a craggy hill beyond the cottage. A gust of wind scattered a yellow fluttering of oak leaves onto the crooked canopy of Rhys' front door.

'There's one condition,' Rhys said. 'We bring the defaid through the hotel for real.'

'Defaid?'

'You need to learn a bit of Welsh. Sheep. A whole load of sheep.'

Gordon chuckled. 'Well, that's the problem. The payoff would mean we don't do it.'

Rhys pursed his lips.

'But if your brother decides he wants some of that land back, we can try bluffing.' He opened the car door, then reached into the glove compartment. 'Here,' he said, scribbling his number on the back of a petrol receipt. 'Talk to him. If you can convince him, phone me.'

Gordon got into his car and switched on the ignition. As he revved the car forward, a white blob of fluff jumped from the bushes right in front of the bonnet.

Gordon slammed his foot on the brakes.

The animal bleated as Gordon pulled up the handbrake.

'What the hell are you doing?' A red-faced woman with wild frizzy hair rushed towards him, then slapped her palms on the car's bonnet.

Gordon opened the car door and stepped out. 'Why can't you control your animals?'

'This is a god damn sheep farm,' she said. 'Not a race track. Why don't you control your driving?'

The fury in her eyes and the anger in her unusual, possibly Canadian, accent shook him. He breathed in, then muttered, 'Sorry.'

She pushed the sheep away, then stood tall, scowling.

Gordon narrowed his eyes, and said, 'I did apologise.' He stepped back into his car, then inched the vehicle slowly down the gravel path. In his rearview mirror, he spotted the woman, probably around mid-thirties, glaring towards his car before shaking her head.

He drove down the winding hills and through the small villages, the frustration from the failed mission squeezing tighter around his ribs. At last, he saw signs towards the motorway.

The weight of the aborted covenant plan pressed harder as he drove along the M54. This was his last hope. What would his grandfather do? Gordon needed to think. He should stop, stretch, breathe in some colder, fresher air. He eyed each motorway sign searching for the next service station.

The mobile on his passenger seat flashed.

He glimpsed across. An unknown number. His heart thumped with a tinge of excitement. Perhaps it was that sheep headed brother of Alan's.

Gordon pressed the hands free on his steering wheel.

'Maybe I'll do it,' the male voice said.

'Rhys?' Gordon asked.

'No, it's Alan.'

Gordon nearly swerved the car into the next lane. Yes!

Thank you, Rhys! You convinced him, you crazy white-haired sheepman.

'But I can't do it,' said Alan.

'You just said maybe you'll do it.'

'I'll go along with the plan but I can't physically do the shepherding. Not anymore. I've got a shepherdess, but I doubt she'll go along with the plan.'

'No, wait. You're getting this mixed up. We're not actually going to run the sheep through the hotel. You're just going to threaten it.'

'Rhys said we would run the sheep through,' said Alan.

'No, that's not what's going to happen.'

'What's going to happen?'

There was a turnoff for the services just ahead. 'Wait, I'm going to phone you back.' He indicated, then swerved off to the service road, and up into the car park near a burger joint. Leaving the engine running, he pressed the number for the last received call.

'What's your plan?' Alan said.

'We'll tell them you're going to do it, but trust me, it's never going to get that far.'

'You want to pretend?'

'Yes.'

'And what if they tell me to run the sheep?'

'They won't.'

'They will. They already did before.'

Gordon sat staring at the golden arches engraved on the fast-food door. His stomach rumbled. 'I tell you what, if it comes to it, we can scare them. If the written notice you give isn't enough, we'll get someone to drive a dozen sheep down in a trailer or something and sit outside the hotel. I'll make sure I'm there to mediate. They'll cave in.'

'No serious- minded shepherd is going to agree to run sheep through a London Hotel.'

'We're not going to….' Gordon sighed. 'Look, I'll do it all myself.' His mouth dried. There was no way he could be the one behind the wheel of the sheep trailer, but of course, it would never get that far.

'You?' Alan laughed, then coughed for several seconds before laughing again.

'I'll find you a shepherd if I have to,' Gordon said, 'and I'll get the hotel to agree to buy the Right.'

'You're a determined bastard, aren't you?.' Alan said. 'I have one more question.'

'Yes?'

'What's in it for you?'

'I already said. I don't want anything. I just want to see justice done.' His heart thumped at the guilty fib.

After a pause, Alan said, 'Tell you what, make your way back to Wales. I think you're right. You can take the sheep. You'll have some training to do first with getting used to these animals. I'll get my shepherdess to help you.'

Jesus. This was getting out of proportion. He didn't need training for a bluff. 'It's not necessary.'

'Are we doing this or not, Mr. Slee? If you're thinking of accompanying a few of my sheep into London, I need to trust you.'

'Right.' He turned off the ignition. He'd need to go along with this for a little bit until communications were exchanged between the Priddys and the Remblents. 'I'll come back towards the end of the week. Even stay overnight if you put me up.'

'Overnight?' Alan laughed again. 'You best pack a bag for a couple of weeks, son.'

'Of course.' Gordon ended the call and strode out across the concrete car park, making his way towards the eatery.

He wouldn't need weeks. He'd tell Edward he'd need a few days in the Welsh hills to firm up this deal with Alan Priddy, and all would be sorted.

He pulled his phone from his pocket and dialled Edward's number.

'I think I can sort this. Purchase the Right for you for practically pennies.'

'Pennies?'

'You know what I mean. The ten thousand I mentioned.'

'Hmmm.'

'Look, I'll need some time off work.'

'You'll have all the time you need if you take the redundancy.'

Adrenaline pulsed through Gordon. 'No, I'll need a salary in the meantime.'

'With all due respect, that's not my problem,' Edward said. 'The deal is the role in six months. Look… I'm sorry, You know we're dealing with redundancies. I can't do the impossible for you. But if you help me, then I'll help you with the possible.'

Gordon breathed out in relief. He'd sort something, somehow. Six months wasn't forever.

'But Gordon…'

'Yes?'

'I'm still waiting for that evidence of Mr Priddy's threat.'

His stomach clenched as he swallowed back his creeping panic. 'Of course. I'll get that over to you. As soon as I return to Wales.'

Chapter Four

At the Brixton flat, something felt different. Yet everything looked the same. In the kitchen, he spotted he'd left a half-filled coffee mug in the gleaming stainless steel sink before rushing out at the crack of dawn. A few stale toast crumbs decorated the counter, and he quickly scooped them into his palm, and brushed them into the shiny waste bin. To think he judged the Priddys on their ramshackle cottage. He may as well have six shabby sofas in this place.

Striding towards the bedroom, he stood outside the door then squeezed his eyes shut. *You're at Eleven Downing Street about to enter your private office.*

He turned the chrome doorknob, and a trace of Stacey's Chanel Mademoiselle perfume greeted him. His heartbeat picked up as he opened his eyes. 'Stacey?'

He switched on the light. Everything appeared exactly as he left it this morning; the thick white duvet with its corner turned back on his side of the bed, his half empty water glass on the bedside table.

No Stacey.

But she'd been here.

He stepped towards the wardrobe and opened its door. His heart stilled. Stacey had removed some of the clothes she had kept in this closet. Next to his shirts hung lonely wooden hangers.

He crashed down onto the rumbled corner of the duvet. Rubbing his face, he turned and looked towards the dressing table. There was an envelope propped against the mirror with his name on it.

He stood and moved slowly towards the dresser. With hesitant fingers, he tore open the envelope. Inside, two keys to the apartment. Along with a note. He unfolded the paper and Stacey's large curly penmanship spoke out to him:

'Sorry, Gordon, but we both know this isn't working. It's my fault. I've been meaning to end things for months. I've just been too

much of a coward. Take care of yourself.'

For months? He pulled his mobile from his pocket and hit her number.

She answered on the first ring with a tentative hello.

'Hey,' Gordon said, aiming to keep his voice calm. 'I got your note. Look. We should talk. It seems like there are things you've been wanting to tell me. For months obviously.'

She sighed. 'It doesn't matter.'

'I think it does. Stacey, you were unhappy for all that time? How could I not have known that? We laughed together, made dinner together, had sex most nights. Okay, lately you've had a lot of work stress, you keep telling me how maddening PR is, but…'

'It wasn't work stress.'

'What was it?'

'Don't make me do this.'

'Stacey, I asked you to marry me and you walked out on me.'

'Sorry.'

'No, I'm sorry. I'm sorry I didn't see the signs. I'm sorry I was so off base that I bought a ring for a woman who was planning an escape. What happened? When did this all change for you?'

'I've got to go.'

'Don't go, I need to understand –'

'Goodbye, Gordon.'

With a click, she was gone.

He stood, his breath quickening.

The mobile buzzed in his hand and he quickly looked at the screen. His heart shrunk with disappointment when he saw Edward's name.

With a huge exhale, he opened the text message.

I have informed the board of Mr Priddy's threat and your proposed negotiations. I suggest you contact Mr Priddy and instruct him to email me with his intentions to run the sheep. The board meeting is at 8.30am. Get him to send this over to me asap.

Gordon sat on the bed again and held his face in his hands. There's no way Alan Priddy can be in direct touch with Edward.

His fingers shook as he texted back yet another lie. *He's an old man. He doesn't do email. But don't worry, he's seeing his solicitor in the next few days. I'll get a letter for you.*

Gordon's breath shortened. Surely he could convince Alan to see his solicitor to request a brief letter? If Gordon could shove a third party between Edward and Alan Priddy, there should be less chance of exposure.

His stomach hardened. This wasn't him. All this scheming and lying spiralling his self-respect further and further down a hole. He steadied his breath. *It's okay. This is what business is about. It will all be worth it because in six months time…*

He stopped breathing. Jesus, he'd forgotten. He hadn't shown up for the HR meetings. He might be out of a job until that director position opened up.

Dread descended. He only had one more pay cheque coming in. The dread pushed down harder when he realised what he might have to do next.

He picked up his phone, scrolled to 'D' and pressed to call. It answered after four rings.

'Hi Dad, it's me,' Gordon said in a quiet voice.

'Mark?'

Gordon winced. 'Don't you have my name on your phone?'

'It says Samsung.'

He pressed his lips together before breathing out. 'Dad, I need to ask you something. It's possible I might be a little short of cash.'

'Oh, it's Gordon then.'

His chest squeezed. 'You say that like it's a constant occurrence.'

'Isn't it?'

'No.'

His father gave a sarcastic laugh. 'You've got a convenient memory. What about that time you owed three months' rent for that house share in Wandsworth or wherever it was?'

'Dad, that was fifteen years ago.'

His father sighed. 'What's the problem now?'

'I'm probably going to be made redundant.'

'Lost your job, you mean?'

'It's only a temporary situation. They're opening up another position for me, but it will take six months. I'll look for something else in the meantime, but just in case, I might need a little to tide me over for maybe a month, or two at most —'

'You still haven't paid back the money from the house share.'

His cheeks burned. 'Forget I asked, Dad.'

'Your brother and sister never asked me for a penny once they each left university.'

'I know.'

'You're forty-three years old.'

He swallowed. 'Forty-two.'

'Whatever. Still old enough for you not to be relying on me.'

'You're right.' Gordon said. 'Forget I asked, okay? I'll work something out.'

He ended the call then lay on the bed with his shoes on and stared at the cracks that crawled like spider's legs from the ceiling corner. Hmmm, so that's what Stacey had been staring at the last time they shagged.

He lay pondering how far the cracks would grow if he spent his lifetime in this flat. That's if he could even afford to stay.

He sat up. That was it. He couldn't afford to stay. Not until he fixed this mess with his job. He'd need to sublet this place. Temporarily. No more than six months.

He rubbed his cheek, then checked his watch. Eight pm. He'd eaten nothing except that burger at the service station earlier this afternoon.

The empty churning in his stomach felt sickening. To hell with food. What he needed was a drink. He went to the cupboard in the sitting room. The whiskey bottle was empty. He stormed into the kitchen, then opened and closed the cupboards, swearing under his breath as he pushed aside pasta packets and tins of tomatoes. He and Stacey must have kept another bottle of something somewhere. He opened the cupboard above the sink and his heart stilled.

Stacey's favourite mug. The silly green one with the scratchy gold lettering that read *'I'd rather be drinking Prosecco.'* He'd bought that for her over a year ago. Her adoring smile had greeted him as he brought her a coffee on that first Sunday morning. She'd sat up in bed, naked, to take the steaming cup from him.

'I thought you'd need your own mug at weekends,' he said to her.

'I love it,' she said, tracing her finger around the large swirly P.

'Because you love Prosecco,' he said.

'No,' she said. 'It's because this P reminds me of words I associate with you.'

'Such as?'

'Precious,' she said, still tracing the P.

He smiled.

'And then there's my favourite word for you.' She set the mug down on the bedside table, then grabbed the folds of his dressing gown as she pulled him towards her.

'What's that?' He whispered, his heart beating faster.

'Passionate,' she whispered.

He allowed her to slip his robe down his shoulders as he climbed on top of her.

The memory stabbed at his heart. He held his breath. It would be an excuse for him to see her. For them to talk.

He picked up his mobile.

It rang at Stacey's end five times before going to voice mail.

He exhaled. *No, don't give up.* He tried again.

This time, she answered. 'Hi Gordon.' Her voice was monotone.

He breathed in. 'Hi,' he said, drawing the greeting out in a low, tender voice. 'I just realised I've still got your favourite mug here.'

'I don't have a favourite mug.'

His heart thudded. 'Your Prosecco mug. I just thought you might want it.'

'No, you keep it.'

'Okay. So it's an excuse. I thought if I came over, gave you your mug, it would give us a chance to talk. Briefly.'

'This really isn't necessary.' She huffed. 'Look, I'm sorry. I'm meant to be going out shortly.'

'I see.' He picked the mug off the shelf and held it, staring at the swirly gold of the P.

'Look, it's been over for me for a while ...' she said.

His fingers around the mug shook. 'I realise that now. That's what I wanted to talk about. Find out where it all went wrong. When. Why I was so blindsided…. Look Stacey, I can make things better for us. I'm going up to Wales to do something—'

A buzzer sounded from where Stacey was speaking from. 'That's my date. I've got to go.'

'Date? Fuck me, Stacey. You have a date already?'

'It's not any of your business now.'

His heart pounded. 'But I mean, come on. So soon? We only split up last week. Don't you even want time to grieve losing us?'

'It's not like you died, Gordon.'

He swallowed down the speeding mass of pain in his chest. 'Who is he?'

'If you must know,' she said, 'It's someone I've been seeing for a little while.'

'Little while?' he shouted. He breathed slowly to calm

his voice. 'Why, Stacey?'

'He's someone I have much more in common with. Pragmatic… and successful.'

'And I'm not, or can't be?'

He gazed at the Prosecco mug on the counter. Tell her. Show her you're pragmatic. How you're going to be a success. 'Look, Stacey, I've got a plan. I've just come back from Wales—'

'He's outside the flat door now. Bye.'

Gordon stood, his heart racing as the phone went silent. He dropped his mobile on the counter and reached his hand towards the Prosecco mug, tracing his finger along the letters. Then he placed his palm behind the mug, as a fantasy emerged of him as an ill-tempered rock star, who would grab the mug and smash it to floor, then watch the ceramic pieces skitter along these white tiles.

Instead, he took the mug and placed it on the cupboard shelf, his chest squeezing as he closed the cupboard door.

One day, Stacey would be one more person sorry she didn't believe in him.

Chapter Five

Gordon drove back to Wales, passing the white dots of sheep on the hills. Dapples of paint on a canvas, my arse. More like careless splatters of neglectful decorators hurrying to get onto their next job.

He followed the sign to Bryn Nefyn. Minutes later, the car chugged up the Priddy's bumpy drive, the yellowed oak leaves blanketing the entrance to the farm.

'Helloooo.' Rhys bellowed as he strode out from the open door of his cottage. The crooked roof canopy seemed to have survived another few days.

Gordon lowered the passenger window. 'Which way to the guesthouse?'

Rhys cackled, then spread his arms wide. 'This is it.' He turned and pointed to a small sign near the foot of the path. 'Can't you read? It says Gwesty. That means guesthouse.'

Gordon's shoulders sunk as he sat behind the steering wheel. Alan never mentioned he'd have a sheep-headed housemate. Reluctantly, he stepped out of the car, then walked towards the boot to grab his bag.

Rhys bowed, extending his arm towards the cottage. 'I'll show you to your room, sir.'

Gordon stood with his duffle bag dangling from his hand. It was too late to think about driving back to London. Tej had already convinced him to sublet his flat to that over-enamoured barista, while also offering to store a few of Gordon's things if necessary. Unfortunately, the barista only wanted it for three months, not six. Out of desperation, Gordon agreed.

A crow cawed overhead as he stood.

'Come on, friend,' Rhys said as he pranced towards the front door.

Gordon exhaled, then followed him.

Rhys was already inside, making his way up the whining stairs covered in a mud-stained, balding carpet. Gordon followed. When they reached the landing, the smell of musty laundry wafted towards him. Gordon turned.

Rhys had strewn what looked like dozens of faded wet T-shirts over the banister, one on top of the other, as if they were going to dry through some weird Rhys-world osmosis.

'Your room,' Rhys said, creaking open a yellowed, paint-chipped door.

Gordon stepped through into the room. A single bed with a bare mattress. A faded brown-rimmed stain covered the bottom end.

'Bedding and towels on the floor over there.' Rhys said, pointing to a jumbled pile.

Gordon picked up a stiff, thin towel. Parts of it were so worn the cloth was transparent. 'How often do you have guests?'

Rhys scratched his neck. 'Let me see. Oh.' He smiled. 'Why, you're the first one ever.'

Gordon dropped his bag to the floor, his stomach knotting with regret.

'I'll leave you to it,' Rhys said. He swaggered out the door, whistling.

Minutes later, music banged through the walls. Rhy's strained singing accompanied the blues song. Some old tune about seeing rain.

Gordon's bedroom door pushed open.

'Almost forgot,' Rhys shouted over the music from the hallway. 'Jenna's expecting you out at Willowherb field. Next to the one where the sheep are grazing.'

'Okay, but which one's the grazing field?'

Rhys rolled his eyes. 'You don't know what grazing is? Eating. Where sheep are standing around eating.'

'I know what grazing is, but where's the field?'

'Next to the tupping field.'

Gordon's brows pinched. 'Tupping? What's—'

'Never mind. I suppose I'll have to take you there. Let me turn Creedence off.'

'Who?'

'Don't you know anything? Creedence Clearwater Revival. American Band. Bad Moon Rising? Have you Ever Seen the Rain?'

'Yeah, okay.'

'Okay? They're more than okay. If I'm sharing this house with a philistine over the next week or two, you'll need an education in music.'

Gordon pulled the new wellington boots he'd purchased yesterday up over the legs of his jeans. He clomped down the stairs in the stiff rubber to find Rhys outside the front door, smoking a rolled-up cigarette.

Rhys stood in waterproof trousers pulled down to the ankles of his mud-caked boots. He looked at Gordon's pristine boots and laughed.

'Yeah, okay, they're brand new,' Gordon said.

'It's not that I'm laughing at.'

'What then?'

Rhys shrugged. 'Londoners. Just pray it doesn't rain.'

Gordon followed him to an ivy-clad gate, then stopped. His heart tapped against his ribcage. Just a few feet from the other side of the gate stood several huge cows, swishing their tails furiously, noses pushed into the grass, peaceful one moment and then… his breath quickened.

Rhys whistled as he pushed open the gate. 'Come on,' he said, holding the wooden door wide.

'You have cows,' said Gordon. The beating of his heart rose to the base of his throat.

'Well done,' Rhys said. 'You know what cows are.'

'But not dangerous ones?' He winced. *You're making a fool of yourself. Stop.*

Rhys let go of the gate, then doubled over and howled until his laughter became more like a high-pitched hiss. 'These cows?' He slapped his thigh before finally standing up again.

The cows stood motionless apart from the billowing

cheeks from chewing cud and the odd swishing of a tail. They looked calm enough, although one shouldn't be fooled. Gordon had experienced firsthand the menace hidden inside these creatures' minds. 'I'm just surprised,' he said. 'I thought you only had sheep in these fields.'

'The cows belong to Pete over at the next farm. We rent out our field to him. Come on. They won't hurt you.'

Gordon followed closely behind Rhys, his heart stupidly thumping in his chest. *Don't look at them.* Jamming his slightly shaking hands into his pockets, he willed Rhys to hurry. He clenched his fingers in anger with himself. *No one else is scared of cows.* Stumbling over a stone in the damp grass, he and Rhys finally reached the gate to the next field.

'Cows.' Rhys sniggered as he pulled the lever to let them through into the next field. 'You better be careful of the rabbits hiding beneath bushes.' He turned and jerked his palms out towards Gordon. 'Boo! They might jump at you.' He tittered again.

Gordon followed Rhys through the squelching mud. Brambles pulled at the sleeve of his jacket as they walked along the edge of the field. They passed a small barn type structure with splintering worn-out timber. Just beyond the old building, a woman dressed in waterproofs and with a blonde, frizzy ponytail dribbled a sack of pellets of some sort along a feeder. Gordon stopped. Of course. She was the shepherdess. The one livid with him for nearly driving into one of her sheep. Several fat, filthy ewes pushed between her arms and the trough as she poured.

'Jenna,' Rhys said, 'I got an apprentice for you.' He beckoned Gordon over.

As he stepped closer, the odour of animal dung rose from the sheep.

The woman stood and turned. She had a rosy complexion and wide eyes. Gordon surveyed her baggy jeans and oversized waterproof jacket, both of which were streaked with mud.

Recognition deepened in her eyes. 'Him?'

Rhys shrugged.

'I've already got four of the college students working with me.' She turned back towards the sheep.

'Alan's idea he comes to work here for a bit.' Rhys said.

Jenna turned again then looked Gordon up and down. Her eyes rested on the pristine boots with a ridge of mud around the toes. 'What for?'

Gordon swallowed back his awkwardness and forced a smile. 'I think you and I need to start again. I mean, draw a line under the other day.' He held his hand out towards her. 'I'm Gordon.'

She glared at his hand, then held up gloved palms. 'What do you want me to do? Take these gloves off?'

Whad d'ya. Not 'what do you.' His eyebrows pinched. Not Canadian. American maybe. 'You're the shepherdess, I gather. Where are you from originally?'

She narrowed her eyes. 'New York.'

He laughed. Another joker, like Rhys. He'd have to get used to this North Welsh banter.

'What's so funny?' she asked.

'A New Yorker? Shepherding sheep? Okay.'

Jenna looked at Rhys. 'Great. Another ignorant Brit who thinks New York is fifty-five thousand square miles of skyscrapers.' She turned to Gordon. 'Never heard of upstate New York?'

Gordon stiffened. Of course he knew about upstate New York. Although not much. He remembered reading the government office was upstate, nearer Canada. Government… he breathed in… didn't she know he was the chancellor…. No, stop it, get on with hoping to charm her. It would keep Alan on his side. 'Upstate New York is where the capital is, right?' he asked.

She gazed at him. 'I'm almost impressed.'

He stood taller and smiled. 'Buffalo.'

'Albany.'

'What?'

'Albany is the state capital. Anyway, I was brought up

on a sheep farm. Believe it or not, we've got some of those over there.' She smirked at him and raised an eyebrow.

Oh Christ, just like his brother, Mark. That stupid affectation of raising one eyebrow. Still, if his sheep plan depended on getting along with this Jenna, he'd do his best. He slipped his hands into his pockets and gave her an apologetic smile. 'Are you willing to teach this ignorant Brit about sheep?'

She looked at Rhys.

'Alan wants him to learn how to handle y defaid so he can bring them to London.'

Jenna's eyes widened. 'London?' She shook her head. 'That's not gonna happen. Alan wouldn't—'

'No,' Gordon said. 'I was just about to say that. It won't *actually* happen.'

Rhys hooted a laugh. 'Oh yes, it will. It's a secret plan,' Rhys said, his eyes gleaming. 'Alan's way of stopping them villagers gossiping about how his sheep can't follow directions for a show. You can go ask him if you don't believe me.'

'He's joking,' Gordon said. 'There's no secret plan. But Alan does want you to help me.'

Jenna stared at the ground, then shrugged. When she looked up again, Gordon repositioned his lips to what he hoped was a trusting smile.

'Wipe that stupid grin off your face,' she said, 'and follow me.'

Chapter Six

Gordon marched behind Jenna as she strode up the hill. Her hands were shoved into the pockets of her puffy anorak, her hay-coloured ponytail growing wider and frizzier as misty grey drizzle turned to fat, cold raindrops.

'Hang on,' Gordon shouted. The mud sucked at the heels of his formerly pristine boots as he attempted to keep up. Twig branches from overgrown evergreens along the side of the path tugged at his jacket.

She quickened her pace. 'Walk faster,' she said, turning over her shoulder. 'It's not like I have all day, you know.' She opened the gate in front of her in a smooth motion, then strode through it, letting it bang shut before Gordon approached.

'Moooooo,' Rhys said, then laughed.

Gordon froze. 'Are there cows in the next field?'

Rhys shook his head and smiled. 'No. There are no cows, you twyllo, but if you keep on about them, I'll make sure there's one in your bedroom when we get back.'

They stopped when they reached the wooden turnstile. A thorny bramble grabbed his jacket shoulder as he reached forward to put his hand on the metal lever. 'Which way do I pull this thing?' He reached out, pulled the lever and trapped the heel of his hand between the metal and the wood. 'Oww, shit,' he said, letting go of the lever.

Rhys chuckled. 'Okay, watch me.' He glided the lever into the metal catch and pushed open the gate. With an outstretch of his arm, he stepped back and bowed. 'After you, sir.'

Jenna stood further up the field, hands on hips. 'Come on, I have other stuff to do around here.'

As Gordon stepped through the gate, the thorny bramble tore a piece from his jacket. 'Oh shit,' he muttered.

'What are you doing wearing a smart London jacket up on a sheep farm?' Rhys said. 'You need to get yourself a thick waterproof.'

Gordon stepped past the brambles into the open space, then stopped, his breath halting. Before him stood a tableau of woolly animals grazing in an emerald field. There were about a hundred sheep, maybe more. The back-drop of halo-white mountains reminded him of a painting he'd seen in the window of a fine art gallery in London. Except this was real. For a moment, the scene of the peacefully grazing sheep against the background of hills and mountains swayed his body with awe. 'This is just beautiful' he said.

He looked at Jenna and she half smiled. A small gleam teased in her eyes before she turned away.

'Keep walking,' Jenna said. 'This is the tupping field. I'm taking you into the next one.'

He looked around at the grazing sheep. Most had a splash of marking near their hind legs, like some farmer went mad with a wide paintbrush. 'What are the coloured markings for?'

'So we know which rams have impregnated which ewes.'

Gordon laughed. 'Is it like speed dating? You chuck them all in a field together and they choose their partners?'

Rhys stopped walking. 'Look around. How many rams do you see?'

Gordon glanced around the field. 'I don't know what I'm looking at.'

'The ones with the black harnesses. They're the rams.'

Gordon stood surveying the animals. 'I can only see one.'

'There are five.'

'How many female sheep?'

'Ewes. About two hundred.'

'Bloody hell.' Gordon continued surveying the sheep. 'Old Red Ram's been a busy boy. Looks like he got most of them.'

'Oh my God,' Jenna called out, 'Will you guys hurry

up? I've got dagging to do.'

'Dagging?' Gordon turned to Rhys.

Rhys grinned. 'You don't want to know. And don't ask or she'll get you doing it.'

They climbed, boot soles crunching into stones, then squelching into moss. As they approached the next gate, Gordon edged himself away from the towering nettles to his side.

Jenna pushed the lever and flung open the gate.

Gordon stepped through and looked around at the wide sweeping field by a forest of evergreen. Dozens more woolly sheep grazed, except these animals had no paint marks. 'Is this all they do? Stand around and eat all day?'

'Whaddya think they do?' Jenna said.

'He's upset,' Rhys said to Jenna, 'that these ones don't get a shag.'

'Whatever,' Jenna said. 'Rhys, come talk to me for a second.'

Gordon watched as they strode towards the gate. Jenna leaned towards Rhys and laughed, then they shook hands.

Jenna put her hand on the gate and shouted out, 'I'll be back in about two hours.'

'Wait. What do I do?' Gordon said.

Jenna shrugged. 'Get to know the sheep.'

'What?'

'Observe. Learn what's normal about them. This way, if they do anything different one day, you'll know something's up.'

'Why can't you stay?'

'I told you,' she said over her shoulder as she slipped through the turnstile, avoiding the six-foot nettles near her face. 'I have things to do. Lambs to weigh. Sheep heads to get out of fences.'

'What?'

'You'll learn. They get up to all kinds of mischief.' She smiled as she closed the gate behind her. The dimples from her smile made her look … pretty.

Gordon looked around at the sheep munching on grass. Surely, this isn't what Alan meant.

Gordon turned towards Rhys. 'Are you going to help me?'

'Jenna said you're to observe them, get a little acquainted with the fluffy ladies. I'll leave you to it, but don't get up to any mischief, if you know what I mean.' Rhys winked.

'So you're not going to help at all?'

'You're fine. They just need to trust you. Feel comfortable around you.'

'By me just standing here?' Gordon's shoulders stiffened.

Rhys smiled. 'Okay, I will help you, Mr Gordon Slee.' He leant in towards Gordon. 'I'll tell you the shepherd's secret.'

Gordon stared at the muddy grass. 'What's that then?'

'Sing to them.'

'Don't be daft.'

'I'm telling you the secret. I promise you it works, makes them feel good around you.'

Gordon glanced up at Rhy's earnest face. Perhaps if he could prove to Alan that he had a bit of a shepherd in him, it might help these negotiations go more quickly.

Gordon studied him.

Rhys' eyes grew dark and serious.

Hell, Gordon thought. This guy lived all his life on a sheep farm and, as he said, Gordon knew absolutely nothing about sheep. Or defaid as Rhys referred to them.

'I like singing Pink Floyd to them,' Rhys said as he watched the grazing animals. 'They have a song called *Sheep*. Try singing it to them.'

'I don't know that song.'

'You know Baa Baa Black Sheep?'

'Come on Rhys. You're not suggesting I sing that.'

Rhys smiled. 'Unless you know any others?'

Chapter Seven

Gordon sat in the field on his own, his arse dampening from the wet ground. He hummed the tune of Baa Baa Black Sheep. The bastard sheep barely moved, not even a glance at him.

He picked at the grass, scrunching cold wet blades between his fingers while singing under his breath. 'Baa baa black sheep, have you any wool?'

A ewe baa-d.

Then baa-d again.

Jesus, he was getting somewhere.

He sang louder, 'Yes sir, yes sir, three bags full.'

Another baa, this time from the other side of the field.

Gordon belted out the next line in a deep baritone. 'One for the master, one for the–'

'What the hell are you doing?' Jenna's voice came up behind him.

He turned.

Her brows furrowed in confusion.

'Rhys told me to sing Baa Baa Black Sheep to them.'

She stared at him, then tilted her head back and laughed. A loud, bubbly laugh.

Heat rose in his face.

She wiped a tear from her eye. 'I'm sorry. You have to learn that Rhys is a bit of a joker.'

He exhaled heavily, then bit back a smile. The bastard. But, he was a clever one.

'Hey,' Jenna said. 'I brought you this. It might come in handy.' She held out a cane. A bloody long cane.

'Have you got an eight-foot man living on the farm, too?'

She wrinkled her nose at him.

'I'm only joking. It's a shepherd's staff, right? But you don't actually use those things, do you?'

She took a deep breath. 'It's called a crook and yes, we really use these.'

'You can't blame me for asking. Between you and Rhys, you seem to be having a bit of fun with me.'

She gave him a small grin, then held out the crook to the side. 'It's used sometimes if a sheep is in danger, you know, to pull them back, hook them around the neck. But most of the time, it's just used to make yourself look bigger. Like this….' She stood arms wide, the crook an extension of her right arm.

'You're not playing with me like Rhys did?'

'No. Here, have a go. Herd a few of them up.'

'How?'

'Walk to the side of them slowly.'

Gordon stood, wiping the mud off the back of his jeans. He took the crook and made a few steps towards the sheep. The animals sprinted a few feet away from him.

'Slowly, you don't want them to run. Get them to that corner over there,' Jenna said, pointing towards the far side of the field. 'Let's see how you go.'

He turned towards her. 'I don't know what I'm doing.'

'It's okay. Just step towards them, arms wide. But approach them gently from the side, not from the back, otherwise they'll run.'

He stepped towards them, holding his arms out, the crook in one hand. Stupid sheep. Can't they see one arm is normal sized, and the other is like a Stretch Armstrong toy? The sheep edged away a few feet, moving as one giant woollen entity.

'That's it,' Jenna said. 'Just keep moving around them until they walk in the direction you want them to.'

They gently trotted as Gordon moved in closer, then around them.

'Slowly. Calmly,' Jenna said. 'You've got it.'

He kept moving towards and around them, guiding the woolly animals nearer the edge of the field, alongside the hedges. They gently trotted as one group towards the corner Gordon had determined. A light wave of something peculiar, something alien, took over his body. Not quite happiness, something more pure. Mixed with a wave of something else.

Pride.

'They're responding,' Gordon called out to Jenna.

'Well, isn't that a thing?' Jenna said, then smiled.

Encouraged, he moved the sheep into a huddle in the corner. Puffing out his chest, he held the crook upright, then pushed its base into the ground.

Jenna strode towards him and grinned. 'You could be a natural.'

'You think so?' His body grew taller.

She pursed her lips. 'Well, strangely enough, yes. I'd say you've definitely got some potential.' She glanced down at the base of the crook, stuck half an inch in the mud and wrinkled her nose. 'But don't do that. Now you'll need to clean it.'

He pulled up the crook. 'Is that it? I've learned how to do it?'

'It's a start. Tiny start.' She turned and nodded towards the opposite end of the field where a lone sheep stood butting its head against the fence.

'Why's it doing that?'

'That's Molly. She's stubborn.'

Gordon held out the crook and strode across the grass. When he reached the butting sheep, he walked to the side of the animal to edge it away from the fence.

It trotted sideways and butted its head again against a further part of the fence.

Jenna walked over to him, laughing. 'It's okay. This one is a bit of a rascal.' She grabbed the sheep from behind and pulled it back. 'Go on,' she said to the ewe, pushing into its side with both hands. 'Go join your friends.'

Gordon watched as the ewe trotted off towards the others.

Jenna eyed him with a teasing grin. 'So, London city shepherd. I think that will do for a herding introduction.' She turned and jaunted towards the gate.

A white fluffy head on a skinny male body came whistling up the path as Jenna pulled the gate closed behind them.

Jenna giggled as he neared. 'Hey Rhys,' she said. 'You got our London guy singing Baa Baa Black Sheep in the fields.'

Rhys bent over, cackling. 'I told you. You owe me a tenner, Jenna.'

She grinned, then shook her head. 'Wrong song,' she said as she walked past Rhys and down the hill.

Gordon looked at Rhys, 'She put you up to it?'

'What? No one puts me up to anything. I said I'd get you to sing 'And Dream of Sheep' by Kate Bush. Until I decided Baa Baa Black Sheep was funnier.' He chuckled.

'It's not funny, Rhys.'

Rhys continued to laugh.

'Okay, maybe it was, a little bit,' Gordon said. They strode down the hill following Jenna. 'So,' Gordon said to Rhys, 'It's all bullshit that they know the word sheep?'

Rhys cackled. 'If you ever listened to Pink Floyd music, you'd know the word sheep doesn't even come up in those lyrics. You see, if you knew about music, you would have caught the trick. Music is an education.'

'I know about music. I used to play the guitar.'

Rhys stopped and eyed Gordon in wonder. 'What sort of music?'

Gordon shrugged. He couldn't admit to the crap of his own songwriting attempts when, in his teens, he daydreamed daily that he was part of a famous pop group. The song lyrics in his head were phenomenal. The problem only happened when he put the words to paper, then strummed the tune on his guitar. All the magic created in his head got lost by the time it got to his fingers.

'Music,' Rhys said in a sombre tone as they walked, 'is interlinked with everything. Like, it controls the universe. Even flowers make a sound as they open their petals. Only other flowers can hear it. That's their music.'

'That's very poetic, Rhys.'

'Of course it is. I write haikus.'

'Do you? That's impressive.'

'I'll show you some later. Or maybe,' he smiled. 'I'll wait until you're worthy of hearing them.'

Gordon laughed. 'I'll look forward to it.'

Ahead, Jenna stopped and turned towards them both. 'Hey Gordon? You know I didn't want you, but I think we can actually make something of you.' She smiled before turning back to walk down the hill.

Gordon's heart stilled. He stopped walking.

'Come on,' Rhys said. 'Time for a brew.'

Gordon held his breath, attempting to push down the pain growing in his chest.

'Are you okay?' Rhys asked.

Gordon breathed out heavily. 'Yes, I'm fine.'

The pain in his chest threatened to reach his throat and he began walking again briskly, leaving Rhys behind. Jenna's words. They were only words. Plus, she was joking. Wasn't she? Unlike that time he first heard that awful thing said about him.

His throat squeezed tight and he swallowed. Face it. Jenna wasn't actually joking. Even if she only half meant it, the words were there. He wasn't wanted. His breath quickened… he had to get out of here.

He turned back towards Rhys. 'I might head back to London tonight. Start negotiations tomorrow.' Christ, where would he stay? Maybe Charlotte would put him up? No, he couldn't tell his family he'd sublet his flat because he'd got himself involved in some crazy sheep scheme.

'Hey, is this because I was winding you up?' Rhys pranced down the hill to catch up with him. 'Look. I'll tell you something that will help you out for real with those animals. If you play the right music, you can get them defaid to dance.'

'Very funny, Rhys.' His heart pounded in his chest.

'This one isn't a joke. Think about it. Ever see them

dancing dogs on shows like Britain's Got Talent? I keep telling you. Sheep aren't all that different from dogs.'

'Right.' Gordon shoved his hands into his pockets. Breathe, it doesn't matter. It's a stupid, pointless memory. He looked down the path towards Alan's cottage.

'These sheep here, they're what I call high achievers.'

'Okay, enough Rhys.' He waved as he walked on.

'When are you going to start listening to me?' Rhys called out as Gordon trudged down the path.

Chapter Eight

He breathed in the air as his boots crunched along the gravel towards Alan's stone cottage. Gazing towards the scenery behind Alan's home, small blobs of white sheep stood grazing on a hill. The peaceful sight couldn't calm the thudding in his chest. Jenna's unexpected words had dug into a memory he'd long buried beneath the deep terrain of passing years. How could four small words wrench it up to the surface? *I didn't want you…* He swallowed to push the memory down. The memory pushed back.

The one from thirty-four years ago. The day he found out the truth about his existence.

How he was never meant to have one.

Eight years old. Aunt Sarah had come to visit and Gordon's mother had shooed the three of them, him and his two older siblings, up the stairs. Gordon's grandfather was there too.

Gordon was certain Granddad would want to play with him instead of talking with his mother and his aunt. 'Where are the water guns Granddad gave us last time he came here?' he asked his sister, who sat rummaging through their mother's nail varnish drawer.

'Mum hid them,' Charlotte said.

'Where?' Gordon nagged. 'Let's ask Granddad to play in the garden with us and the water guns.'

'I don't know where they are,' Charlotte said, pulling out a beige bottle and testing the liquid on her fingernail.

His brother, Mark, strode towards their parent's wardrobe and slid open the door. 'Up here,' he said, reaching towards a shelf. He pulled three plastic guns down and dropped them on the bed. 'I know where everything is. Even Dad's Playboy magazines.'

'You're gross!' said Charlotte.

'I've got an idea,' Mark said. 'You should both sneak up on Mum and Aunt Sarah. I'll fill up the water guns in the bathroom first.'

Gordon grinned. 'And squirt them while they're sitting in the kitchen.'

'I'm not doing it, but I'll watch,' Charlotte said.

The three of them crept down the stairs, Gordon carrying the filled water gun. They tip-toed through the sitting room and into the dining room, stopping just outside the doorway to the kitchen. They stood for a moment grinning at each other while Mark raised a finger to his lips.

Aunt Sarah's voice travelled through the open door. 'Mary, I'm no spring chicken. Thirty-four years old and I still want to have a baby. Although, I shouldn't worry, right? I mean, look how fertile you were in your thirties. You didn't even want a third child, and it happened anyway.'

Gordon's grip on the plastic gun loosened as a strange, watery feeling churned through his stomach.

Aunt Sarah chuckled. 'What woman wants another baby with a two-month-old in their arms?'

A huge invisible ball slammed into Gordon's chest.

Numb, he counted out the months on his fingers. He was born the end of November. Charlotte, on the New Year's Eve the year before. That made Charlotte eleven months older. Babies grew inside their mothers for nine months. That's what Mark had said when he told Gordon what parents had to do to make babies.

'I didn't want another baby. But it was too late for me to do anything but have him,' Gordon's mother said. 'By the time I found out, I was too far gone. I'd put the extra weight and lack of periods down to having Charlotte.'

Charlotte looked at Gordon. 'I bet you don't even know what periods are,' she whispered.

'Shut up, Charlotte,' Mark said. 'This is serious.' He looked at Gordon with sad eyes. 'Mum's saying they never wanted you. You weren't ever supposed to be here.'

The water gun dropped from Gordon's hand with a

clatter.

'What was that?' his mother said as Gordon rushed through the dining room and into the sitting room. Panting with shock, he squashed himself behind the sofa. Pulling his knees as close as possible to his chest, he couldn't get one of his feet in behind the sofa with him.

'Gordon?' His mother called out.

He held himself rigid.

'Gordon,' she said, gently kicking the sole of his trainer. Her voice moved close to the sofa back. 'Whatever you think you've heard, you heard it wrong.'

'We all heard it.' Gordon said through sobs.

'No, you didn't,' his mother said, her voice stern. 'You and Charlotte and Mark have no idea what you heard, so don't you make up stories in your head.'

Gordon pressed his fist to his mouth.

'Gordon,' she said again, then sighed. A moment later, her footsteps echoed from the room.

He heard it.

The three of them heard it.

He squeezed out from behind the sofa and rushed upstairs to his bedroom.

'Let's go up to the High Street,' Granddad said when he found Gordon sniffling on the end of his bed with his Action Man toy in his lap.

They walked to the High Street in silence until Gordon said, 'Mum said to Aunt Sarah—'

'Shhh, I heard them. I was in the kitchen too.'

'But Granddad—'

'We'll talk once we have our milkshakes.'

Gordon sat at a table sipping the strawberry drink, the tightness in his throat making it hard for the frozen cream to slip down.

Granddad leant forward over the table. 'Gordon, there are no accidents. Everyone has a reason why they exist.'

His breath fluttered as hope rose in his small chest. 'What's my reason?'

'You'll figure it out.'

'No, Granddad, tell me. How do I find the reason?'

'It will find you.'

This stupid, pointless childhood memory. If he allowed it to rise, it had this unstoppable power to halt his breath, make him want to run away, hide in a tight space behind a sofa. He forced a hurt smile as he carried on walking towards Alan's cottage. As his footsteps crunched along the path, he conjured up a joke for himself that if he turned around and went back to Rhys' place, he'd at least have a choice of sofas to hide behind. His silent attempts at self-deprecation left a hollowness in his chest.

Alan's cottage was just ahead and he stopped walking. He pulled his phone from his pocket and dialled Charlotte's number.

'You're right,' he said. 'It still bothers me.'

'What does?'

'The stuff about Mum not wanting me.'

Charlotte gasped. 'Where are you? Come over. I'd come to you, but the boys will be home from school shortly...'

'I'm not in London right now, but I wanted to ask, can I stay with you for a few days?'

'Stay?' she hesitated. 'Oh, right…umm…poor you. It must be horrid going home to that empty flat with Stacey gone.'

He hadn't told her about the sublet, how he currently wasn't living there. Coming to stay would inconvenience his sister, upset her careful family routine. Maybe Tej would put him up.

'No, forget it,' he said. 'I shouldn't have asked.'

'Gordon, if you need to, of course you can stay. You're upset.' She sighed. 'I do feel guilty sometimes.'

'About what?'

'When we were kids… Mark used to play that stupid song over and over again on his stereo, *Gordon is a Moron.*

You were so sensitive, yet I still let Mark convince me to tease you as well sometimes. Like when I used to sing that other song to you.'

Gordon laughed softly. 'You mean the Mary had a Little Lamb song?' Charlotte's childhood voice drifted back to him, "*Gordon had a little plan, but his dreams were just for show…*"

'I knew it,' said Charlotte. 'It hurt you.'

'You're wrong,' Gordon said. 'That never bothered me. I knew Mark put you up to it. Look, don't worry about this stuff, I'll text you later.'

'I am worried… about you,' she said. 'You phoned to tell me you were upset about the past and now you're trying to brush it off.' She sighed. 'I go into denial too about our childhood.'

'What do you mean? Yours was idyllic.'

'Do you honestly believe that?' said Charlotte. 'Look, all us kids felt it. Mum was a force to be reckoned with. She wanted to get back to her law firm job when we were all still young. Practically toddlers.'

Gordon gazed at the soft hills beyond Alan's cottage. 'I was a baby.'

'You were. But don't think it was that much easier for me. Or Mark, I imagine.' She was silent for a moment. 'You don't know what it was like to be the daughter who was supposed to emulate her. The way she went nuts if I didn't get top grades at school because I was supposed to grow up to be a top-notch lawyer.'

'Instead you married one,' Gordon said.

'Oh my God, and how angry she was with me when I was content working as a paralegal and then committed the ultimate crime of giving up that job when the twins were born.'

'Well, at least you weren't unwanted.'

Charlotte was silent.

'I always felt it. Well, not always.' He swallowed. 'Did I seem different to you when I was really young, like at age five or six?'

'I'm not sure.'

'I seem to remember I felt different then. Bolder somehow. Trusting that the world was full of hope.' He rubbed the back of his neck. 'It was probably good though that I learned the truth by the time I was eight. Otherwise, it would have been too confusing for me as the years went on.'

'What would have been confusing?' asked Charlotte.

His exhaled slowly. 'Despite Mum's job, she still seemed to have time for you and Mark when she was at home. I was always the nuisance.'

'That's not true.'

'It is.' A sheep bleated nearby and Gordon covered the bottom of his phone.

Charlotte's voice broke. 'I should have been kinder to you growing up. I knew you had all these insecurities, and I still let Mark goad me into teasing you. We made it worse.'

'It's not your fault,' Gordon said. 'We were all just kids.'

She sighed. 'Did you hate me growing up?'

Gordon looked down at the stones on the path. 'No. I didn't hate you. You were kind.... sometimes.'

'Was I?'

'Yes,' Gordon said. 'Remember when Mum asked me if my science paper was marked and I lied? Year five. I said I hadn't had it back yet? She asked for my schoolbag and I felt my face go bright red. You stood from the table and shouted "I'll get it!" I was furious with you.'

Charlotte chuckled.

Gordon continued, 'When you came back into the room with my schoolbag and Mum opened it, I sat glaring at you, waiting for Mum to punish me not only for failing the paper but for lying about getting it back. But there was no paper in there.'

'Yes,' Charlotte said. 'I didn't want you to get in

trouble.'

'I never said thank you.'

'Okay, stop it. Or you'll make me go all tearful. Text me later, like you said.'

When he reached Alan's cottage, he found the older farmer outside, repairing a panel to one of the paddocks. Gordon inhaled sharply. The warming conversation with his sister couldn't erase this current predicament. Imposing himself on a place where he wasn't truly wanted.

'Alan, I'm going to head off to London tonight. I'd like to arrange a meeting with the hotel group and start negotiations. The only thing you'll need to do is get me a brief letter from your solicitor stating your intention to run the sheep. A quick email maybe.'

'No.'

'I'm sorry?'

'You said you would spend time in Wales, learn how to handle the sheep in case you need to take them to London.'

Gordon's heart quickened. 'This way could be easier.'

'Easier for who? You? What is it again you actually want out of this?'

Gordon breathed in, then exhaled slowly. 'To do the right thing by you.'

'That's all? You barely know me.'

'Okay, I admit it. The hotel might give me a fee for brokering the deal.' He swallowed back the lie. 'But that's not going to affect how much they give you. You have my word.'

Alan sighed. 'Look. I'd like you to stay. I need you here.'

'For what?'

'Help with the farm. I've not been all that well recently and the truth is, I was looking forward to having you here. Just for a little while, until I can get around to hiring another set of hands.' He sighed. 'I'm having to admit to myself that I'm not getting any younger, am I?' He grimaced. 'I know I'm not paying you right now, but will that fee for brokering this deal make up for it?'

Gordon pressed his lips together and nodded. 'If you truly want me here, sir.'

Alan held out his hand for Gordon to shake. 'I want you.'

A warmth tingled through Gordon's limbs. He shook Alan's hand, then headed back towards Rhys cottage. Pulling the phone from his pocket, he sent Charlotte a text.

Silly pity party over. Gordon has a little plan and he still has far to go. :-) x

Chapter Nine

Jenna stood facing him, the back half of a sheep between her legs. Rhys crouched behind the sheep, stroking its head, attempting to hold it still while slipping its face through a metal brace attached to the fence.

'Hang on,' Rhys said. 'Let me fasten the hurdle.' Tying a rope, he secured the brace, then leant forward and crooned a Black Sabbath tune to the sheep.

'He really does sing to them?' Gordon asked, his eyes widening.

'Only during dagging. It calms them.'

She switched on the clippers and bent over the back of the animal, shaving the fur around its bottom, making almost a horseshoe shape against its skin. Tufts of wool with dangling turds dropped to the ground. The smell of sheep dung mixed with something like faint petrol and a million wet dogs rose from the ground where the turd wool dropped.

'Why are you doing this?' Gordon asked.

'Keeps the flies off them,' said Jenna.

'You're very considerate towards these sheep, aren't you?'

She glanced up at Gordon and shrugged. 'The alternative is they get maggots eating away at their skin.'

His stomach lurched, and he stepped back. 'Why do they smell like that? I mean, I expected the manure smell, but there's something else.'

'Trace of lanolin maybe,' Jenna said. 'It's secreted from their skin. Sort of waxy, It's what keeps their coats dry in the rain or snow. Although you can smell it more when we shear them.' She pushed the damp hair from her face as she bent again. 'People pay good money for pure lanolin. Useful for things like leather shoes and boots.' She stood, taking a step forward, releasing the back of the sheep. 'Next.'

'Hang on,' Rhys said, untying the brace rope. 'Let me

get its head out of here first.'

Gordon moved closer. 'Want me to help?'

Jenna smiled. 'Not yet. The sheep don't trust you yet.'

He looked at the ground. 'So, is that how you make money from them?' he asked. 'Selling lanolin?'

Jenna furrowed her brows at him. 'We sell the sheep's wool. Look, if you want to do something useful, have a walk around the fields. Tell me if you see any sheep getting up to mischief. Let me know if any have escaped, are on the other side of the fences, near the roads.'

'Or if any of them have their heads stuck in gaps,' Rhys said as he guided another sheep's face along the top of the brace. 'These defaid stick their noses everywhere they can.'

'Right.' Gordon sighed. 'And then I'll unstick their heads and chase them back into the fields?'

'No!' Jenna and Rhys shouted in unison.

Jenna moved her legs so she could straddle the next animal Rhys had braced. 'The sheep don't know you, Gordon,' Jenna said a little more quietly.

This would be a long few days, standing around watching Jenna and Rhys work. 'Maybe I can help with shearing them,' Gordon said. 'I mean, if one of you teaches me?'

Rhys hooted with laughter. 'In November? You'll have them freezing their little tails off. That's a summer job. Not that Jenna would let you try it, anyway.'

Gordon flushed with embarrassment. How was he supposed to know a sheep farm calendar?

'Crazy Londoners,' Rhys muttered.

Gordon shoved his hands in his pockets, then trudged towards the fields as grey mists of rain whispered in the air. Fine. He'd walk around for the rest of the afternoon, keep out of Jenna's and Rhys's way. Alan might need him, but it was clear his existence was useless right now to Rhys and Jenna.

'Gordon,' Jenna called out.

He turned.

'Thank you. I know it doesn't seem like it, but you roaming the fields and checking they're all okay is more helpful than you think.'

Early the next morning, Rhys blasted the same Creedence Clearwater Revival song from the sitting room over and over again. The lead vocalist screeched out the tune of '*Have You Ever Seen the Rain*' as huffing winds and seething rain lashed against Gordon's bedroom window. He pushed off the duvet with the scratchy cover and looked at his phone.

Six am.

He sat up. His lower back and shoulders ached from carrying hay in the drizzly rain yesterday afternoon. Nearly two hours of lifting and dragging, then carrying the huge bales over muddy puddles. Still, he remembered Alan's words to him, how he was needed, and in order to get the job done, he imagined himself as an Olympic athlete pushing through the pain and training for gold.

Afterwards, in one of the fields, he'd felt a pride stirring as his subtle shepherding skills improved. With measured steps and his crook held wide, he got twenty-odd sheep to move into an adjacent field. Apart from Molly. Once again she took to butting her head against the fence in protest. Gordon tried Jenna's trick of pulling her back, but when he grabbed her back flanks, the stubborn bitch kicked him in the thigh, causing a shock of pain to run through his groin right up towards his chest. He abandoned her and found Rhys, who of course cackled and had great pleasure in telling him half an hour later that Molly had 'danced' for him into the next field 'as graceful as a ballerina.'

Alan had stood in front of the hedgerow in the misty drizzle as Gordon strode to the next field and moved another twenty sheep. Thankfully, this herd didn't include Molly. Alan gave a slow clap when Gordon closed the gate on the adjoining field with the sheep on the other side, munching on the newer grass.

Gordon strode towards Alan. 'So tell me, what's the point of all this sheep moving? One field seems as good as the other. Is it just to get me used to the sheep? Or them to me?'

Alan looked at him with thoughtful grey eyes. 'That and the fact it needs doing. You've got to lead them on over to the good grass. They'd end up going hungry if you just kept them on the same field. It's a year-round job, moving them to the next area.'

A strange feeling of pride flushed through Gordon. Alan's confirmation that he had actually done something useful with these sheep. He stood taller. In his mind, he saw Gordon, the Chancellor of the Exchequer, slamming his briefcase shut and marching out of the office for the last time. In the next imagined scene, Gordon stood in an arena with a dozen sheep around him and a dog, bowing to a standing ovation from the crowd for winning this year's national sheep trials.

'You've ripped your jacket,' Alan said, gazing at the shoulder of Gordon's anorak.

Gordon shrugged. 'Doesn't matter. It's old.'

'It will matter when this drizzle decides to start pissing down, which it's due to this week. I'm sure Rhys can lend you something else.'

The next morning, rain pelted against the bedroom window as the music from downstairs banged out louder. Gordon pushed himself up from the saggy mattress.

Rhys's footsteps pounded up the stairs while the lead vocalist howled out the chorus again.

'Yes, I can see the bloody rain,' Gordon called out. 'More than I need to see in a lifetime.'

Cackling bellowed outside on the landing. The bedroom door swung open. 'Brought you a panad,' Rhys said, plonking the mug of tea on the floor next to the bed.

'That's so kind of you,' Gordon said.

Rhys grinned. 'Don't get used to being waited on. It's

just that I need to ask a favour today.'

'Oh… no milk?' Gordon asked as he lifted the mug from the floor.

'I can put some brandy in it if you like. That's how I have mine.' Rhys took a gulp from his own mug. 'I don't drink milk. Not fair on the calves. I don't share my brandy with them, so why should I take their milk?'

Gordon took a sip of his tea and winced. 'It's fine. What's the favour, dare I ask?'

'Jenna. It's the anniversary of Dylan's death. Two years. I want to get her some flowers. You know she's a widow, right?'

'No. I'm sorry. I didn't know that.'

Rhys shrugged. 'Just telling you, as I thought you might want to take a little interest in the people you're working for.'

Gordon stared into his mug of dark tea, then placed it back on the dusty floor. 'How old was her husband?'

'Young. Not even forty,' Rhys said. 'Dylan was my cousin. Died of cancer.'

'I'm sorry. Really, I am. What's the favour you're after from me?'

Rhys sighed. 'My car's not working. Tom, who sometimes works at the post office, is coming around to have a look but he can't get over until after five pm and the florist closes—'

'I'll drive you there.'

'Okay, but not till late morning. You've got more hale bales to carry and troughs to fill and heads in fences to check and —'

'I know, I know, sheep in roads to search for. I'm getting up.' He said, pulling the duvet back. He grabbed a stiff towel from the floor and made his way towards the shower.

'Here,' Rhys said, standing in front of the stairway banister still overhung with laundry. His hand reached under the rumpled shirts and pulled out a pair of waterproof trousers. Shirts tumbled over the banister and soared down the stairs. 'A present for you,' Rhys said, tossing him the thin polyester trousers.

Gordon bent and caught the rain trousers. He held them up. 'There's a huge rip down the side.'

'You prefer to get the whole of the legs of your jeans wet then?' Rhys shrugged. 'Suit yourself.'

'No, you're right. Thanks, Rhys.'

'Just for the farm. Not when we go into town. You'll look a right twmffat.' Rhys sauntered down the stairs, bending to pick up the fallen shirts and throwing them back up over the banister.

'Oh, and Alan said you might have a spare jacket for me. My other one is ripped.'

Rhys furrowed his brows. 'No time to look for that now. I'll sort it later. At least your jacket rip will match your rain trousers and you can pretend you're in a suit.'

At around 10.30 am, Gordon stood in the florist shop. Scents of carnations, roses and whatever you call the other flowers filled the room. The rain outside had slowed to a thick drizzle.

'How's your brother?' The woman shopkeeper said to Rhys. She looked about mid-thirties, and had an infectious grin. 'I never see him.'

Rhys leant his elbows on the counter, smiling while shaking his head. 'You know he won't come in here. You or one of your customers will bring it up again.' He turned to look over his shoulder, out towards the street.

'What?' the woman said. 'You mean nineteen-ninety-six? Everyone's forgotten about that.'

Rhys chortled. 'No, they haven't.' He glanced over his shoulder again.

'True,' the shopkeeper said. 'My mam still talks about it. Says your brother's never had the nerve to enter his sheep into another trial. That true?'

Gordon looked at his watch. 'Can we get a move on?

Alan's expecting me to move about fifty sheep into the next field.'

'Ah, you've plenty of time,' Rhys said. He turned back to the shopkeeper. 'How's that sister of yours?'

'She and her wife moved way down south to Brighton. She'd been talking about it for years.'

'Rhys,' Gordon interrupted. 'I told Alan I'd have the sheep moved before lunch.'

Rhys chuckled to the shopkeeper. 'He'll be lucky to get them defaid where they need to be by bedtime.' He grinned. 'Londoner.'

'Hey,' Gordon said. 'I moved about forty sheep yesterday.'

The shopkeeper raised her eyebrows and looked at Rhys. They both burst out laughing. 'That many?' The woman said.

Gordon looked at his watch again. 'Rhys, can you hurry with the flowers?'

Rhys' eyes narrowed as he gazed past Gordon's shoulder. 'Ah, wait. My mate's over there. You choose the flowers, Gordon.'

Rhys skipped towards the door and called back, 'Oh, and pay for me? I forgot my wallet. I'll pay you when we get back.'

Gordon stood open-mouthed.

'I'm good for it,' Rhys said.

Gordon stared after him as Rhys jaunted across the road. A young lad with a hoody pulled up over his head stood waiting with his hands in his pockets.

'I've got some nice cream roses just in,' the shopkeeper said.

Gordon turned and looked at her. 'I don't know anything about flowers, but could you please make something beautiful? It's marking the anniversary of a death.'

'Of course. The roses will look nice with some of these blue hydrangeas.'

He nodded, then glanced back at Rhys and the hoody lad. Rhys was taking a wad of cash from his front pocket.

Bastard.

'I can add some trailing eucalyptus.'

Gordon pressed his lips together and turned towards the shopkeeper. 'Whatever you think.'

While the woman busied herself with wrapping and cutting a length of straw-like ribbon, Gordon stood watching Rhys. He and the young lad were chatting and laughing. With a quick glance around, the lad handed Rhys a small envelope. Rhys shoved it into his back pocket.

'Seventy pounds please.' The shopkeeper said.

'What?' Gordon turned back to the florist.

'These cream roses don't come cheap and I assumed you'd want a dozen of them.'

Gordon stared at her wide-eyed. 'This is a tiny shop in bloody Wales, not some luxury florist to the royal family.'

She stood back and crossed her arms. 'This tiny shop in bloody Wales has won an award.'

Rhys came jaunting back into the shop as Gordon picked up the flowers.

'Whoa, that's over the top.' Rhys laughed. 'What's wrong with a few carnations?'

'I'm not doing that again,' Gordon said as he drove them back to the farm.

'What? Taking me into town?'

'Taking you on a drug run.'

Rhys cackled. 'Drug run.' He shook his head. 'It's just weed. That's practically legal.'

'It isn't. If the cops suddenly stopped me and found you with that envelope in your back pocket—'

Rhys howled with laughter. 'You watch too many cop films. Everyone around here knows me. Besides,' he waved his hand towards the windscreen. 'Do you see any heddlu around Bryn Nefyn? There's Hari the Heddwas over in the next village but he's not going to bother us.'

'Harry the head what?'

'Heddwas. Welsh for policeman.'

'Well, you owe me seventy pounds,' Gordon said.

'Seventy fucking quid! Have you gone mad?' Rhys' eyes widened, then softened as his lips curled into a smile. 'Oh, I get it. You see her as your lyle.'

'I don't know what that means, but unless it's Welsh for ball-breaking shepherdess the way she has me lugging the bales around, you're wrong.'

Rhys chuckled. 'Alan won't like it, you fancying her. He's protective of our Jenna.'

'He doesn't need to worry about me. I don't fancy her. In any case, Jenna doesn't strike me as someone who needs protecting.'

'Ah, it's just a Priddy tradition. Looking out for our family members. Alan takes it very seriously.'

Gordon glanced across as Rhys nodded.

'You know,' Rhys said, 'that tradition's the origin of why you're here in Wales right now?'

'Why would that be?' Gordon said.

'Hen daid. My great granddad. The one who owned that bit of land in London. He sold it to help his sister Mari and her kids. She'd been living in South Wales where her husband was a miner. He was killed, sadly. Along with over four hundred of his colleagues.'

Gordon glanced across again. 'That's very sad.'

Rhys' eyes softened. 'It is. The Senghenydd 1913 colliery explosion is still the worst mining disaster in British history. Did you know that?'

'No.'

'After the tragedy, Hen daid wanted his widowed sister and her kids near, so his family could look after them. Help them deal with the shock and the grief. He used the money from that small piece of London land to support her, and to also buy her a house up here near Bryn Nefyn. He knew that she and her kids needed to be near family.'

Gordon nodded. They drove in silence for several

minutes. Gordon made a mental note to research more about Senghenydd when he had the chance. This family had layers of loyalty he hadn't appreciated.

Rhys broke the silence with a chuckle.

'What's so funny?' Gordon said.

'Bronwen in the flower shop. She's still going on about that local newspaper contest from three years ago? It was only her and the supermarket flower stall that were entered. And she got you to pay her seventy fucking quid.'

Chapter Ten

They pulled up outside Rhys' cottage. Rhys jumped out and headed towards the house.

Gordon pushed open the driver's door and called out, 'Aren't you going to take those flowers you left on the back seat?'

Rhys turned. 'Nah, I've got stuff to do. You take them, bring them to Jenna. She'll be up that path there, by the folding.'

Gordon's brows pinched in confusion.

'Sheep pen,' Rhys said.

Gordon peered towards where Rhys pointed, up the path towards a larger stone cottage. He shook his head. 'I can't take them. On a day like today, she needs a family member to take these flowers.'

Rhys narrowed his eyes. 'A day like today?'

'The anniversary of her husband's death.'

Rhys looked down and kicked an imaginary stone. 'Ah, yeah. That was last week. I'd forgotten. But Jenna won't mind. She knows I can be forgetful.' Rhys turned and skipped back into the house. Seconds later, Creedence Clearwater Revival blasted from the front room.

Gordon found Jenna inside the pen on a stool, trimming the foot of a lamb. She looked up and her eyes widened at the enormous bouquet. She switched off the clippers.

'They're from Rhys,' Gordon said.

'No, they're not.' She sat back, as if terrified by the bouquet. 'Rhys never buys me flowers like that. I'm lucky to get a few carnations from him.' She glared at Gordon. 'What is this about? You think I might be one of your London conquests or something?'

Still holding the enormous flowers, Gordon stepped back. Embarrassed, he laughed. 'No. Honestly, no. No way.'

'No way? I don't know if I should be more insulted

now.' She switched on the clippers again.

'Will you take the flowers?' Gordon said. 'I think they'd be wasted in Rhys' room of sofas.'

She dropped the lamb's foot and the clippers, then stood, brushing down her jeans as the lamb skittered away. She reached for the bouquet, then eventually pressed her nose to the flowers. 'This is how I know they're not from Rhys. He doesn't buy anything with a scent.'

'Unless it's weed,' Gordon said.

Jenna laughed. 'These certainly are gorgeous, if not a little too much,' she said, smelling the flowers again. 'Listen, as I said. This isn't the way to go about it.'

'Go about what?'

'Winning me over to help you. That is, if it isn't because you've got other intentions.'

'I'm not trying to win you over. They're not even from me.'

'Oh, stop it with trying to tell me it was Rhys.' She lowered the flowers and narrowed her eyes at him. 'And if it's other intentions, I am not looking for a relationship with a guy, okay? If you want me to help you, maybe try just being a friend.'

'Fine by me,' Gordon said.

She laid the bouquet on the stool and strode towards the barn opposite. 'You can help by bringing some hay up to the paddock in Clover field. It's two fields from the tupping area.' She dragged a heavy wheelbarrow from the side of the barn, then grabbed a huge bale from the top of the stack leaning against the barn wall. She threw it next to the wheelbarrow where it thudded to the ground. 'Take some of that hay up the hill.'

He looked at the huge bale dwarfing the size of the barrow. 'The whole thing?' he said.

She grinned, tiny dimples forming in her cheeks. 'Up to you. If it were me, I'd break it up. Use a hoe.'

He strode towards the barn to find a hoe. 'Seems like this new friendship we're forging is a bit one-sided.'

'Oh yeah?'

He came out of the barn with the hoe and stabbed it into the hay bale. 'Yeah,' he said, attempting to imitate her New York accent.

'Tell you what. I'm making a lasagne later. If you fill all the troughs in the fields beyond the tupping, I'll let you try some. I make real lasagne. New York style.'

'New York style? How is that real lasagne?'

She grinned. 'How did I know you'd have that reaction? For your information, Italian immigrants like my great grandmother used a different recipe.'

She turned and glanced over her shoulder towards the stone cottage behind. 'That's my house. Come over about seven?'

'It's really kind of you.'

'Not really.' She grabbed the clippers while holding onto the lamb. 'Maybe I just want to get to know the guy who'll be spending time with my sheep. Who is this crazy Londoner who's willing to wheel barrows of hay up and around the hills just so I can teach him to shepherd? At least you'll get a decent supper out of it. I can't imagine Rhys is much of a host.'

He watched as she pulled the lamb closer and moved the clippers around its back foot. She wanted to be friends. This was a good thing.

'No need to bring anything tonight,' Jenna said as she grimaced towards the flowers.

'Jenna, those flowers. It really was…'

She switched off the clippers again. 'What?' Her brows furrowed in annoyance.

'Great getting an invitation from you. For us to be friends.'

Troughs filled, he'd just about got all the sheep into the next field, until he saw one stubborn bitch-of-a-ewe facing the fence with her back to him, refusing to follow the others. Oh Jesus, not another Molly. He exhaled and walked towards her. The rain lashed against the ripped waterproofs over his jeans, the water so heavy it ran down the polyester leggings and into his wellies. His feet squelched in sodden socks as the water built up inside his boots. He reached the ewe and moved to the side of her to coax and that's when he saw it.

Her head stuck through the fence.

Oh Jesus. He'd have to get Alan. Unless….

Gordon stood for a moment and stared at the trapped ewe. It wriggled in panic. Poor stupid thing, obviously scared. Think. They put blinders on horses to stop them from panicking.

He crouched to the side of the ewe and pushed the brambles aside with his gloved fingers. Next, he slid a hand through the wire to cover the sheep's eyes. 'I know, I know,' Gordon said. 'You just thought the grass was greener on the other side.' He pushed his other hand through and brushed the ewe's ears back, holding them down flat, while he gently eased the head back through the hole.

His heart expanded with joy as he let go, and the sheep trotted away.

He'd done it.

He needed to tell Alan. After, of course, he finished his chores. Then took the empty feed bags back to the barn and stowed away the wheel barrow and the hoe. He began to whistle as he strode towards a trough and grabbed an empty feed bag from the ground. Once he explained to Alan how he'd just got the approval of one sheep, Alan would agree that the rest would surely follow. If Alan believed Gordon capable of taking sheep on a little road trip to London, he would trust him to start negotiations. Maybe now he could also convince Alan to get that solicitor's letter.

His chores completed, he walked down to Alan's cottage and banged on the door, then stood waiting for several minutes. No answer. Perhaps Alan had gone to see

Rhys.

Gordon made his way to the guesthouse, anxious to tell Alan he was ready to move to the next stage of their plan.

He strode through Rhys' front door. A haze of pungent weed drifted from the room of sofas. Gordon stood in the room's doorway to find Rhys lying on a sofa, Black Sabbath's Iron Man pulsing from the speaker.

'Where's Alan?' Gordon said.

Rhys looked at him, heavy lidded. 'Don't know. Maybe at Jenna's.'

Gordon strode out, then trudged up towards Jenna's cottage. When he arrived, the back door was open. He stepped through into what looked like a utility room area, closing the door behind him to stop the rain from coming in on the tiled floor.

Two sets of wellington boots stood against a wall, wet mud around the heels.

His heart lifted. Alan must be here. He bent to remove his own filthy boots.

Alan's voice boomed from the open doorway leading to the next room. 'I don't trust that Londoner.'

Gordon froze. Without removing his boots, he slowly stood, then edged towards the crack of the open door.

Alan sat at a kitchen table, a mug of something, presumably tea, in front of him. The huge bouquet of flowers were shoved in a glass vase on the table. Jenna had her back to Alan as she whisked eggs in a glass bowl near the stove.

She glanced over her shoulder. 'Pass me that tub of ricotta cheese.'

Alan reached out across the table and handed her the round tub.

'I know what you mean about not trusting Gordon,' Jenna said as she scraped the ricotta cheese into the egg bowl. 'I thought the same thing that first day he came here. But maybe he's not so bad. He can be kind of sweet really.' She chuckled 'He might have a bit of a crush on me. Gave me those flowers.'

'He what?' Alan said.

'Oh, don't worry,' said Jenna. 'I can handle myself around him. Made it clear I'm not interested. But I did invite him over to dinner so I could find out a little more about him.'

'Jenna.' Alan said in a stern voice.

Gordon's mouth dried, and he forced a swallow. He peered closer through the open door crack.

'Be careful,' Alan said.

'Of what?' She laughed again. 'An opinionated Londoner who not only believed there were no sheep farms in New York, he also thinks we can't make real lasagne?'

'Jenna,' Alan said again. 'This isn't a good idea.'

'Oh, it's fine.'

'What I meant was, your American lasagne recipe….' Alan picked up his mug, then set it down again, shaking his head. 'We both know that dish was Dylan's favourite.'

She stood rigid. 'What has this got to do with Dylan?' Ricotta mixture dribbled onto the counter. She dropped the spoon. It clanged to the floor.

'I told you. I don't trust that Londoner,' Alan said.

She bent, picked up the spoon, then threw it into the sink. She turned towards a drawer and gave it a forceful tug, rattling the utensils in their tray, then grabbed a whisk and whipped the ricotta and egg into a frenzy. 'Come on, Alan. I think he's pretty harmless in his own way.'

'No. Something's not right. I feel it. Not sure he's who he says he is.'

Gordon's heart thumped.

Jenna laughed. 'You're only thinking like that because he's from London. Remember how you were unsure of me when Dylan first brought me here, all the way from New York?'

'No. I was unsure before you came over. But it only took me seconds once we met to see you were genuine.

Him?' Alan shook his head.

'Well, we'll just have to see then, won't we?'

Alan sat in silence as she removed a lid from the pot on the stove. The aroma of simmering tomatoes and beef wafted through towards where Gordon stood.

Alan sighed. 'Okay, I'll leave you to it.' He pushed his chair back, and it screeched along the stone floor.

Gordon stepped backwards towards the outside door. He turned and tugged on the handle. The top of the door shuddered while the bottom stayed stubbornly put.

Swollen wood.

Alan entered the utility room. 'What the hell?' he whispered.

With a heavy pull, Gordon yanked the back door open and stepped out into the chilly November air. 'I didn't hear a thing,' he said over his shoulder to Alan. He shoved his hands into his jacket pockets and marched down the muddy path. *Didn't hear a thing, didn't hear a thing. How bloody stupid.*

Footsteps fell in behind him. 'You wait. I want to talk to you.'

Gordon stopped. He hunched his shoulders and breathed in before turning to face Alan.

The old man's face held a mixture of anger and hurt.

'It's not what you think,' Gordon said. 'I mean the flowers.'

'You think I can't read people?' Alan said. 'What are you trying to get out of her? You trying to wrangle a bigger commission for yourself from my Right money? Get to *me* through her?'

'No, never. It's not about money.'

'But the hotel are paying you a fee.'

He swallowed. He'd forgotten that lie. 'Yes.'

'So, of course ultimately, it's coming from my money. The extra they might give to me.'

Gordon inhaled sharply.

Alan stepped forward. 'You work for the hotel, don't

you? You're one of their employees.'

Gordon's heart thudded. If he told Alan the truth now, the whole deal would collapse.

'And if you're not working for the hotel,' Alan said, 'and this isn't about money, it can only be my other suspicion. You're trying to charm my niece.'

Gordon forced a laugh. 'Why would I do that? I barely know her and I know she's grieving for her husband.'

Alan exhaled as he looked to the ground. 'Truth is, I don't think she's still grieving for Dylan. Not like how she was. But she is missing her daughter, who's just gone off to uni, so that makes her vulnerable.'

Godon blinked. His stupid eye twitch was threatening. 'Jenna doesn't look old enough to have a daughter at uni,' he said, hoping to lighten the mood.

Alan breathed out a long sigh.

'I'm sorry about your cousin,' Gordon said, attempting a truce. 'She must have really loved him. Moving all the way from New York for him.'

'Oh, that she did.' Alan said. He pressed his lips together as he stared at the muddy ground. 'She and Dylan didn't waste any time. Married at twenty-one so she could live here in Wales with him.' Alan turned to gaze towards the hills.

Gordon waited. The water from his plastic trousers trickled down the legs, into his boots, the chilly rain numbing his toes.

'That's the thing with a woman like Jenna. When she's ready to be with another man, it won't be for a fling or a one-night stand. You got me?'

'Alan, I have no intention—'

Alan stepped to walk away, then stopped. 'So why are you bringing her flowers?'

'That's the thing. I didn't. They were from Rhys. He used it as an excuse for me to drive him into town.'

'To the florist? Opposite that alleyway?' Alan's eyes narrowed. 'If I find out you're enabling my brother with his drug purchasing…'

Gordon held his palms out. 'I wouldn't…'

'He's been in trouble with the law smoking that stuff.'

'I had no idea what he was up to until it was too late. I've told him I won't do it again.'

Alan stared at him again, his lips pressing into a thin line. 'Make sure of it. Listen, I've let you onto my land, trusted you with my sheep, put you up with my brother and introduced you to my nephew's wife.'

Gordon swallowed. 'Have I got this wrong? I thought it was your cousin's son, not nephew?' he said, hoping his voice had a respectful tone.

'He called me and Rhys *Uncle*, so that makes him my nephew.' Alan stepped nearer. 'Do not romance my niece-in-law.'

'I won't. You have my word.'

'If I can't trust you,' Alan said, 'then this whole sheep in the hotel deal? That's completely off.'

Gordon breathed heavily. 'The deal is about to happen, I promise. It's going to happen before there's even any chance of me doing anything with Jenna or Rhys, not that I would anyway. Either of those things.'

Alan stared at him.

'It's what I came to tell you. The sheep trust me. There was this ewe with her head stuck in the wire fence, and she let me guide her out, didn't fight me or anything—'

'I decide when you're ready.'

'Okay, but, at least let me start negotiations. And at the same time maybe you can get a letter for me from your solicitor, because you know, these sheep never need get to London if I can just—'

'I'm the Right owner. I make the decisions about when you start negotiations.' He turned and glanced back at Jenna's home. 'And what you do with your time on my farm.'

Gordon exhaled, then nodded towards the cottage. 'She's cooking for me tonight,' he said.

'I know.'

'I promise you, I'm not looking to get involved in any way with Jenna, apart from working together on getting justice for your grandfather's land. You have my word.'

Alan stared at him.

'My word is good, I promise you.' His heart rate rose again as he willed Alan not to read the guilt in his eyes. He wasn't out for Alan's money, he wasn't after the man's niece, and he wasn't intending for the hotel to totally rip the farmers off. His heart thudded in protest. Wasn't he?

Alan nodded, then moved his gaze to Gordon's boots. 'Your socks wet?'

'Soaking wet.'

Alan chuckled. 'Why do Londoners put the legs of the waterproofs inside their wellies? Rain just runs down the trousers right into the boot.'

'Oh,' Gordon's face reddened. 'What do I do?'

'Wear them outside the boots.' He patted Gordon's wet shoulder. His eyes narrowed at the tear in Gordon's jacket as he pulled his hand away. 'Rhys not given you a different one yet?'

The rain plunked in puddles around Gordon's boots. He wiped beads of water from his face. 'Not yet. I'm surprised Rhys can find his own clothes in that house.'

Alan laughed. 'I have a spare one you can borrow.' He turned and strode back to Jenna's cottage. 'I'll get Rhys to fetch it over to you,' he called out before disappearing through Jenna's back door.

Chapter Eleven

At five minutes to seven that evening, Gordon rushed from the freezing cold shower, barely able to dry himself with another threadbare excuse of a towel Rhys had left in his room. He dressed hurriedly in a clean pair of jeans and grabbed a ball of thin socks from his duffel bag from under his bed before realizing, no, this isn't a real dinner, it's a quick, casual supper. No need to dress up. His suede trainers could get caked in mud on the way to Jenna's cottage.

He stepped towards the window. Dark and misty outside, although the mist could be an illusion created by the filthy window. Rhys probably hadn't wiped it in years.

Barefoot, he tramped down the stairs to the utility room. He retrieved some thick socks from the bundle of wet clothes he'd thrown into the dryer an hour before. As he pulled on a sock, Rhys' voice bellowed from the kitchen, 'Shall I sing for you? Get you in the mood for a romantic dinner?'

'Are you talking to me or to one of the sheep?'

Loud guffawing from the kitchen. 'How about a little Nat King Cole? When I Fall in Love?'

Gordon grabbed another sock as Rhys appeared in the doorway, holding a wax coat and small rucksack.

He fixed Gordon with a serious stare. 'Are we expecting you home tonight?'

Gordon shoved his feet into boots then grabbed his jacket from the hook behind the washing machine. 'Rhys. You know I don't fancy her.'

'Hmmm. You haven't got a woman in your life, have you?'

'I haven't got time working on this farm, have I?' Gordon said. 'Same as you, I imagine.'

'Ah, I've got my fill of ladies,' Rhys said, leaning against the doorway. 'I go down to the Ty Coch Inn just to have a quiet pint and they don't leave me alone. Have tons after me, I do. I don't let them stay here though. Learned my lesson.'

'Don't they like the sofas?' Gordon joked.

Rhys pursed his lips. 'They seem to like different ones. I just got fed up with the sneaky things they do if you let them stay overnight. Leaving stuff in your bathroom cabinet, marking their territory in case another woman comes into the house. They do that, look to see what's in your cabinet. Been enough arguments about makeup and face creams being found there.'

Gordon stood holding his jacket.

'Here,' Rhys said holding out the wax coat. 'From Alan. Oh, and he gave me this rucksack to give you as well. I guess he doesn't think you're working hard enough. Said you should put your sandwiches in here at lunchtime so you don't have to leave the fields and come back to the gwesty during the day.'

'Thanks, I guess.'

Rhys shrugged before leaning against the door frame. 'Just as well you don't fancy our Jenna, you know. She's way out of your league.'

'Is she now?' This man had obviously never seen a woman like Stacey. Nor any of the other women who had rejected him.

'Punching above your weight, you would be—'

'Okay Rhys,' Gordon said as he grabbed a torch from a shelf. 'I'll be about an hour. Leave the door unlocked.'

'Leave it unlocked? It's not been locked since nineteen-eighty-five.'

'Why? What happened in nineteen-eighty-five?'

'I lost the key,' Rhys said, lighting up a joint.

'Oh and thanks for getting me into trouble with your brother, for taking you to buy weed. I don't want Alan to blame me for your drug habit.'

'Listen. My brother is an uptight bastard. Haven't you realised that yet? This little smoke has never done me any harm.'

'Alan mentioned something about you getting into trouble with the police?'

Rhys coughed midway through a drag, then laughed. 'He's just making a great big mountain out of a molehill. I never got in any trouble.' He grinned. 'You need to go before you're late for your dinner date.'

Gordon trudged up the path towards Jenna's. He breathed in the coldness, his lungs enjoying the escape from the weed infused air of the guesthouse.

The rain stopped, but the wind made his teeth chatter. The air had a strong touch of winter about it. As he neared Jenna's house, his eye twitch started. Nerves. At least he would be out of the guest house for an hour, if Jenna would put up with him for that long. She didn't seem like someone who would spend time with fools like him for longer than necessary. He'd need to be careful. Not slip up and say anything stupid about being an employee of the Remblents Group.

He stepped towards the back door to go through the utility area, then stopped. No, he was a guest, not family like Alan. She probably expected him to knock at the front.

He stepped around the side of the cottage, brushing past evergreens with bright berries. Of course, someone like Jenna would have shrubs against her home that one could visually enjoy during all seasons. Not like the street he lived on in London, where the November flower boxes on neighbours' windowsills draped dead weeds and flower skeletons.

He knocked on the front door. A few seconds later, it opened. Jenna appeared from behind it wearing a smile, dark jeans and a soft v-neck top.

'Come in,' she said. Her hair fell into soft curls, freshly washed and hanging loose around her shoulders.

'You want me to take these boots off?' he asked.

She laughed. 'Well, yeah. Put them behind the door

here.'

She watched as he leant against a wall and stumbled before finally pulling both rubber boots off.

'Is that the London look?' she asked.

Gordon looked at his feet. Jesus. One red sock and one black. 'It's the Gordon Slee look.'

She smiled and a dimple appeared.

He felt his cheeks redden. 'The last time I wore mismatched socks, I lost my job,' he joked.

Her brows pinched. 'Really? Was that with the insurance company?'

'Insurance company?'

'The one you were working at when you found out about Alan's Right.'

'Oh yeah.' The heat in his cheeks intensified. 'No, not that job. A different one. Long time ago. When I was a teenager.' He glanced around the narrow hallway, looking for a reason to change the subject and finally said. 'Something smells good. Is that the lasagne?'

'Come through to the kitchen.' She led him through a low-ceilinged sitting room. Dark oak beams stretched above. He ducked his head as he stepped beneath the one nearest the kitchen. He turned again to face the sitting room and admired its charm. Jenna had it lit by low table lamps. An oval candle flickered in its glass holder on the coffee table. A few feet from the sofa, the glowing flames of an open log fire danced in a wide stone hearth, creating shadows along the opposite walls.

'A bit different to Rhys's place.' He stood, drinking in the room's cosiness. It was also a stark contrast to the bright white and chrome look he had in his own flat. Maybe one day when he was a success, instead of the minimal look, he'd choose this, within an older house. One of those large Victorians like his sister had in Southwest London. Or even a smaller cottage. He smiled at the multi-coloured crochet throw that had been draped elegantly over the sofa. Plump cushions rested against each arm. He imagined if he settled himself there, the springs in the furniture's frame wouldn't whine in protest like in Rhys' room of sofas. 'I bet you made that throw,' he said.

'I did.'

'Where do you find the time? I mean, with all the work you do with the sheep?'

He turned towards her as she stood in the kitchen doorway. The bright kitchen light framed her golden curls like a halo.

'Long winter evenings. It's nice sitting near the fire and doing some needlework.'

'I bet it is,' he said, turning to admire the wide stone hearth. He breathed in as the warm amber flames crackled through a log.

'You've got a real fireplace.' he said.

She laughed. 'What? You thought I'd have some electric storage heater in there instead?'

'No. Just that in London, most people have gas points fitted next to their fireplaces. With fake coals. So you know, you flip a switch and have an instant fire.' The sweet aroma of the burning timber wafted through the room. 'Ah, but it's not really the same, is it? Where do you get the wood. Do you buy it in?'

'Buy it in?' She laughed. 'No, of course I don't buy it in. I chop it myself.' She turned and ambled towards the stove.

The smell of fried onions, roasted garlic, and simmering tomatoes filled the kitchen area. His heart warmed when he caught sight of the flowers he'd bought her, still standing proud in their tall vase in the centre of the table. He chuckled to himself. No. The flowers *Rhys* had bought her, and not yet paid him back for.

'Something funny?' she turned before she bent to pull a tray from the oven.

'Just thinking about Rhys,' he said.

'He's such a character. I adore him.' She looked over her shoulder to give him a smirk. 'You'll get used to him.'

He stood looking at the place settings of delicate rose-patterned crockery, flanked by mismatched cutlery. 'Yes….. umm, which seat is mine?' he asked.

'Don't be so formal. You choose.'

An awkward silence settled between them in the kitchen while Jenna stood at the counter clanging spatulas full of meaty sauce and pasta onto plates. She brought the steaming lasagne dishes over and placed one in front of him and the other opposite.

She plonked a glass bowl on the table filled with salad leaves. 'Help yourself.'

He waited for her to sit before he tucked into the creamy lasagne. 'Mmmm… this is gorgeous.'

She smiled. 'Even without bechamel sauce?'

'I like it. Is this creamy stuff the egg and ricotta mixture you used instead?'

Her eyebrows pinched together as she set her fork down. 'How did you know that's what I used?'

Heat rose from his neck. 'Alan told me. I saw him earlier.'

She nodded, then grinned. 'Oh, right. It was supposed to be a secret, my recipe.' She picked up her fork then said, 'Oh. I forgot. Do you want some wine?' She got up and strode towards a pine dresser, then came back with a bottle of red and two glasses. 'Screw top,' she said. 'Don't expect anything fancy.'

Gordon unscrewed the cap and poured some red liquid into each glass.

'Talk to me about your family,' Jenna said as she sat down again. 'Are you close to your parents?'

'I see them fairly regularly. Birthdays, Christmas, the occasional supper.'

She frowned. 'That's regularly?'

'Probably more regularly than you see yours.' He smiled.

'Not really. I see them at least once a year for several weeks. My parents come here in the summer.' She nudged the salad bowl towards him with clean, unmanicured fingers. 'Here, have some more.'

His fingers touched hers as he took hold of the bowl. A twinge of something awkward rushed through him.

Two bright pink dots appeared on her cheeks.

'Sorry,' he mumbled. Jesus, of course, this was bloody uncomfortable. He shouldn't have agreed to this embarrassing 'getting to know you' meal.

'I'm sensing you're not very close to your parents,' Jenna said, the pink dots fading.

'Oh, we get along okay. On the surface, but I don't know.'

She watched him, waiting for him to continue.

'There's this distance that's hard to measure,' he said.

She smiled as if understanding, like she'd already caught some glimpse of that hurt little boy hiding inside of him.

'I don't know what I'm saying.'

She shrugged. 'You do. And it's okay. I'm a good listener.'

He couldn't hold her gaze. Instead, he allowed his eyes to travel the length of her hair hanging loosely over her shoulders.

'My family stuff is boring,' he said, reaching for his wineglass. 'Tell me about your daughter.'

That did the trick. For the next half an hour, she eagerly sipped her wine as she talked about her daughter, Emma, aged eighteen and studying zoology down in Bristol. Gordon topped up her glass when the subject led naturally on to Dylan. How they met when he came to work on her parents' sheep farm in upstate New York. Her parents apparently were aghast when she ran off to Wales with him two years later, already pregnant with their daughter, a detail Alan had left out earlier today. Her face softened when she spoke about Dylan. She described the simple but tender life-style they once shared, lowering her eyes when she admitted how she had hoped they would share it together for at least a few decades more than they were given.

'The thing about Dylan and me,' she said as she finished the wine in her glass. 'It's like some couples need to busy themselves with fancy restaurants and parties at weekends. Or big expensive vacations on a Caribbean Island somewhere.'

A rush of defensiveness jerked through him. 'Don't knock it until you've tried it.'

She reached for the bottle of red wine on the table.

'I don't normally drink,' said Jenna. 'But I figured as a Londoner you'd want a glass of wine with your supper. I dug that out from the cupboard earlier today. Something Alan brought around when Emma was last here for a Sunday lunch.' She took a sip from her glass. 'This is pretty good, though, isn't it?'

Gordon smiled.

She set the glass down. 'What I meant before, when I was telling you about me and Dylan. I think when you're happy with someone, really in harmony, you can just sit in a room together. Maybe one person reading, the other doing something like… crochet, I don't know, and you can just look across at each other and know.'

'Know what?'

'That's what happiness is. That harmonious energy between you. And you don't need the distractions of expensive outings or other people to try to make you feel that way.'

A twinge of envy passed through him. He hadn't ever shared something that simple, that pure, with a partner, not in the way she seemed to have experienced with Dylan.

'Oh, I almost forgot,' she said. 'Dessert. Don't get too excited. It's only ice cream.'

'I adore ice cream.' Gordon smiled.

'Aha, I've found something you're passionate about.' She laughed.

Gordon's cheeks reddened. Of course, he was

passionate. Although it wasn't her fault she couldn't see this. He'd been concealing his directorship ambition since he arrived on this farm.

She placed a bowl with two scoops of ice cream in front of him.

He forced a wide smile. 'I'm certainly passionate about eating it.' He dug his spoon into the pink swirly dessert. 'Especially strawberry.'

She grinned. As their spoons clinked against the porcelain bowls, a silence fell between them.

'Tell me more what happened with the insurance company?' she asked.

'The insurance company, why?'

'I think you lied to me about your employment with them.'

His breath halted. Placing his spoon into the empty bowl, he picked up the wine bottle. They'd drank pretty much all of it. 'Have you got any more wine?'

'Really?' She laughed. 'Okay, then. Let's go for it. I can't wait to hear the real story of Gordon Slee. There's another bottle in the left-hand side of that Welsh dresser over there.'

His mouth dried as he scraped back his chair and rose to his feet. She was a nice woman. It felt wrong to lie to her. Yet, if she told Alan it was the hotel he'd been working for, he'd get thrown off the farm and the deal would be off.

He strode towards the pine dresser and found another bottle. Unscrewing the cap, he sat down opposite and held it towards her glass.

'Just a tiny bit of wine. Then tell me the truth.' She grinned.

He breathed out. Should he tell her? No, he shouldn't, but… He poured a small amount into her glass then filled his own halfway.

'I'll make it easy for you,' she said. 'You weren't sacked from your fictitious job as a teenager. I could tell from your face that was a lie.' She leaned forward and touched his fingers for a brief second, then sat back. 'You got sacked from your insurance role because you didn't convince your client, the hotel group, to take out that expensive, but necessary policy.'

Gordon held his breath.

'How close am I?' she asked.

'Hmmm,' he said. 'Close. You're quite perceptive that no, there wasn't a job I lost as a teenager on the day I wore mismatched socks.'

She laughed. 'I knew it.'

'Can I ask you something?' Gordon said, eager to change the subject.

'Okay.'

'Why did Alan sell the land? I mean, I know it's because he had debts, but why the debts?'

'Oh,' a shadow passed across her face. She grabbed her wineglass and sipped. 'I guess it's not a secret. Although, I don't think Rhys is aware of the extent of the debts.'

'Is it bad? The debts, I mean.'

She stared at the table, then slowly nodded.

'Ten thousand.' Gordon sighed. 'Are you going to tell me it's not enough to get him out of trouble?'

She shook her head. 'It's not Alan's fault.'

'What isn't?'

She shoved her glass towards him. 'Oh hell, you might as well fill it to the top before I tell you this.'

Gordon poured more wine, and she continued.

'Alan had a life partner. His name was Evan. Great guy. A little older than Alan. Died twelve years ago. He had Parkinsons.'

'I'm sorry.'

'Yeah, we all were. They were together for nearly thirty years. Although Alan told me how in the early days they kept their relationship hidden. Pretended Evan was a friend, a farmhand. Evan hated all that, but back then the villagers weren't as open-minded about these things.'

'Was Evan from around here?'

She pursed her lips. 'Cardiff. South Wales. To you, that's probably near enough to here, but to Bryn Nefyn people it was almost a different world, a big city, you know. Anyway, you asked about the debts. Before Evan died, he wanted to do something locally. Set up an LGBTQ+ community centre. Sort of a Pride club. He told Alan he never wanted anyone else to ever feel they weren't accepted for who they loved. Alan, of course, agreed to back this project. He understood Evan wanted to leave this legacy.'

'So Alan sold some land?'

'He took a loan against the farm. Things were okay for a while, but Alan found it difficult keeping up with the interest rates, fell behind on a few payments. Suddenly, there were financial penalties. Alan hid all the problems from Evan, especially in the last few months. In the end, he sold off some of the land to clear the debts.'

'But he still has debts?'

She nodded, then rubbed her face. 'Sorry, do we have to keep talking about this?' She looked at the clock on the wall behind Gordon. 'Hey, it's getting late.' She stood and gathered the plates.

He turned to look at the clock. 'Oh. Wow. Have we really been sitting here for three hours?'

She opened the dishwasher to load the plates, stumbling slightly as she bent. 'Don't tell Alan I told you that stuff, okay?'

'No, of course not. You can trust me.' His throat tightened. 'Hey, do you want some help?'

'No, I've got it. I'm a little tipsy, but not falling down drunk.' She giggled before she turned and held his gaze. 'You know something? I enjoyed your company tonight.'

'Not that you expected to?' He gave her a small grin. 'I'm joking. And I must admit it was easier for me sitting here talking with you than with my sheep-headed housemate.'

Her dimples deepened as she laughed. 'Sheep-headed? I never thought of him like that, but yeah, I can see it.' She grabbed the empty wine glasses from the table and brought them to the open dishwasher, turning them upside down on the top rack.

'I guess I should go… oh, but wait.' said Gordon.

'What?'

'I can't believe I didn't tell you. Guess what I did earlier today?'

Jenna closed the dishwasher door, then turned, pushing the curls from her face. 'Don't make me guess. I've had too much wine.'

'I actually pulled, very gently, a ewe's trapped head from the fence. All on my own. She let me do it.'

Jenna's mouth opened. Then her eyes filled with tears. She wiped a finger under her eye. 'Sorry, I'm being silly.' She looked at him and held his gaze. 'Dylan was great with that, too.' Her chin trembled as a lone tear slithered down her cheek.

His mouth went dry. He'd never spent time with a widow. What was the protocol when a person started crying over her dead husband? Hug her? He pushed his chair back. 'Umm. Right. What can I ….' he glanced around, looking for words to finish the sentence.

'Ignore me,' she said. 'Wine does this to me. But hey, it's been good talking with you. Really good. We've moved on to another level tonight, right?' She grabbed a tea towel and began wiping the draining board next to the sink.

He blinked rapidly. 'Have we? Oh, you mean friends? I've actually passed the Jenna Priddy buddy exam?'

She turned and shrugged. 'I wouldn't go that far.' Then she smiled. 'But you've got through the first round.'

He couldn't explain how, but as her grin broadened, the deepening dimples in her face warmed his heart. Maybe this was what it was like to have a real friend.

'I'll walk you to the front door.' She dropped the tea towel onto the counter, then lead him through the sitting room.

She opened the front door while he balanced awkwardly against a wall, tugging on his boots.

'Look, it's a clear night.' She pointed at the dark sky.

He zipped up his coat and stood next to her in the doorway. 'Wow,' he said, staring up at the shimmering stars. Sequined-silver dots hugged the outline of hilltops, as glittering constellations stretched above the farm. 'You barely get to see the stars like this in London.'

'Too much artificial light,' Jenna said.

'Look at it.' His lips broadened into a smile. 'It's like someone threw a handful of moondust over a black canvas.'

'Listen to you,' Jenna said. 'You sound like a poet.'

'What?' Heat rose to his cheeks. 'You think that sounds stupid?'

'No. Not stupid at all. I like it.' She elbowed him playfully. 'You should get together with Rhys. He writes haikus.'

'So he says,'

Jenna laughed. 'So he says is right. He never lets anyone see them.'

Gordon smiled and a silence fell between them.

'Right,' he said, turning towards her. What was the convention? Kiss her on the cheek? To play it safe, he held out his hand. 'Thanks again for dinner.'

'You're welcome. And I'll see you out in the fields tomorrow. Bright and early.' She gripped his hand and gave it a firm shake.

'Oww, you're strong.' He pulled his hand back jokingly.

She laughed. 'We'll toughen you up pretty soon, London boy.'

He nodded, then switched on his phone light to walk down the path. As his boots crushed into the gravel, he breathed in the chilled night air. Then he glanced up again to admire the moondust scattered night sky.

Chapter Twelve

Gordon stood nervously in Alan's sitting room. The November morning sun picked out sparkles of dust in the stale air between where Gordon stood and where Alan sat in his fraying arm chair.

'What is it?' Alan said.

'I know you told me yesterday that you'll decide when I'm ready to approach the hotel group.'

'That's right.'

Gordon removed his hands from his pockets and flumped onto the sofa opposite. 'Alan, I know what these people are like. What their limits are. And it's not a case that I'm even going to drive these sheep to London, let alone bring them inside a hotel.'

'What are you saying?'

'Trust me. I want to send them an email today. One that will get an urgent response. It's time to start negotiations.'

Alan picked up a lighter from the side table and flicked it to a flame.

'I didn't know you smoked,' said Gordon.

'I light candles sometimes. For Jenna's Dylan and for….'

Gordon waited.

'Someone else who used to live here,' said Alan. He placed the lighter gently back on the table. 'I can guess why you're rushing. You frightened of hanging around too long?'

'I already told you. I want to help.'

He smirked. 'Yes. With getting me a mere ten thousand pounds. You're working for the hotel, aren't you?'

Gordon reddened. His heart picked up several beats.

'You're still working as their insurance broker,' said Alan. 'Am I right? You trying to please your client, get more business from them by promising to sort this little mess out for them? Something like that?'

Gordon gazed towards the floor. 'No. I absolutely do not work for that insurance company.' He swallowed, adding the lie, 'What I mean is, not anymore.'

'So this is all out of the goodness of your heart and a small percentage from the ten grand?'

Gordon's throat tightened as he nodded.

'I don't know what you're up to, but you must be pretty desperate to do all this for so little.'

'I want to help.' Gordon's heart lightened with the realisation that he meant it. He then swallowed back the guilt of knowing that ten thousand wasn't a fair deal for the Priddys. 'Look, I'm in a tight spot myself, so my percentage helps me out a little bit too.'

The slow dripping of a tap echoed from the kitchen into the corridor. On the side table next to Alan's chair there was a dark wood photo frame. Inside the frame was a picture of Alan standing with another man. Black and white, taken maybe twenty-odd years ago. Before time and grief had etched the lines into Alan's face and erased the muscle from his stature.

'Jenna told me you lived with someone.' Gordon said.

'That's right. Twenty-eight years.'

'That's a long time,' Gordon said. He gestured towards the photo. 'I guess you couldn't tell too many people about it back then.'

'Nope.'

'Or marry.'

Alan shook his head. 'Law passed not long after he died that we could have done.'

'Life's a bitch.'

'No. It isn't. I had twenty-eight years of happiness. That's more than many people seem to get these days.'

Gordon nodded. 'Jenna mentioned last night about…. Evan was his name?'

'Yes.'

'He opened some sort of community centre? LGBTQ+?'

Alan nodded. 'Some of the locals weren't thrilled about it. But in the end they were outnumbered by those who supported us. Word spread and members joined us from different part of Wales.'

Alan flicked his lighter again, then moved the flame towards the candle in front of Evan's photograph. 'Had a little social club set up in the village,' he said as he lit the wick. 'Hired an events manager who would organise excursions, social outings and such for the younger members. We used to organise trips to London too for the Pride march. Paid for the members who couldn't afford it to have the weekend there. It was a good thing Evan did.' Alan sighed. 'Couldn't keep it going, though. Cost too much.'

Gordon thought about the loan against the farm, the debts Jenna said piled up. The guilt from his offer of a mere ten thousand tightened in his chest.

'Well go on, then,' Alan said.

'Go on?' Gordon gazed at him.

'Go send your email and let me know what they say.'

A tingle of excitement rose in Gordon's chest. 'Can I tell them to expect a letter from your solicitor?'

'Why do I need a solicitor when I have you?'

The tingle thudded.

'You're supposed to be the negotiator,' Alan said. 'So, go. Negotiate.'

Chapter Thirteen

He strode out to the fields, the adrenaline pumping through him. This wouldn't be as smooth as he thought, but he'd have to do it. Edward would have to understand they weren't dealing with business people. Letter or no letter, Edward would have to accept that Gordon needed to negotiate this fast or the Priddys would rush ahead with bringing sheep into London. Ten thousand pounds. No. The hotel had to be a little more fair to the Priddys. It wasn't like The Remblents Group couldn't afford it. In truth, they should have coughed up nearly forty thousand for a policy to protect them from this Right.

A layer of guilt mixed in with the adrenaline. He'd made a promise to Edward, his soon to be fellow board member with any luck. Edward was about to agree to pull out all the stops to swing the directorship for Gordon, yet here was Gordon sneakily planning to give the Priddys more.

Whose side was he on? Could he be a little bit on both without letting on to either? A superb politician would play it that way. His Chancellor of the Exchequer fantasy resurfaced: Gordon Slee in a suit and tie instead of jeans and wellington boots, striding along Downing Street instead of this field of grassy dew. He'd have to secretly help both sides. What other choice did he have?

He moved between the woolly sheep, their thick fleeces almost a chalk-white in the mid-morning sun. A ewe baa-d at him as he walked, and the fantasy changed to that other one fighting to emerge; Gordon in farming clothes, bowing to the applause of a crowd at the sheep trials, with his animals in their flour-white coats gleaming in the sunlight as he stood in an emerald-coloured field. He sucked in the crisp air.

Boots squelched in the mud behind him, and he turned. Jenna.

He stopped and smiled, allowing her to catch up to

him.

'Thanks again for last night,' he said.

'Yeah, sorry. I got a little weird, I think. I'm not used to drinking wine.'

He turned and ambled towards the guesthouse, allowing Jenna to fall in beside him as they stepped through the bracken reaching into the path. 'Weird?' he said. 'No. It was…Nice. I enjoyed talking with you.'

'And me crying over Dylan because you got a sheep's head out of a fence?'

'I think you're allowed. You and Dylan, you seemed to have something special.' The twinge of envy squeezed his ribs again.

'Have you been out rotating yet today?' She asked.

'I've got to do something for Alan first. Draft an email.'

'Noo,' she drawled. 'The animals always come first.'

'Right,' he chuckled, then stopped to give her a quick salute. 'Doing it now, then. I'll whizz around and do some rotating while checking no heads in fences.'

'Check the ditches, too. Behind the hedges.'

'What for?'

'Check there aren't any sheep upside down in them.'

Gordon laughed.

'I'm serious. Maybe I should come with you.'

'It's okay. I can handle it, and I know you've got your own chores.'

'Yes, but I think I'd like to come with you,' she said. 'After what you told me last night about rescuing the one with her head caught in the fence, I'd like to observe you some more with the sheep.'

'Okay then.'

They trudged through the mossy green grass towards the next field. The wild hedgerows scraped harmlessly against the sleeves of the wax coat Alan had lent him, while the short, high-pitched burst of a jackdaw chacked overhead as he and Jenna walked.

They reached the top of the hill and Jenna slid open the metal latch of the turnstile. She let herself through first, then held the gate open for him. They strode along the sunlit grass amongst the dozens of heavy fleeced sheep who were contentedly pushing their muzzles into the grass and munching.

'I'm curious,' Gordon said. 'What do you do weekends?'

'Weekends? I work.'

'What? When do you take time off?'

'Sheep don't know what weekends are. Funnily enough, they still want to eat.'

'You never take time off?'

'Of course I do. Two or three mornings a week, the college apprentices take over for me.'

A ewe skittered to the side as Gordon marched past, then skipped towards some of its flock.

'Don't you do things like go out on a Saturday night?' asked Gordon.

She chuckled as she shook her head. 'What am I, eighteen? Yeah, I go down the clubs in Bangor and Pwllheli every chance I get.'

Gordon winced with embarrassment. 'Sorry, stupid question. I guess I was just thinking about how I still meet up with my friends from university sometimes. About twenty of us. We still get together and have a laugh occasionally.'

'Twenty of you. That's a big group.'

Gordon shrugged. 'I guess you could say I've always liked having a flock around me.'

She moved closer to playfully elbow him in his side.

He gazed around at the animals who stood peacefully motionless apart from the chomping muzzles and quietly twitching ears. 'They all seem fine here.' He swept his arm out in a gesture.

'Shall we have a quick check over there?' he said, pointing to the next field, before shoving his hands into his coat pockets.

They arrived at the next gate. He stood back to allow Jenna to open it, then stepped forward again. 'Let me… oww!' He released his trapped hand from the metal catch and sucked his palm. 'Why does my hand keep getting caught?' He shook it at the wrist to flick the pain from it.

Jenna laughed, her giggles rising, then falling to a low chuckle.

She pushed open the gate into the tall grass, and he followed.

They strolled around the extensive field. Halo-white mountains peeked through the distant hills. They ambled through happily grazing sheep, either still or merely shuffling an inch or so as Gordon and Jenna trudged past. No one up to any mischief yet, from what Gordon could fathom.

'This is going to sound strange,' Gordon said, 'but I get this peaceful feeling being around the sheep.'

'Nothing strange about that. I've found that some people who choose to be around sheep aren't always sure of themselves. Then, they get a feeling of calm because these animals are so sweet and gentle. It's probably why you're good with the sheep,' said Jenna. 'You needed them to help you shake off your London stress.'

'Stress? Was I that obvious?' He forced a chuckle. If she only knew how much stress. 'You actually think I'm good with these sheep?' He gave her knowing grin. 'You're being kind. Remember, I'm a city boy at heart.'

She shrugged. 'It's like what I said to you that first day. You've got some potential.'

'If you say so,' he laughed. Then he stopped and looked at her. 'You love what you do, don't you?'

She smiled. 'Well, yeah, I wouldn't do it otherwise.' She brushed a wisp of hair from her face. 'But you know, there's this thing about life. What keeps you going is having new goals too.'

'Such as?'

'I'd love to have a little cheese making business one day. Using sheep's milk. I can picture a shop in Portmerion.'

'Ah, cheese.' He laughed, then shook his head. 'Oh no.'

'What do you mean, "Oh no"?'

He grinned. 'Cheese is disgusting. It smells of feet.'

'Oh, stop it.' She pushed his shoulder.

He laughed again. 'Okay, I'll let you have your cheese dream. I'll even come visit if you promise to make ice cream too.'

'Okay, deal. But, first you'll have to tell me your dream?'

He breathed in, then sighed. Fixing his gaze towards the lambs, he said, 'Successful businessman. Director within the Rem...' he stopped. 'Within a big organization. Nice house.' He shrugged.

'Hmmm,' she said, then started walking. Glancing over her shoulder, she said, 'Come on, I'll walk you towards the guesthouse so you can send your email or whatever it was you needed to do.'

He trudged down the path, his boots crunching through the taller grass, crackling the twigs hidden beneath. 'So this goal, this cheese shop,' he said, catching up with her.

She looked at him, and he wrinkled his nose.

Jenna giggled.

'When's it happening?' Gordon asked.

'Oh, it's not. It's still a dream. I'm nowhere near ready to let go of the shepherding yet. Not full time anyway.'

'Yeah. I can see you're not someone who would easily let go.'

She stopped. 'Hey. What's that supposed to mean?' Her eyes widened and she blinked. 'Is this about me getting emotional last night? Because of Dylan?'

Gordon stood open-mouthed. 'No, that's not what I meant. I meant how you're devoted, determined, and you love these sheep.'

'But, you see me as someone who has a problem with letting go?'

He looked at her, his heart pounding. Was there an inkling of truth in what she assumed he meant? The way she talked about Dylan, the perfect harmony they had shared. The prick of jealousy that surprised him when she said it.

She turned and tramped down the hill, the gravel spitting behind her heels.

'Jenna.' He quickened his steps to catch up.

She stopped and turned. Her eyes glistening, expectant.

Tell her. Tell her how she made you feel last night. The light warmth from her smile … how it inexplicably stirred something…

She narrowed her eyes, waiting.

No. She said she just wanted friendship. Don't make this whole sheep scheme even more complicated. 'Maybe I'm not always good with expressing myself. I don't even know myself what I was trying to say back there. But I know I'm really happy we've agreed to be friends.'

'Are you? Why? You've only known me a week.'

He blushed. 'Can't explain it. Just felt last night, I don't know…' The heat in his cheeks intensified.

'Felt what?'

He swallowed. 'Accepted?'

She laughed, then stopped. 'Sorry, I just can't imagine why you would worry about that.'

'I'm more sensitive than I let on.' His fingers froze, stunned by his own admission.

Her eyes widened before she gazed down at the weeds pushing through the gravel near her feet. After a few seconds she looked up and gave him a small smile. 'Okay. Maybe, just maybe, I overreacted.' She took a deep breath. 'I admit I can also get a bit sensitive when people talk about me losing Dylan. I am coping okay, you know. You'll just have to get used to being friends with a –'

'Mad New Yorker?'

'I was going to say widow, but yeah, crazy New Yorker

will do.'

On Rhys's orders, Gordon lugged heavy hay bales for the rest of the morning. In the afternoon, he stomped the fields to check the electricity in every single fence. It was evening before he was back to his cramped, musty bedroom in the guesthouse.

Rhys must have been in a post dope haze as there was no Black Sabbath, no Creedence Clearwater Revival or any other music blasting through the corridors.

Great. It would give him clear thinking time. He grabbed the mobile from his back pocket and bounced down onto the bed. The rusty springs creaked in defiance.

He rested his head back onto the damp, lumpy pillow, closing his eyes in a moment of anticipation.

Time to set in motion the resolution for Priddy versus Creaton.

Gordon opened his email app and thumbed a message.

Dear Edward,

I'm still up in Wales with the Priddys. I know you want the written proof of their threat, but the thing is, they're a little more stubborn than I anticipated. I'm not sure why, but instead of sending you a letter, they seem dead set on just bringing these sheep into London and marching them through the hotel. It has something to do with proving themselves to people in this village.

But here's the good news. They seem to trust me. I'm certain I can get them to see reason, but my guess is that it's going to take a little bit more than the ten thousand figure I originally anticipated.

Seeing as we would have needed to pay those insurers about four times that, what if we offered something a little more than halfway? I'm thinking £25,000 and then Remblents owns the Right and all of this is behind us.

Seems like a win-win to me. I'm sure you'll agree.

Regards,
Gordon

He exhaled a nervous sigh as he re-read the message. It's okay, it was good. Pragmatic. Yet, something was missing. Where was Gordon's job guarantee? He dropped the phone to the floor and rubbed his face. Come on, he could trust Edward. The guy had a reputation for being a little ruthless at times, but Gordon knew when it came to it, Edward would do the right thing by him. Edward owed it to Gordon's grandfather. If it wasn't for Granddad, Edward wouldn't have risen so quickly in his own career.

Gordon's heart thudded. What would his grandfather say to him now? *Don't be foolish, Gordon. There's too much at stake.*

Base music thudded against the wall, signalling Rhys wasn't comatose after all. Gordon grabbed the phone from the floor. Come on. He had the brainpower to pull this off. Hadn't Tej called him a business athlete? That couldn't be much different to people like footballers and rugby players who kept pushing on until they achieved their goal. Hell, Gordon had even imagined himself as an amazing football star in his twenties.

He added a PS.

Of course, we can't complete on this Right sale until my director's position is in writing.

No. That's no good. Too blunt. He typed a new sentence softening the statement.

Of course, the Right purchase can't be fully completed until that other matter we discussed is resolved and put into place in approximately six months' time.

Chapter Fourteen

The next day, Gordon found Alan and Rhys in the barn.

Alan stood, opening the latch to a pen filled with half a dozen lambs shuffling over dirty clumps of straw. 'Maybe you can clear this out for us once I get all the lambs through onto the trailer.' He said to Gordon. 'Put some fresh straw down.'

Gordon nodded while Alan lead one of the lambs out of the pen and into a steel cage beside Rhys. The rough wooden walls of the barn behind the pen climbed towards heavy rafters where several spiders had created sticky nets, no doubt in hope of trapping the flies that currently buzzed near the mouldering straw.

Rhys peered at a metal box near the side of the cage and made a note in a booklet with a pencil. He waved his hand towards Alan, mumbling, 'Next.'

Alan lead the small animal out onto the back of a trailer, and up the ramp, then pulled back a metal gate so it could join another lamb. He hitched it shut, then returned to the indoor pen to lead another lamb into the cage next to Rhys.

'What are you doing?' Gordon said.

'Recording their weight. We're taking these ones to market this morning,' said Alan.

Gordon's breath caught. His legs went weak as Alan shooed the next lamb onto the weighing scale and Rhys scribbled into the notebook.

'But....,' said Gordon, 'how can you do this? After looking after them, feeding them...'

'This is a business,' Alan said. The lamb flicked its ears while it stood on the sleek metal plate of the scale.

Gordon gulped down a breath. The smell of urine and manure from the pen suddenly made him queasy. 'I still don't understand. Isn't it hard sending them to market?'

'Why?' said Alan.

'Because you've nurtured them, fed them....'

'They're not being sold for slaughter,' said Alan. 'These are Llyen sheep. Sold for breeding. They make good mums. You want to help us weigh? Record some figures?'

Relief flooded through his limbs, strengthening his stance. 'Umm, Jenna wants me to rotate some sheep in the fields. But after that I'll come clean out the stalls here.'

'Thank you,' Alan said. 'I've got a small list for you too when you're done doing Jenna's jobs and mucking out the stall here.' He nodded at Rhys, who pulled a folded paper from his pocket before handing it to Gordon.

'No problem,' Gordon said, shoving the list into his coat pocket. 'I just wanted to come by to tell you something before starting my chores. I sent an email to the finance director at Remblents.'

'Uh huh,' Alan said, opening the weighing pen and allowing the next lamb through. 'You really think that arsehole ex-client of yours is going to negotiate?'

'I'm fairly certain,' Gordon said.

'Only fairly?'

'Let's wait and see,' Gordon said, running a hand through his hair. It might be best to play it cool with the Priddys, and then present them with the increased offer out of the blue. Blindside them with the higher offer, so that they're immediate response was a resounding yes. 'I think I know what I'm doing.' He attempted a joke, 'An ex-colleague of mine once said I was a business athlete. Let's see if he was right.'

Rhys chuckled. 'Business athlete,' he repeated under his breath while he scribbled another figure in his notebook.

Alan opened the gate to lead the lamb onto the trailer. 'What exactly do you believe is going to happen once you arrive in London with a few sheep?'

Gordon pressed his lips together. They still thought this would need a ridiculous display in London. Maybe he was playing it too cool. 'I don't even think it's going to get that far, Alan. I expect to hear today from Edward Creaton, phoning me with an opening offer to put a stop to the entire plan.'

'And if they don't phone?'

'Don't worry.' Gordon smiled. 'Trust me. They will. That Right puts you in a position of power. What you might even call an impenetrable power.'

Alan looked at him, his narrowed eyes uncertain.

Rhys broke the silence with his cackle. 'I guess that's what you'd call your super power. Bullshitting.'

Gordon looks at Rhys. 'Who says I'm bullshitting?'

'I prefer my super power if you ask me,' Rhys said.

'Okay, so what's your superpower?' asked Gordon. 'If it's something that you think would help, I'll use it.'

Rhys shrugged. 'Not giving a shit what other people think.' He looked at Gordon and grinned. 'I'm lucky. It's the most powerful superpower there is.'

Lunchtime, Gordon dashed back to the guesthouse. He still hadn't got around to taking a packed lunch to the fields, but just as well. He wanted to sit in the stillness of his musty room when he got the triumphant email. Not have Rhys tramping up behind him, or Jenna calling for him to grab a feed bag. No, he wanted to sit here and savour the moment when his dreams finally transformed into reality. The hotel group elated he'd solved the overhanging threat of a sheep run; the promise of a directorship making his parents and sister proud, and his older brother possibly envious; plus now there was the huge added bonus of helping the Priddys. He would be a hero.

The bed sagged beneath him as he sat. In the next few seconds, he'd see it in writing. Pulling the phone from his pocket, he opened his email app. He scanned through the new messages. Nervous excitement stilled while he searched through the notifications of supermarket points, and the spam offers for dating sites, or weird medical products he'd never consider purchasing. His rapidly beating heart slowed to disappointment. He scrolled up, then down again, in case he missed it. Breathing in, he then huffed out a frustrated breath. Nothing from Creaton.

He clenched his teeth. *Don't get despondent. Perhaps this isn't surprising.* He warmed to a newly forming theory in his head. If the negotiations were an outright 'no,' Edward would have responded straight away.

Instead, Edward was probably stuck in an urgent board meeting with the others, getting them to agree to the sensible figure of twenty-five thousand. Although, the board might initially force Edward to come back with a counteroffer.

Resolve flickered through him. He had to be fair to the Priddys.

Chapter Fifteen

Gordon spent the rest of the afternoon ploughing his nervous energy, his anticipation, into chores. He stomped through the fields carrying the crook Jenna had given him and rotated the herds on today's list. Late afternoon, before the sun set, he clomped in his muddy boots back to the empty barn to clear out the pen as Alan had instructed. The dry taste of chaff tickled his throat as he stirred up the new hay and laid it on the concrete floor. He allowed the sweet smell of the fresh straw to soothe him as he breathed in.

Next, he referred to the next item on Alan's list and set about checking the electricity within the roadside fences, torch in hand as the November dusk drew in. As he checked each fence with his thick gloves, he occasionally pulled a thorny bramble from the wires, his heart momentarily pinging as he imagined a little lamb's face getting an unexpected prick.

When he'd finished checking the electrics, he turned and stomped up the hill towards the last field, remembering the troughs needed checking and possibly filling.

He pushed through the hedgerows, into a moss covered clearing, then shone his torch around the fences. That's when he saw it. The ewe banging her head against the timber fence in front of the spruce trees. She must have got out somehow. He looked past the five-bar gate where he imagined the rest of the sheep were grazing.

'Okay, Molly,' Gordon said. 'No time for games. Get with the others.' He stepped around to the side of her. She trotted a few feet away, then started her head banging again.

'Need some help?' A voice called out.

Gordon turned to see Jenna's outline against the darkening hills as she opened the gate and strode towards them. He stepped back from the ewe and said, 'I still can't get this one to listen to me.'

Jenna laughed. 'Sheep don't obey. They follow. There's a difference.' She stomped over towards the butting ewe. 'This one still needs to learn to trust you.' She reached down and pulled Molly backwards, then gave her a smack on her side to send her off towards the open gate. Jenna followed the ewe, then closed the gate after Molly scuttled through.

With her head down and hands in pockets, Jenna sauntered back towards Gordon, her boots squelching in the grass. She gave him a shy smile. 'Don't worry. You'll get there. You're picking this up a lot more quickly than I imagined you would.'

'Really?'

'Really. You're better than any of the college apprentices we have at the moment.'

His chest swelled with pride. 'I'd like to think that's true.'

'Hey,' she said. 'You're talking to a New Yorker, remember? We never bullshit. Never mislead or even practice that lovely British ritual called lies of omission.'

'Lies of omission? I don't think that's a British…' He stopped.

'What?'

Gordon sighed. He surveyed the darkening hills in the distance, at the forest green bands brushed along their bases, and at one hill in particular with a jagged stripe of trees climbing towards it's craggy peak. The brisk wind carried with it a whiff of the Scotch pines from the field behind. The words in his heart bravely rose. *Tell her the truth. How you're with the hotel, but you're trying to be fair to Alan.*

He turned 'Look, I need to tell you something,' he said. 'There's something I've … well, a lie of omission, you could say.'

She looked at him, a panic rising in her eyes. 'What haven't you been honest about?'

He breathed in.

'Gordon, if we're going to be friends. There's something you should know. Honesty is really important to me. It's like, the most important aspect of any relationship to me.'

Shit. Running his hand through his hair he exhaled heavily. 'Umm…' stalling, he glanced around, and then towards her cottage. He was stuck now. He had to tell her. He looked at her again, at her bright trusting eyes. 'Something I allowed you to believe…' he said.

Her eyes widened with fearful worry.

No. This was a mistake. He couldn't tell her about working for Edward Creaton. Not yet. She might tell Alan, he'd insist the deal was off and that would not be the best thing for them all. He'd tell Jenna after, sit her down and explain everything, but after the deal was done.

'You're scaring me,' she said.

'Sorry, it's stupid. I was thinking about the flowers,' he lied. 'The day I brought you flowers. It was actually Rhys's idea.'

She let out a peal of laughter. 'Oh please! Would you stop talking about the goddam flowers already?'

'But….'

She put a hand in the air and giggled. 'No. Do not mention the word flowers again. Ever.'

'Okay, but one day I'm going to tell you the truth.' His increased heartbeat told him he meant it. One day, he would tell her all about his role with the Remblents Group, how he made up the story to his boss that he already knew Alan, about how his whole livelihood had rode entirely on this one deal, and how he realised he needed to keep the deal, and the lies, going to help the Priddys' livelihood too.

'I already know the truth about the flowers.' She gave him a mock smile. 'You bought them because you're madly in love with me? Aren't you?' She elbowed him.

He grinned. 'No. You'd know if I was.'

He followed her through the next gate, then froze.

She walked ahead, then turned and stopped. 'What is

it?'

'Sorry. I've just got this thing about....cows.'

'Oh, come on. They won't hurt you.'

The blood pounded in his temples as his mouth dried.

'Gordon.' Jenna laughed. 'Come on.'

He ignored the tremble in his legs and moved forward.

Jenna stomped back towards him and grinned. 'Come on, silly. Where does this fear of cows come from?'

He exhaled. 'From when I was little. I was walking through a field down in Surrey with my grandfather.'

She nodded. 'How old were you?'

'About six. His dog was with us, on a lead. I was holding the lead.'

'I think I know what's coming,' Jenna said. 'There were calves in the field?'

'Must have been. I didn't see them, but Granddad told me afterwards there were.'

'What happened?'

Gordon swallowed. 'The dog wasn't even paying attention to them, but suddenly the cows had moved and grouped together and then were behind us, following. I could hear them.'

'Walking?'

He nodded. 'The cows. I heard them behind me. They weren't stampeding yet, but when I turned and looked over my shoulder, they were in that big group—'

'Herd.'

'Whatever. Every time I took a step, they took a step, like in unison. Granddad told me to drop the lead and let the dog run out of the field. I turned and looked at the cows again, standing in this menacing group staring at me. They were just a few feet behind me. No way was I going to let go of the dog.'

'Gordon. The dogs usually get away.'

'I know. That's what Granddad said to me after. I wouldn't let go of the lead. I kept walking as calmly as I could, listening to the cows stepping right behind me. My heart beat so fast. I didn't know about stampeding, but I felt something from them. Something that wasn't good. Next thing I knew, my grandfather had stood right behind me. He faced the cows with his arms outstretched and just shouted, "stop."

'I walked a few more steps. I heard the cows step forward again. I turned and looked at my grandfather, who stepped backwards and shouted again, 'stop.' The weird thing was, every time he did that, they stopped.'

'A cow whisperer. So tell me what happened next,' she said.

'We got out of the field and my grandfather sat me down in the car and told me about stampeding. How the cows protect their young. He apologised, said he hadn't seen the calves at first.'

Gordon laughed nervously. 'My heart is beating now, thinking about it. I nearly got us both killed that day. And every so often I read about it. Someone getting trampled in a cow field.'

'It doesn't happen that often. Once every several years you might read something?'

'But my eyes always seem to find those stories and every time I do, I feel sick.'

She looked at him. 'It would be dangerous if the dog was out of control, chasing or barking, but it's actually quite rare for cows to stampede.' She gave him a small smile. 'Cows are curious creatures. If they were matching their pace to yours, it's more likely they were just checking you out.'

The adrenaline in his body slowed. He had to trust her. She knew a lot more about these animals than he did. He exhaled heavily and forced a smile. 'Thank you.'

Her eyes softened as she returned his smile. 'Thank you, for being so open. I really value that in a person.'

They walked through the field before reaching the next gate. She pushed the lever and allowed him to follow through.

'What about you?' Gordon said. 'Anything you're scared of?'

She looked down at the path as they walked. Then she shrugged. 'Ending up on this farm all alone, I guess. Alan and Rhys are much older than me. My daughter's moved down south. The rest of my family are over three thousand miles away.'

Gordon stopped walking. 'Jenna. You wouldn't end up alone.'

She stopped alongside him and forced a smile. 'I'm fussy. Rhys and Alan don't know this. Last summer, I nearly got involved with someone. Luckily, I put a halt to things before they ever got started.'

Gordon pressed his lips together and nodded, his ribs tightening ever so slightly. 'What happened?'

'He was one of the lecturers at the local college. Seemed a nice straight forward guy. Until I found out he was a fantasist.'

'Fantasist?' Gordon's heart beat a little quicker. Surely, having the odd fantasy was normal?

'Liar. Told stories. Claimed his father was an Earl, but he'd turned his back on his inheritance. I believed him until Bronwen at the flower shop took me aside one day when I was in there. Said he'd been in and asked her in confidence if she knew what flowers I liked.' Jenna laughed, then shook her head. 'You never tell Bronwen anything in confidence. Anyway, she knew his reputation better than I did and she warned me off him.'

'I don't think you were being fussy,' Gordon said. 'You deserve better.' His own lies poked him in the heart, but surely, his were different. His didn't tell stories to impress people, his current tales were necessary strategies to help everyone concerned in this Right deal. His cheeks reddened. A strategy to help everyone, including himself.

'Hey,' she said. 'Did you send that mega important email of yours?'

He grinned. 'I know you're being sarcastic, but let me

tell you that there's a good chance when I get back to the guesthouse tonight, and bring up my phone messages, I'll have an email from the hotel with an offer for Alan.'

'Well, check your phone now, don't you have it with you?'

Leaves swished in the wind as the chak-chak-chak of a magpie swooned above. The sound of footsteps plopped through the field behind him. He turned to see Alan and Rhys approaching.

'Gordon's getting an email from the hotel,' Jenna said to them. 'They're gonna make you an offer, Alan.'

Alan grimaced. 'Ten thousand? Is that really all the Right is worth?'

Guilt burned in Gordon's stomach as he said, 'It will be more. I've asked for more.'

'How much more?' asked Alan.

Gordon breathed in. 'Twenty-five thousand.'

Alan reached out and squeezed Gordon's shoulder. 'Thanks, son.'

'Go on, check your email now,' Jenna said again.

The trees rustled above as Gordon gazed towards the darkened field. 'Okay, but the odds are this first offer will be below what they'll actually pay.' He pulled out his phone, then scrolled through his emails. He felt the eyes of the Priddys upon him as he continued scrolling. Disappointment hardened in his stomach. Nothing from Edward.

'You're so clever,' Jenna said before turning towards Alan. 'Isn't he?'

'A business athlete,' Rhys chuckled. 'I'll believe it when I see it.'

Gordon sighed. 'No response yet, but that doesn't mean anything. The business day isn't over. But, my guess is this will all be sorted by this time tomorrow.' He swallowed, praying his words would make it true.

An hour later, he strode back to the guesthouse, the thick

soles of his boots slipping slightly on the gravel as he neared. Dusk was turning to evening, and his heart lifted at the thought that back in London, the business day would be over. The email will have surely arrived on Gordon's phone, waiting to be opened and read.

Closing the cottage door behind him, he switched on the hall light. A single lightbulb, its hanging wire strewn with cobwebs, flickered before it stilled. The corridor was blissfully silent without Rhys's music blasting through the walls.

Exhilaration pumped through his veins as he leant against the front door and tugged off his boots. Throwing them to the floor, he pounded up the stairs to his bedroom.

He sat on the bed, then lowered his face against the thumbs of his prayer-like hands. He couldn't explain it, but he had this sudden instinct, a strong one, that there wouldn't be a need for further negotiations. His heart pounded with an excited realisation. The board would only have held one meeting. It would have been totally clear to them all that what the Priddys were planning to carry out would be catastrophic for the hotel, and to make this go away for twenty-five thousand pounds was nothing to them. Why even bother with a negotiation game? As long as Edward also got them all to agree that the Right would be signed over after Gordon got his new role.

He pulled the phone from his pocket and sat on the bed. His heart beat faster as he stared at his email app. This might be it. Closing his eyes, he breathed in. No, he shouldn't get ahead of himself. They would most likely offer to pay the amount to the Priddys but it was just possible that for Gordon, they would suggest a compromise. The mattress squeaked as he took a few steady breaths. He had to be realistic. They might not give him a board position, or even an executive director title. Instead, they might start with a lower regional director role.

He exhaled slowly.

Okay.

Gordon would accept that compromise.

With a shaking thumb, he opened the email app.

There it was.

In bold.

Edward Creaton.

Downstairs, the front door whined open, then slammed shut. Rhys whistled as his heavy footsteps echoed through the corridor.

Gordon sat on the bed staring at the unopened email. Tingling ran through his fingers, and up through his arm as he held the phone.

The smell of a lit joint wafted up from the corridor. Gordon stood, then reached over and quietly pushed his bedroom door closed.

He sat down on the bed again, the mattress springs groaning in protest.

Taking a long breath in, he held it for one, two, three seconds.

Okay. Here we go.

He breathed out and pressed his finger on the email.

Dear Gordon,

Thank you so much for offering to broker a deal between Mr Priddy and the hotel group. Here's my response: Go to hell.

Regards,

Edward

Chapter Sixteen

Gordon woke in the darkness of the early hours. He lay on his back, perspiration beading his upper lip. Sweat from his body seeped into the T-shirt he'd worn to bed. The cotton material stuck to his back, to his chest. He tossed over onto his side.

What the hell had gone wrong?

Edward probably hadn't even told the board about Gordon in Wales, brokering this deal.

Gordon's eyes blinked in the darkness.

Tej.

Tej might know if a sudden directors' meeting occurred yesterday. He'd contact him in the morning. Gordon turned over onto his other side and willed himself to get some sleep. Fear and frustration twisted inside him. There would be no new role waiting for him. No money, as he assured the Priddys. He exhaled heavily, dizzy with exhaustion. His middle aged body was used to desk sitting and central heating, not the hefty physical work of lugging hay bales and feed bags day after day.

He turned again and the saggy mattress whined in protest. He didn't even have his flat to go back to currently. The clean bedroom with the memory foam bedding and a freshly laundered duvet set. He reminded himself that was a fortuitous thing. Someone to pay his rent for a few months at least. In the meantime, he was stuck here in Wales, yet with these kind farmers who trusted he would come up with a resolution for them.

He had failed.

When the dull light of morning peeked through the curtains, Gordon slumped over the bed to grab his phone from the floor.

He scrolled for Tej's name, then thumbed a text. 'Hey mate, how's it going? I really need to talk to you. Phone me when you have a minute.'

He showered and dressed quickly, before Rhys could

catch hold of him, and left the guesthouse to head towards a field. One that would hopefully have heads caught in fences or tangled in wires with sheep butting themselves in the face alongside the trapped ones. Anything to stop him from thinking about what the hell he was supposed to come up with next.

He arrived at the first field, and his heart shrunk. Alan's frail figure stood just inside the gate, checking some wiring near the top of the fence. Gordon stopped, then turned to step quietly towards a different field.

'Gordon,' Alan called out. 'Come look at this wiring. One of them has chewed right through it. The electricity must have been off. Did you check this one recently?'

Gordon shook his head. 'Can't remember. I think so.'

'Can't remember?' Alan frowned.

Gordon stared at the ground. 'I'm sorry, my mind's been—'

'It's okay, son.' Alan sighed. 'Rhys should have been helping out more, not leaving it all to you.'

Gordon's phone rang, and he pulled it from his back pocket.

Tej.

'I've got to take this,' Gordon said, trudging back down the path towards a smaller field. 'Business. Research to do with our hotel negotiations.'

'Hey, Gordon. What's up?' Tej's jubilant voice rang out. 'You still a man of leisure or have you found a new job?'

'I'm in Wales.'

'Wales?' Tej chortled over the phone. 'Lucky you. Those Welsh ladies with their sweet accents? They drive me a bit wild, you know? Not like that crazy barista who stalked me for weeks. Wish I could be there in Wales with a nice Welsh lass.'

'Listen,' Gordon said. 'This isn't a pleasure trip I'm on.'

'Oh hey, speaking of that barista, did she contact you? She said she had to move out of your flat.'

'She what?'

'Oh don't worry. She said she left it tidy. Gave me the key so I could give it back to you.'

'What?' Gordon said. He stopped walking. 'But my rent…'

'What, you didn't take a month up front?'

'I took a week's deposit, she said she'd pay the rest at the end of the month when she got paid.'

'Ah well, she only stayed a week, so you're good.'

His heart thudded with a dreaded panic. There would be no money to pay his rent after this month's final pay cheque. He would lose his home completely. A vision of himself in a red Big Issue jacket selling their homeless magazines took hold. Standing on a street corner, desperate to sell enough issues to sleep in a bug infested hostel that evening. He shook the vision from his head. 'Tej, look. I need you to find something out for me. I sent this email to Edward Creaton yesterday. You have your finger on the pulse with everything that goes on in that office. Did Edward seem different yesterday? Maybe locked in a meeting with the other directors?'

'I wouldn't know,' said Tej. 'I left The Remblents Group.'

'Left? When?'

'The very next day after you! Creaton called me in for a redundancy meeting and I took the package. Jumped at it, to be honest. I'd been there eight years, so it was worth it.'

Gordon pressed his lips together, the frustration of losing this connection with that office. He breathed out. At least his friend had come out of the redundancy unscathed. 'Oh, hey. Good for you. What are you going to do now?'

'Starting my new job on Monday.'

'Well,' Gordon said, as he surveyed the mud caked to his boots. 'Can't say I'm not envious. How did you get a new job so fast?'

'What can I say, don't you know what my name means

in India?' Tej laughed. 'Lustrous, power.'

'Yeah, you've told us that many times at the pub.' Gordon said.

'Okay, but seriously,' Tej said. 'The Cardman Group has been trying to get me to join them for years. As soon as I saw the figures for my redundancy package, I thought, wow, this is like a lottery win. Not a huge one, but nice. I asked Creaton if it meant I could leave straight away, like go on gardening leave.'

Gordon fought back the stab of envy attempting to lodge in his gut. Tej deserved this.

'So you know the first thing I did, of course,' Tej said. 'I phoned the other company and,' he laughed. 'What can I say? They set up an interview that afternoon.'

'Yeah, that's great, Tej,' Gordon said.

'It's a manager's role,' said Tej. 'With prospects to rise to director level within a year. I told them I'd take it if I could start next week.'

Gordon was silent as he looked around at the sheep grazing in the next field. What the hell was he still doing here? He needed to get back to London as soon as possible and look for a job himself.

'You still there?' asked Tej.

'Yeah.... I'm here. Congratulations on the new job.'

'Gordon.' Tej whispered. 'They're a big company. Can I put in a word for you? Would love to have you here, mate.'

'Would you? Wow. Although, I'm still trying to work something out with Remblents...' He paused. Edward's *go to hell* email flashed through his mind. He gave a defeated sigh. 'Yeah. Okay,' Gordon said. 'That would be great. Thanks.'

'No problem. Mates look after each other, right?'

Gordon smiled. 'I really appreciate that.'

'What was the email?' Tej asked.

'The what? Oh, to Edward you mean.' He kicked at a tuft of grass.

A ewe a few feet away *baahhed* almost as if rebuking him.

Tej chuckled. 'Are you up there sorting out those sheep, Gordon? Is that what your email to Creaton was about?'

'I probably shouldn't say.'

Tej guffawed through the phone. 'Okay, I'll take that as a yes. Let me know how you get on. But knowing Creaton, that guy's never going to rise to any farmer threat.'

Gordon was silent.

'He got that scar,' Tej said, 'from some frustrated bastard glassing him in the face for his smugness.'

'Really?'

'No. Just kidding, but wouldn't surprise me if it were something like that, you know?'

Gordon exhaled heavily.

'Hey, mate. Let me settle into my new role for a week or two, and then I'll start sniffing around for an opening for you. If there's nothing at my new company, then maybe somewhere else. In the meantime, I wouldn't tell too many people what you're doing, messing around with some crazy covenant. If word got around, it could close doors for you.'

Gordon nodded while staring at a ewe trotting towards an empty trough. 'Thanks for the advice… and for asking around about jobs.'

'Chin up as they say,' said Tej, 'and catch you again soon.'

Gordon clicked off and looked at the empty trough. Rhys was due to fill the ones in this field shortly. Maybe he should just go down and grab a feed bag. He stood for a moment, staring out towards the hilltops, towards the grey leaden clouds moving closer. He looked at his feet, then tugged the leggings of his waterproofs up from inside his wellies, and rolled the polyester fabric outside the boots, down towards the heels.

One ewe moved closer to his feet, still grazing. He bent

to stroke its soft head. It skittered back a few inches, then stopped and continued grazing. He stared at its ears, gently flicking as the raindrops fell. Gordon pulled the hood of Alan's wax coat over his head, then exhaled heavily.

He pulled his phone from his pocket as he walked down the hill. He stopped as he dialled Edward's number. It rang twice and went to voicemail, as if deliberately diverted. Come on, what's going on, Edward? He rang the office number and Bethany answered.

'Oh hey, Gordon. Sorry to hear you lost your job.'

'Lost it?' Anger built in his chest. How could it be official without an HR meeting? Official enough for everyone to know about it? 'Look… I need to speak with Edward.'

'He's in his office, I'll put you through.'

Gordon's heart beat a little quicker.

Bethany came back on the line. 'Sorry Gordon, he said to tell you he's not here and won't be here the rest of the day and every day after. Although I'm probably supposed to dress it up to sound convincing.'

Gordon's teeth clenched. He breathed in, then exhaled heavily. 'No need to dress it up.'

'Gordon!' A voice called out from behind. Gordon turned to see Alan trudging down the path behind him.

'Take care, Beth.'

Alan panted as he approached. 'You've got a busy day ahead. That fool of a brother of mine has done something to his ankle.' Alan's face reddened with anger. 'That bloody stuff he smokes. Told me he climbed on his roof to recite a haiku to a magpie. Had a fall as he was climbing back down.'

Guilt pounded in Gordon's chest. Alan probably thought this was his fault. He'd taken Rhys to buy that weed, even if he hadn't been aware of it at the time. 'You want me to take him to a doctor?'

'No, it's a sprained ankle. Jenna's over there putting an ice pack on it. The bigger emergency is some of our sheep have got out on the road and he's in no fit state to get them. I need you to help me. That mindless brother of mine needs to stay off his feet for a good few days at least.'

Gordon shoved his phone into his pocket. Adrenaline rushed through him as he strode down the path and towards the main road with Alan. The directorship couldn't be his priority. Not right now. There were people here who had grown to trust him, and at every turn he was letting them down. It had to stop. These people, Alan, Rhys, Jenna, they needed Gordon's help to preserve this farm and Evan's memory, and he needed to step up with getting this Right sorted.

He strode with determination. Whatever Creaton was up to, he wouldn't get rid of Gordon easily.

Chapter Seventeen

To: Edward Creaton
From: Gordon Slee
Subject: Alan Priddy

Dear Edward,

I am completely dumbfounded by your last email. I'm here in Wales trying my best to protect the hotel from serious danger. Is twenty-five thousand that much of a barrier to this? Do you want me to try for a lower figure? Twenty thousand?

Perhaps we can discuss this by phone. You have my number. I'll await your call.

Regards,
Gordon

In Rhys' room of many sofas, Gordon sank low on a front row green one, opposite the two farmers on their faded brown couch. Rhys's injured foot was propped up at an angle on the beige sofa to the side that had been edged forward.

Alan shook his head. 'Not good, the fact you haven't heard from that director. When did you send your email? Two days ago?'

Gordon swallowed, as if he could push down the omission of Creaton's 'go to hell' response, along with his follow-up email of this morning that remained unanswered.

'I did warn you,' Alan said. 'Your Creaton fellow is waiting to see if we actually do it. Bring the sheep to the hotel. This is why I've had you doing the training. Face it, you're taking these sheep to London.'

'I'll send another email. What's today, Thursday? I'll give them a week to stop the sheep coming to London. I'll tell them Jenna's arriving next Thursday at noon to run the sheep through their foyer.'

Alan's face hardened. 'You're going with her. She

doesn't know her way to London.'

Rhys sat forward. 'I'll drive.'

'Not with that ankle,' said Alan. He looked to Gordon. 'Can I rely on you to bring Jenna?'

Rhys grimaced. 'Careful, Alan. He's been looking to make her his lyle.'

'I don't even know what lyle is,' said Gordon.

'Girlfriend, sweetheart.' Rhys said. 'Learn some Welsh.'

Alan cleared his throat. 'Is there something going on with you and Jenna?' he said to Gordon.

Uneasiness swirled in Gordon's stomach as he sat forward. 'No. I'm a man of my word, Alan.' The layers of lies laid heavy in his gut. He'd lied to Alan about his connection to the Remblents Group. He had not been completely open with the directors who would be shocked to find Gordon turning up with the sheep.

Alan pursed his lips. 'You'll need to work together with Jenna. You're talking a twelve hour round-trip journey. Longer when you add the rest stops for the sheep. And she needs to drive the vehicle. You need authorisaton to transport animals to drive the trailer which you don't have.'

Gordon nodded slowly.

'And I want Jenna to help you in case you have to bring the sheep inside the hotel.'

Gordon pushed out a heavy breath. 'I'm hoping it won't get to that. We might not even need to leave Bryn Nefyn.' He peered at Alan. There was something different about him. He seemed thinner, his pallor more grey than usual. Perhaps it was the stress of worrying about this scheme Gordon had set in motion.

Guilt squeezed around his chest. He stared at the carpet, at the various cigarette burns, almost forming a constellation pattern. The Little Dipper fallen from the sky and burning itself into Rhys' filthy carpet. Rhys didn't smoke cigarettes, so the burns must have been weed souvenirs.

He glanced up again at Alan. The kind thing to do would be to give this all up, walk away, save Alan the stress of worrying about his sheep and whether the hotel would negotiate. Yet Alan needed the money, and Gordon had already made too many promises.

He looked at the carpet constellation again, forcing a fantasy of himself in Parliament defending against rebel backbenchers. A row of Creatons. A minister worth his weight would fight them.

His eye ticked. He was no minister, no unflinching chancellor, and it seemed not even a lowly hotel negotiator.

Fuck it.

'Alan, do you want to abandon the whole thing?'

'What?' said Alan. 'Are you out of your mind? What on earth have you been doing here for the past ten days?'

'I just thought —'

'Don't you dare back out of this. You're getting me that justice for my great grandfather's agreement. Or are you not a man of your word?'

He gazed again at the carpet burns and slowly nodded. 'Okay. We need to do this right. Not just turn up at the hotel. I need that letter from your solicitor. Something I can email over to Creaton.'

Alan stood and nodded. 'That can be done. I'll get you your letter. Let me make a call. But I'm telling you now, you'll still be going to London next week.'

Later that afternoon, Gordon composed a third email in response to Creaton. He sunk down onto the bed and put his face in his hands. *You're a business athlete in a position of impenetrable power.* He grabbed his phone from his back pocket, opened his email app, and typed.

Dear Edward,

I am sorry it appears The Remblents Group is not willing to negotiate with Mr. Priddy regarding his Right. I've just had a final meeting with the Priddys. Alan Priddy is in the process of having his solicitor write to you, confirming the permission for his sheep to run through the foyer of the Remblents London as early as next Thursday.

We need to stop this before it's too late.

Regards,
Gordon

Gordon checked the email on his phone several times during Friday morning while out in the fields. He then busied himself getting sixty-four sheep into the adjoining field for new grazing.

At lunchtime he went back to the guesthouse and made himself some toast, forcing himself to eat, despite the dread that built in his stomach. The rucksack Alan had passed on to him through Rhys still lay on the floor in the utility room. He ought to get into the habit of bringing lunch out on the fields with him to keep Alan happy for the next few days.

He checked his phone again. Still nothing from Creaton.

Granddad's pen. Gordon could certainly use the good luck. If that sort of thing was real. Before returning to the fields, he went up to his room and shoved the pen pouch into his shirt pocket.

'Why you taking that fancy pen to the fields?' Rhys said as he hovered on a walking stick in the doorway.

Gordon raised his eyebrows to him.

'I know what a Mont Blanc is. I seen it there in its case when I brought you tea the other day. You worried about leaving it here on its own? You don't trust me?'

'I totally trust you,' Gordon said. 'I just wanted to have it with me this afternoon.'

Rhys pursed his lips, before shaking his head. 'Londoners.'

During the afternoon, while Gordon moved the hay bales, his phone rang. The shock of the ringtone caused him to lose his grip, dropping a bale as it rolled into a thick brown puddle.

He pulled the mobile from his pocket and his heart hammered against his ribcage as the name flashed across the screen.

'Hello, Edward,' he said breathlessly.

Creaton sniffed. 'I don't appreciate being double crossed. We had an agreement. Ten thousand.'

'I know, but it's just… well, Alan told me it's not enough.'

'Who are you acting for? Me? Or your new friend Alan?'

'You obviously. Come on, Edward. What's twenty-five thousand to The Remblents Group? You know the Right is worth a lot more if they plan to use it against you.'

'It's not about the money. It's you. How you're going about things. I'm not happy.'

'Okay. Like I said. I'll get the figure lower. Twenty thousand.'

'And you're going to hold off on the purchase going through until I give you your new director's role?'

Gordon calmed his breath. 'It was just a negotiation. Or rather confirmation of an agreement. Between you and me.' He sighed. 'Twenty thousand. It's a steal, Edward.'

'Fifteen thousand and you'll get the director's position in writing in six months' time. After we've closed the deal.'

Disappointment hardened in his stomach. 'Fifteen thousand,' Gordon whispered.

'Not a penny more,' Edward said. 'You need to trust me, Gordon. Your Grandfather always did.' He clicked off the line.

The following morning, Gordon helped Alan mend some wire fencing. 'I heard back from Edward Creaton.'

Alan stood back, 'And?'

Gordon swallowed. 'It's better than the ten thousand.'

'How much better?'

'Fifteen.'

'No.'

'That's the most they'll pay.'

'What happened to my twenty-five?'

'It's a no.'

'Fine. Then you and Jenna go to London.'

Later that afternoon, Gordon checked the batteries for the electric in every single roadside fence, ensuring none had run out. While Alan went back to his house for lunch, Gordon rang Creaton.

'Edward, I've tried my best, but it's got to be twenty.'

'Why are you bothering me with this on a weekend? I'm out with my granddaughter.'

Gordon heard a little girl giggling in the background.

'I'll come look in second, sweetheart,' Creaton called out, in a voice oddly tender.

'Edward, I won't keep you. I just want to sort this for you quickly. Yes to twenty thousand?'

Creaton sighed. 'Phone me on Monday.'

On Monday morning, Gordon woke early, full of energy and optimism. He shoved Granddad's pen in his shirt pocket, next to his heart. Then he pulled out his phone and dialled Edward.

Straight to voicemail. 'It's Gordon. Phone me. Let's wrap this up.'

During the morning, he busied himself with guiding sheep's heads into braces while Rhys picked up the fleece trimmers to dag. In between each sheep dagging, Gordon fumbled with his phone to check for missed calls. None. He checked his emails. Nothing.

At lunchtime, he rang Creaton's office. 'Bethany, please tell him it's me.'

'Oh,' she said. 'Strangely, he wants to speak with you.'

Gordon's heart lifted as Edward's gruff voice came on

the line. 'Tell that bastard Priddy he can have his twenty thousand, but I want the purchase proposal in our solicitor's hands this week.'

'You got it, Edward.'

He rushed over to Alan's cottage. He found Alan sitting in his kitchen with a mug of tea. Gordon stood opposite him, smiling 'We've got a deal,' he announced, his chest puffed with pride.

'How much?'

'Twenty thousand.'

'No deal.' Alan looked down, then slurped his tea.

Gordon's mouth gaped. 'Alan, come on.' His jaw tightened in frustration. Screw it, once Gordon had the director's job, he'd give Alan the extra five grand himself. 'Okay then. Twenty-five thousand. There's just a delay with the final five.'

Alan looked up again, narrowing his eyes. 'Why?'

'Who knows?' Gordon shrugged. 'Tax reasons? The purchase agreement will say twenty, but you have my word you'll get the other five.'

'I've been thinking,' Alan said. 'They'll pay up a lot more if you go to London. A lot more than twenty-five thousand.'

Gordon breathed out slowly to release the tightness in his chest.

'I'm doing this for them,' Alan said. 'Rhys and Jenna. This is their home too and I don't want to see them losing it.'

'Lose their home? I thought the money was to buy back some land?'

'Well, now you know the truth. Twenty-five thousand isn't enough.' Alan pushed his chair back and stood. Then he patted Gordon's shoulder as he walked past. 'This is why you and Jenna are going to London on Thursday.'

Gordon trudged down the path towards Rhys's cottage. Jesus H Christ. What the hell was he supposed to do now?

His breath shortened as the thoughts in his head blurred. In desperation, he pulled his mobile from his pocket and phoned Edward.

'All agreed?' asked Creaton.

Gordon stopped. Ran a hand through his hair. 'No.'

'No?'

'I did my best.' Damn it Fuck it. 'We underestimated Alan Priddy.'

'You mean you did. Funny how when he came to see me, I got rid of him fairly quickly. I don't think you've ever been up to these negotiations.'

'It isn't that, Edward. I think his situation might be more desperate now than four years ago. You're going to need to pull out all the stops. Meet with the board. Come up with the best possible offer you can.'

'Or what?'

'Or the sheep will be outside our London hotel come Thursday morning.'

The hours ticked by without a word from Creaton. Throughout Tuesday morning, Gordon checked the fields, filled all the troughs. With Rhys still confined to hobbling around the guesthouse, Gordon then helped Alan weigh and record lambs for the market.

Wednesday lunchtime, he went to see Jenna. 'Hey,' she said, zipping up her parka. 'I'm heading into the village. She nodded towards two teenagers, clearing out the pen. 'Apprentices are here, so I've got an actual lunch break today. Want to come with me? We can firm up on the plan for tomorrow.'

His throat tightened as he followed her towards a beat up old truck.

'I have a better idea,' she said. 'Instead of the village, would you like to visit Rhys' favourite pub?'

Why not? He could use a drink.

They drove for about twenty minutes, through a town Gordon didn't recognise, and then to the top of a hill.

As they trudged down the steep hill, rugged rocks off to the left were hugged by the bright blue water.

'Sometimes you get grey seals on those rocks,' Jenna said.

Gordon breathed in the sea air as gulls squawked above. The scenery so beautiful, with the sea along the side of their path, it almost didn't look real. The white tipped waves disappeared behind the golf greens as they continued walking downhill. As they reached a path through some cliffs, the sea came back into view.

'It's just there,' Jenna said. 'Right on the beach.' They climbed down onto the sand, then trudged towards some wooden tables along the front of the pub.

'You okay to sit outside?' Jenna said. 'I like looking at the bay. Oh, and these are on me.'

He watched her disappear inside the pub, then turned to admire the boats bobbing on the bay.

Jenna returned a few minutes later with two dripping pints. 'I've ordered us sandwiches too. I hope you like roast beef.'

'Let me pay,' Gordon said.

She waved her hand. 'No. You're doing enough for us.'

Guilt tightened in Gordon's throat. He took a sip of lager.

'So, it's tomorrow?' Jenna said. 'Our big trip into London? I guess we should leave here by….'

Despite the lager, Gordon's mouth dried. 'Six am. To get there at noon.'

'Five am.'

'What?'

'The sheep will need a few rest breaks. Service areas, check they're okay, give them water.'

'Okay. Five am,' Gordon said. He gazed out at the boats again. Come on, Edward. Phone me. Don't wait until the morning. Do it today.

'Then what?' Jenna asked. 'We bring the sheep in, or do you go talk to the hotel guy first?'

The sickly lager swirled in his stomach. 'I think we just play this all by ear. Chances are, the director will phone as we're heading down the motorway in the morning. If not this evening.'

Her forehead wrinkled as she took a sip from her glass. 'Can I ask you a personal question?'

'Go on.'

'How much are they paying you for this? The hotel group?'

He swallowed. 'Nothing, as it might turn out.'

'So why are you doing this?'

He shrugged. 'I can't stop now, can I? It's to help Alan…. And Rhys.'

She laughed. 'Oh, come on, you didn't even know them until a few weeks ago. Why did you come up here to start all this in the first place? I mean, who are you even working for now? You're an insurance broker, yet you're spending all this time in Wales.'

'The truth is … what I said about being an insurance broker…' He looked at her, at those eyes, trusting, waiting.

'Go on,' she said.

'I'm not actually working at the moment. So yes, I thought I could sort something out for myself by doing this private deal.'

'I knew your motive had to be money. It's pretty obvious how much material stuff means to you. The things you said to me the morning after we had dinner. When we were walking back from the field. The director's job you were dreaming of. The big house you would buy.'

His cheeks flushed. It used to impress Stacey to hear that talk.

'Jenna, it's not really about owning the material stuff.'

'Isn't it?'

'All my life I've wanted to ….'

'What?'

'Prove myself.'

'Who to?'

He shrugged. 'My family, maybe. Just grasp a little piece of success before it whizzed by on its way to someone else.' He tapped the table and forced a grin. 'Like it usually does.'

'And success to you is what?'

'Being settled. In a home. A proper house, I mean, not just a rented flat. A career with prospects. A big enough salary to even support a family one day.'

'How old are you?'

'Forty-two. I'm not over the hill yet.'

She laughed, then looked towards the boats moored along the bay. 'I'm nervous about tomorrow.'

'Me too.' He breathed.

'Ah, our lunch is here. Let's eat up, then get back.'

He walked the fields the rest of the afternoon, unnecessarily checking the batteries in the electric fences for a third time, the adrenaline cursing through him as he stomped through the grass.

'Gordon,' Jenna called out.

He turned.

'One of the silly ewe's has got her head stuck in a wire fence hole in the next field. How about we see if you can manage this one?' She approached him, brushing remnants of straw from her jeans. 'I was filling the trough when she didn't come running with the others. I was gonna free her from the fence, then thought, I wanna see you do it. If you're as good as you say, I might even award you the title of qualified junior shepherd.' She smiled.

They walked together to the far end of the field. When they reached the gate, he grabbed the lever, pinching the flesh of his palm between the metal and the wood.

'Ouch, Jesus. Why don't you get this fixed?' he said, then sucked on the heel of his hand.

Jenna laughed. 'It's not the lever, it's you.'

She pushed the gate forward, and he followed her to the next field. The sun had broken through the afternoon clouds. Its rays streamed across the grass, the tiniest pearls of light clinging to the moist blades as they walked.

'Just over here,' she said. She knelt in the wet grass near some bushes, next to the trapped ewe. 'Gordon's here to get your silly head out,' she said softly.

He crouched near the other side of the sheep and looked at Jenna. Sunlight peeked through the bushes, illuminating her face. As she stroked the ewe's neck, he noticed her eyelashes, so light in colour, a shade paler than her hair and just a little darker than the wisps of straw that were stuck to her jeans. The outer edges of her lashes had a curl. She looked up, her eyes registering his gaze. Two pink dots spread across her cheeks.

His mouth dry, he shoved his hands into the fence wiring, flattening the ewe's ears as he guided her head back.

'Thank you,' Jenna said, as the ewe scuttled backwards, then ran across the field.

He stood and brushed the mud from the knees of his jeans.

'It's rewarding isn't it?' She said as she stood. 'Caring for them.'

'It is,' he said. With a strange mixture of confusion and pride, he nodded. 'Anytime you need me….'

'Lambing season. You should come for lambing season.'

'When's that?'

'Not till Spring. Or actually, January is great too.'

'What happens in January?'

'That's when we scan all those ewes who've been enjoying their time with the rams in the tupping field. See who's carrying how many lambs.'

'And lambing is when?'

'Around March time.' She smiled wistfully. 'It's hard work. Really hard work. Someone's got to be with the pregnant ewes, keeping an eye on them, in case they need you to assist with the birth. Which could mean pulling the lamb out by its hind legs. I usually end up sleeping in the lambing shed overnight during the season.' She turned to gaze towards the next field. 'Dylan and I used to take it in shifts.'

Gordon swallowed. 'Doesn't Rhys help?'

'Rhys, Alan, the local agricultural students. But I like being there. It's the best time of the year. Why should I miss out on watching the result of what we've all worked for throughout the seasons?' She shrugged her shoulders upwards, as if hugging herself. 'Maybe it's how midwives feel. Witnessing that miracle, the cycle of life beginning again. The fact it's happening in Spring when all of nature is coming to life, the flowers, the buds on the trees, and then when I'm holding that slimy, wriggly newborn lamb in my hands, the entire world just feels overwhelmingly beautiful.'

Her eyes sparkled.

He nearly wished he could be here for Spring. But of course, by then, with any luck, Creaton will have phoned him this evening and his renewed life in London will have made Wales a distant memory.

'So, tomorrow, right? We get some of these ridiculous sheep out for their day trip?' She grinned nervously. 'Five am outside the guesthouse?'

Gordon's heart thudded in dread. 'Tomorrow.'

Chapter Eighteen

At five a.m., Gordon stood outside the guesthouse in the heavy darkness. His teeth chattered in the morning air as he shoved his hands into his pockets and attempted to halt the twisting nerves in his stomach. Wearing a baseball cap that he'd found amongst the jumble of clean wrinkled sheets in Rhys' utility room, he pushed back the brim and looked at the black sky. A ghostly silver moon peeked out from behind the dark outline of the lopsided hill.

Ahead, a shadowy figure behind the pin light of a torch appeared. Gravel crunched beneath her boots as she approached. 'Nervous?' she asked.

He shook his head no, then stopped. 'Yes, very.'

She gave him a watery smile. 'What's with the baseball cap?'

He shrugged.

'I'm a Mets fan, not Yankees,' she said. 'Not sure I should let you wear it.'

'I don't know what you're talking about.'

'Of course not. Half the people in the UK who buy that cap don't realise the NY emblem is for New York Yankees. Come on, let's get to the trailer.'

Jenna turned and walked with her torch towards the barn.

Gordon followed. Creaton would phone. He'd do it before nine am. There were still four hours to go.

Alan had parked the trailer inside the barn, leaving the vehicle's back door wide open. A ramp rested against it, reaching to the floor. The nearby pen contained half a dozen sheep.

'Take hold of that loose gate against the pen, then stand back,' Jenna said.

'Why?'

'You think they're just gonna waltz into the back of this trailer? When I open this pen, they'll come out because they're nosey. I need you there with the gate in front of you moving slowly forward so that they turn and get in the trailer instead of walking out past you to the field.'

Gordon grabbed the gate and dragged it in front of his feet. 'At least this one doesn't have a metal lever.' He said, attempting to unknot the nerves in his stomach.

Jenna opened the door to the pen. The six ewes trotted out, straight towards the opposite wall of the barn, then stopped when they could get no further.

'Stupid sheep,' Gordon muttered. 'Staring at a brick wall.'

'They're not stupid. Move forward a bit and they'll turn away, hopefully towards the trailer.' Gordon inched forward with the gate. In unison, like a choreographed dance move, the sheep turned their tails to him to face the open back of the trailer. The ewe at the front stepped onto the ramp and stood at the trailer's back entrance, ears flicking. The other five followed her and pushed her forward inside the trailer. Within seconds, all six were on board.

'They knew to get on the trailer?' Gordon said.

'I told you, they're nosey. Once the first one wanted to see what was in there, the rest had to look too.'

Gordon gazed at their woolly tails and smiled.

'I'll back us out,' Jenna said. 'Then you can drive. I'm not keen on motorway driving. The lanes here in the U.K. are too narrow.'

'You've been here, what? Twenty years? Still not used to our motorways?'

She looked down. Her hair, loose again, obscured her face. 'Dylan always did the motorway driving.'

'But…' his mouth dried. 'Alan said I'm supposed to have a certificate or something like that to drive them.'

Jenna stared at the ground, biting her lip. 'I'll drive until we get to the motorway? We can do the first rest stop for the sheep just before we get on it and then you can take over from there.'

'Gordon, I'm worried,' Jenna said as they entered the motorway with Gordon behind the wheel.

'I know.'

She bounced her knee rapidly as she sat in the passenger seat. 'I'm so stupid. Why did I agree to this? They're probably already nervous in that trailer, us coming down this motorway. It's going to be chaos if we let them run through that building. They'll be scared of the indoor environment, all the people, new noises.'

Gordon swallowed. 'It will be okay. I keep telling you, it won't happen. The sheep will never leave the trailer once we're in London. I know this company. It's a game of bluff.' He reached into his front pocket and tossed his phone into her lap. 'From eight am, keep checking my emails. My passcode on the phone is twenty-nine, eleven, eighty-three.'

'Your birthday?'

He nodded.

'Dangerous.'

'What is?' Gordon asked.

'Sagittarius people.'

He peeked at her again and she was smiling.

'Adventurous, impulsive….' she said.

He shrugged.

'Maybe. Whatever. I don't believe in that stuff. I'm surprised you do.'

'Are you judging me?' she said.

'What?' he said. 'No, I'm not. I just thought you were more sophisticated than that, you know, being a New Yorker.'

'What sort of stereotypical comment is that? You still think I'm from New York City, some Carrie Bradshaw type interested in shoes and rich men, drinking cosmopolitans?'

'That's obviously not you.' He chuckled, but the sound caught in his throat as Stacey appeared in his consciousness.

'You know, I never said I actually believed in astrology but I do believe in social graces and making conversation and we now seem to be stuck together for hours on a motorway—'

'Okay, sorry. Check my email?'

'It's only twenty past seven.'

'Check it anyway.'

'Did you say twenty-ninth of November? Your passcode?'

He nodded.

'Three days after Thanksgiving.'

They drove in silence for several minutes, apart from the baaing of sheep inside the back of the trailer. Gordon switched the radio on to find some music.

'You should come,' Jenna said.

'Where?'

The familiar opening strands of Creedence Clearwater Revival blasted through the speakers.

'Jesus, Rhys,' Gordon said, pressing the CD button to off. The sound switched to a BBC morning show.

'You should come to Thanksgiving,' Jenna said a little louder. 'It's next week. I do a family dinner every year at my house.'

He pressed the radio volume to low. Placing his hand on the wheel again, he glanced at her in confusion. 'You know,' he said. 'I'll be leaving Wales after today. I'm hoping this deal will be done before we even get off the motorway.'

'Oh.' Jenna turned to look out the passenger window. The grey light of morning had started to rise. 'I hadn't thought of that.' She turned back towards him. 'What about Rhys? His foot's still bad and Alan needs you to help out on the farm….'

Gordon swallowed. 'You're right. Maybe I can stay a few days longer.' The anxiety churned in his stomach. Not too much longer. He really needed to sort out a temporary paying job for himself before he lost his home. Lost everything.

They were silent for several minutes. Gordon glanced towards her again. She stared at the slow-moving traffic in front of them. He indicated to overtake the car in front.

'Don't do that,' Jenna said. 'Drive slowly. There's a speed limit for when you're travelling with livestock. Keep below sixty.'

He flicked the indicator off. Nervousness mixed with the anxiety in his stomach. The air in the cab grew heavy with the silence between them.

His mobile buzzed in Jenna's lap, and Gordon bolted upright behind the wheel. 'Answer it!'

'Hello… yes, he's driving but I can pass on a message…… oh, right….'

'What?' Gordon hissed.

'It's your sister. Do you want to go to her place for lunch on your birthday? She says it's a Sunday.'

His heart crushed inwards. He'd have to face his family and what? Tell them the truth about his current lack of job? How he might need to give up his flat?

'I'll phone her later,' he said.

'He's going to phone you back,' Jenna said. 'Oh, me?' She giggled. 'Umm, Jenna… well, I've got work… I'm a shepherdess…. yes really…. It is interesting….'

'Jenna,' Gordon said.

She looked at Gordon. 'Right, sorry, I need to go. We're waiting for another call. It's business…. Yes, with sheep!' she laughed.

'Jenna,' Gordon said, a bit more sternly.

'Okay, bye.' She dropped the phone in her lap and looked at Gordon. 'Your sister sounds really nice.'

'Yeah, wait until you meet her. Well, not that you ever will, but….' He trailed off.

They drove several more miles in silence.

He cleared his throat. 'I can stay in Wales until Sunday. I reckon Rhys will be fine in another three or four days. I caught him yesterday dancing to his favourite Credence song in the kitchen.'

'Really?'

Gordon forced a smile. 'Although he grabbed a chair and plonked himself down moaning as soon as I walked in.'

Jenna laughed.

'What I wanted to say is, I'll still come up for Thanksgiving?' He glanced at her nervously. 'I plan to do some job searching early in the week, but it's not likely I'll have a new job by next Thursday,'

'Yes.' Her voice brightened. 'Yes, you should come. Ever have a real home-made pecan pie? It's not a New York recipe. My aunt from Georgia taught me how to make it.'

He shook his head. 'Not had the real deal, I don't think. I'll look forward to that.'

They passed a sign announcing a service station ahead. 'Do the sheep need another rest break?' he asked. It would be good to stall. Give Creaton just a bit of extra time.

She checked the time on the phone. 'Not yet. Give it another hour.'

His stomach knotted with nerves. He'd been counting on an email before they got nearer to London. Him arriving on the steps instead of one of the farmers would inflame the situation further. Even if the directors were about to offer a deal, Creaton would be so incensed he could withdraw it at the last second.

'Jenna, when we get to the hotel, it might be best if the directors don't see me.'

'What do you mean?'

'They think I'm on their side.'

She turned in her seat, eyes wide. 'Why?'

'Because that's how negotiations work. It's part of the game.'

'Then how do I know that you're on our side?'

'You just have to trust me.'

Five hours later, they arrived at the hotel. As they approached the street of the Remblents London, Gordon's hands on the wheel grew sweaty. He looked across at Jenna. Her complexion had paled to an even whiter shade. He watched as she thumbed in his passcode again to check for an email notification.

'Anything?' Gordon said. He parked the trailer along the side street of the hotel.

Phone in hand, she turned to look out the passenger window. 'Aren't we going around to the front? To make an entrance?'

'Check the emails first. If the offer is there, which I suspect it will be by now, we'll be turning around to get back to Wales.'

'Russian beauties are waiting for you,' she said, and laughed, but it was strained, more of a high-pitched giggle. Her hands trembled as she handed Gordon his phone.

The nerves in his stomach twisted into a solid clump. 'Okay.' He exhaled. 'Maybe I do need to drive us around to the front. Let them see you've arrived with the sheep.

He drove slowly around the corner to the front of the hotel, edging the vehicle into the loading bay near the bottom of the hotel steps. His heart raced as he switched off the ignition and turned his face away from the hotel entrance.

'One of the directors is probably just inside,' he said. 'Waiting to offer us a last-minute settlement.' He swallowed. 'They just wanted to see if we'd actually show up. We'll wait here just for a minute.'

'I'm not sitting around waiting. Let me go up. See what happens.'

The nerves in his stomach twisted further. 'Okay. Just tell them you're here. Then come back down and tell me what they said.'

She stepped out of the trailer and slammed the door behind her.

He pulled the baseball cap further over his face and

peeked from beneath it as she climbed the steps, each footstep she took escalating the panic in his chest. *It's okay, any moment that glass door will open and one of the suited directors would appear and hand her a letter….*

The glass door pushed open.

In the entranceway stood Edward Creaton, arms crossed. He glared at Jenna, his lips pressed tightly, before breaking into a wide grin.

Gordon's heart thudded.

As Jenna reached the top step, Creaton stepped aside and a younger man, bespectacled and wearing a dark suit, walked up to her and handed over a folded sheet of paper. Yes! He knew it! Victory at the very last second! Excitement flooded through him as he held his breath.

He watched then as Creaton leant towards Jenna, smiling as he spoke with her. Gordon breathed out with relief. At last. These weeks in Wales weren't in vain. He was right to suspect this scheme may have been the unusual, yet crazy, sort of thing an up and coming Director had to do to prove his worth.

Jenna stepped back from Edward, her face reddening, her features hardening as she shouted something. A security guard stepped forward and gripped her elbow.

Gordon grabbed the door lever and kicked the driver's side open.

Jenna shook herself free and rushed down the steps with the folded paper in her hand. 'Stay in the goddam van,' she shouted to Gordon, then swung open the passenger door and slumped down into the seat.

'What the hell is going on? Why did that guy touch you?' said Gordon.

'Because I told them to fuck off,' she said.

Gordon grabbed the door handle again. 'If they want to manhandle somebody, they can deal with me…'

'Stop it,' she said. 'You'll make things worse. You said we needed to think of this as a game and that they can't see you. We may have struck out but we still have more innings to play, right?'

He rubbed his face with his hands before slumping against the driver's seat. 'What does that paper say?'

She passed it to him. 'The guy who gave it to me said he was a Health & Safety official. That paper bans us from running sheep through this hotel. Said this order overrides any permission from the Right and he'd have us arrested if we brought even one sheep onto the premises.'

Gordon's heart froze as he took the paper. Unfolding the page with trembling fingers, he couldn't read it. The letters quivered on the page.

'And that creepy older guy,' said Jenna. 'He told me there's a zoo over in Battersea where he takes his granddaughter sometimes to feed the lambs. Suggested I take my sheep over there for a little mingle with their cousins.'

'Bastard.' Gordon whispered, the paper shaking in his hands.

'*Buy them some chocolate ice cream too,*' Jenna mimicked. '*My granddaughter says it's the best.* He was talking to me like I was some stupid airhead. I swear I would have punched him in the face, but I can't get myself arrested with half a dozen sheep waiting to get back to Wales.'

Gordon's heart pounded in anger. 'Fuck this.' He put his hand on the driver's door handle.

'Where are you going? Don't. You said he can't see you.'

Gordon hesitated.

'Don't ruin it by going out there,' Jenna said.

Gordon's hands shook with anger as he placed them on the steering wheel. He rested his forehead on its top. With this insane sheep clause, life had handed him an opportunity on a golden, bloody plate. Yet Gordon had somehow dropped it and witnessed it smash.

He breathed in. A Right, an actual legal Right belonging to a family who gave him permission to exercise it, yet still, he messed it up. Self-loathing crawled along his skin. His father wouldn't have messed up this opportunity. Nor would have Mark.

He pushed the keys into the ignition, willing the torment building in his throat not to rise any further.

'What should we do?' asked Jenna.

He started the engine. 'I don't know yet. But we need to get out of here.'

They drove through the crowded London streets, and on to the road leading towards the motorway.

'But we're not giving up?' Jenna asked.

He swallowed, trying to find the right words. 'Bastard. Fucking… excuse my language… bastard. He lied.'

Jenna sat in silence. After several long minutes, she said, 'Can it be overturned?'

'I'll look into it, but…' he banged the top of the steering wheel.

'What?'

He saw a sign leading towards a slip road. 'Are you hungry?'

'No. I was before, but I'm not now.'

'I need a break.' He turned off at the slip road and eventually pulled up outside a Costa Coffee shop. In silence, he tugged up the handbrake, then switched off the ignition.

'What did you mean when you said Edward Creaton lied?' asked Jenna.

Gordon slumped back against the driver's seat as he gazed out through the windscreen. 'I meant that he hid this tactic from me. We were supposed to be a team.' He glanced towards her. 'I mean, that's what I wanted him to believe.'

'So, it just sounds like he was bluffing you the same as you were bluffing him. Part of the game, right?'

He inhaled sharply.

'You're not giving up, though?' She asked.

'I'm not sure how we move forward. I'm so sorry.'

'I can't see how this is your fault.'

He looked down into his lap. 'It is. You know, I have these stupid fantasy moments when I think I can take on the world, but I seem to cock it up every time.' He shrugged and tried to smile. 'It's like there's this emptiness inside me that I try to fill up with success, like nothing else is enough. And I get so blinded by grasping for it, I trust the wrong people. Then I miss the obvious pitfalls.' He squeezed his hands into fists. They sat in silence again for several long seconds before he finally looked at her.

She stared at him with those wide eyes, filling with something akin to sadness.

'Sorry, stupid thing to say out loud.' He released the fingers digging into his palms, then leaned forward to turn the ignition key. 'There's a drive-through window if you want a coffee.'

'No, turn that off.' she said.

He did as she asked and sat back, his shoulders sagging as he stared out through the windscreen at the Costa Coffee hut.

'Go on,' she whispered. 'Explain it to me. About the emptiness.'

He sighed as he continued to stare ahead at the people leaving the coffee shop carrying tall, white cups. People who had normal, happy lives judging by the way they laughed, or walked with determination, with confidence. People with purpose, a reason to be in this world. He swallowed, the lump in his throat growing.

'Why do you feel empty?' said Jenna.

He winced. 'It's like power is this thing outside of me,' he said. 'I can see it there right in front of me, but when I reach out for it, the power moves, eludes me, like it's playing.' He studied his hands in his lap, fingers still shaking. 'It's supposed to come from within. That's what people say, right? I don't think it is within me or ever was. I've always had to grasp at it from the outside.'

He glimpsed over towards her. She'd turned away and sat looking through the passenger window, her focus on an older couple getting into the car next to them.

'What are you thinking?' Gordon asked.

She turned towards him. 'That I want to help you grasp it.'

Then he saw it, the tiniest curl of her lips as she smiled.

He gazed at her, at the wide eyes, with the lashes just a shade darker than straw. His face moved towards her, just a few inches, and he stopped. Her smile widened, so he moved a little closer and together, they moved towards each other until his lips were on hers and her hands lightly gripped the back of his neck. Then, her delicate fingers pushed up through his hair, sending tingles through his scalp as her mouth pulled him in closer, deeper, into a swirling abyss of desire.

Chapter Nineteen

Jesus, what had he done? He pulled away from her, from her soft lips, and edged himself back in his driver's seat, embarrassed and more than a little… excited.

'Sorry… we….' he said as he looked at her.

'You're sorry?'

He sat back. 'I meant…' he rubbed his hand over his face. 'I don't want… Alan will think….'

'What has this got to do with Alan?'

'He's protective of you. All the stuff Rhys told me about the family tradition.'

'Oh, for God's sake. I'm not a child.' She huffed.

'I know you're not, but I gave him my word.'

'Oh, let's just go.'

He swallowed. 'You don't understand. I'm not…'

'What?'

He turned the key in the ignition and started up the engine. This was not the time to get entangled emotionally with a woman in Wales, not with the mess of these Right negotiations crumbling at his feet. Besides, Alan would probably shoot him if he found out Gordon had kissed his niece in a moment of weakness.

His heart thudded. No. It was more than that. This beautiful farm girl, no not farm girl, woman, shepherdess…and she was beautiful, more so each day it seemed. Why would she want him with his history of screwing up relationships? It had only been weeks since he proposed to Stacey. Plus, his career prospects were currently zero, and Jenna deserved someone with a sold life after the stability she shared with Dylan. No. It was impossible.

He drove onto the motorway, fighting to keep to the livestock speed limit of sixty miles per hour, aching to get back to Wales, to dump the sheep into their paddock and then what? Stay at Rhys's until Sunday? Then head back to London to search for a life?

They drove for miles along the motorway in silence. He pulled into a service area for Jenna to go around to check the sheep and give them water.

As they got nearer to Wales, he glanced towards Jenna, who sat with a tight expression while staring straight ahead.

Regret squeezed around his heart. He peered at the signs towards the M42. It would be an hour before they reached Bryn Nefyn. He sighed, not meaning to, then cleared his throat. 'We should stop again. We've not had anything to eat since breakfast.'

'Okay.' Her voice was low, sad.

'Jenna,' he whispered, as he glanced towards her.

She ignored him and continued to stare straight ahead.

'There's a McDonald's at the next service station,' he said. 'Let's eat something before we get back and maybe… talk.'

He swallowed, not sure what he would actually say to her. He swerved to move towards the slip road. A horn behind blared.

'Careful!' Jenna shouted.

'It's okay. Just some arse behind us.'

Jenna turned. 'Flashing lights.'

'What?'

'Cops.'

Gordon's stomach jolted. 'Shit. What happens to someone driving these animals without a transport certificate?'

'I don't know.'

He glanced at her as he drove towards the service area. 'What do you mean, you don't know?'

'I've never known anyone who drove them without the right paperwork.'

He pulled into a parking space, turned off the ignition, and rested his head on the steering wheel. 'Are the police pulling in behind me?'

Jenna turned in her seat. 'No. They must have been

looking for someone else.'

He sighed. 'You need to take over after we get something to eat.'

'When we're off the motorway. Then I'll drive again.'

At the restaurant table, they sat in strained silence. Gordon struggled to swallow the last bites from his burger, then dropped the remainder into its carton. 'Jenna. About what happened between us earlier. Why I pulled away from you. It's just …. I'm not who you think I am.'

'Oh don't start with this nonsense. Who are you then? The son of an Earl?'

He grimaced. 'It's not nonsense. I would explain it, but I'm not sure how.'

She shook her head. 'Look, I'm tired, Gordon.' She squashed the empty burger carton in front of her, and his heart crushed with it. 'If it makes you feel any better,' she said. 'I agree it was a mistake.'

His breath slowed. 'I see.'

'Can we just get back now?' she said.

As they drove along the motorway, Gordon said, 'I might as well drive us the whole way back. We've come this far. Not long to Bryn Nefyn.'

Jenna nodded before turning away to stare out the darkened passenger window.

An hour later, they reached the turning towards Bryn Nefyn. Another ten minutes and he could escape the tension between them. He put his foot on the gas.

'Hey, slow down,' Jenna said.

A car came up behind them and a blue light blipped.

'Oh Christ,' Gordon said, and pulled the trailer over to the side of the road. He turned off the ignition and sat back, rubbing his hands over his face.

Jenna opened the passenger door.

'What are you doing?' Gordon said.

'It's okay.' She rushed out.

Gordon watched in his wing mirror as Jenna laughed and chatted with the policeman behind the trailer. A few minutes later, she hopped back into the passenger seat and closed the door. 'We're okay. Just drive before he comes over to ask you any questions.'

Gordon turned the key in the ignition and slowly pulled back onto the road. 'What did you say to him?'

'That you were one of our new farm hands. Which is true. How we were just tired from a long trip. He never questioned if you had the authority to drive this thing. Best to just keep driving now.'

'What if he phones it in?'

'Phones what in? He knows me. He's a friend of Rhys.'

Gordon nodded. 'Hari the Heddwas?'

Jenna turned towards him. 'You know Hari?'

He shrugged. 'Someone Rhys mentioned. The day we went to….' He glanced at her and swallowed. 'Get your flowers.'

She nodded and looked away.

They drove for the last eight minutes in silence. Finally, they reached the farm and Gordon steered the trailer into the barn. He turned off the engine and exhaled heavily.

'Who's going to tell Alan?' said Jenna.

He flushed with embarrassment. 'You want to tell Alan that you and I…'

'Oh, for God's sake, not about us kissing. The hotel. The Health and Safety order.'

'I will.' he said.

She opened the passenger door and got out. Then she turned and bent to peer towards him.

'What?' said Gordon.

She pressed her lips together and shook her head. 'Men.'

He stared at her.

'I was pretty sheltered with Dylan and me getting together so young. Now I know why people think relationships are complicated.'

Gordon breathed in and nodded.

'Do me a favour,' she said. 'Look into maybe getting

that Health and Safety order changed. Do it for Alan. You got him all excited about buying his land back. You can't just give up on helping him like this.'

'I'll look into it,' he said.

She stood tall. 'Asshole,' she said under her breath before stomping towards the back to open the pen.

He opened the driver's door. 'I just said I'd look into it. My sister's husband. He's a solicitor. Maybe he knows someone—'

'Whatever.' She pulled the trailer doors open and let the sheep out.

'Oh, Jesus Christ.' He climbed out from the driver's side and trudged towards her. 'Is this about what happened between us earlier? I'm sorry I pulled away from you. But you said it yourself, it was a mistake.'

She ignored him as she picked up the single gate and guided the sheep into the paddock.

Right. She didn't want to talk, and she didn't need him to help with the sheep. He strode out towards the field.

'Where are you going?' Jenna called out.

'To tell Alan things didn't work out with the hotel. And that it was my fault.'

'Stop it. I'm gonna come with you. We have to tell him we're still trying.'

He stopped walking and stood, his shoulders stiffening.

Her footsteps crunched in the gravel behind him. He turned.

'I just don't want to get any more hopes up for anyone,' he said.

'Neither do I, but you know, there's such a thing as not doing things too abruptly. Letting someone down gently.' She stared at him for several long seconds. 'You know what I mean?'

He watched the irritation in her eyes soften to a question. The moonlight picked out the curl at the edges of her lashes and the urge to kiss her again burned within him.

He took a deep breath. 'Okay, we'll let him down gently.'

She bit her lip.

The small action made him breathless for a moment. 'Let's walk together,' he said as he turned towards the path to Alan's cottage.

Chapter Twenty

'So, you're telling me it didn't work?' Alan said. 'What did I say to you the very first day you turned up here? That hotel, and especially that smug director, they're not interested in paying me for that Right.'

'I agree it's a setback,' Gordon said. They sat in Alan's sitting room. Gordon clasped his fingers in his lap until his knuckles turned white. Jenna was right, it would be kinder to let Alan down slowly. Give him time to accept that this Right purchase wouldn't happen.

'Sounds like a great big setback to me,' Rhys said, his legs stretched out, his walking stick lying along the floor. 'But then again, I'm not a business athlete.' He sniggered.

'He's got this,' Jenna said. 'Gordon knows a solicitor who specialises in this sort of thing. Getting Health and Safety orders overturned.'

'You think I don't know about Health and Safety?' Alan said to Gordon. 'I run a farm, employ farmhands.' He looked at Jenna. 'And a shepherdess. I know a bit about Health and Safety legislation and can't imagine what grounds you would have to get an order reversed.'

Rhys smirked at Gordon, then turned towards his brother. 'Don't be so mocking of the man's abilities. He's in a position of impenetrable power, right?' He nodded at Gordon.

Gordon's face reddened. 'Maybe impenetrable was an exaggeration.'

'You actually believe you can get the order overturned?' Alan said.

Gordon swallowed. How many more lies would he have to tell? 'I'll give it my best.'

Rhys laughed. 'Oh man, I love that super power of yours.' He stared at Gordon and silently mouthed, 'Bullshit.'

Gordon, Rhys and Jenna left Alan's cottage and trudged down towards the guesthouse. Rhys swung his walking sick like a baton.

'I'm going home,' Jenna said. 'See you guys in the morning. Rhys, I see that foot's had a miraculously healing. I want you in the field filling the troughs by sunrise.'

'That's Gordon's job,' Rhys said.

'He's leaving tomorrow.'

Both Rhys and Gordon stopped walking.

Jenna looked at Gordon. 'You told me you needed to get back to London, right?'

Gordon gazed at her, then exhaled heavily. 'Yes. I guess I do.'

'Whoa,' said Rhys. 'What was that you just said back there to Alan? You're not even going to try?'

'Of course I am. But the person I need to see, the solicitor, is based in London.'

'What?' said Rhys. 'You suddenly lost your phone? Sorry, but I'm not getting up early tomorrow. I've got things to do.'

'Like what? Lying in bed, rolling a joint, playing Black Sabbath on your Bluetooth speaker?'

Rhys stood tall, puffing out his chest. 'I am,' he bellowed, 'what every man aspires to achieve while he's working day in and day out, slaving away on fields or in stuffy prison cell offices.'

'And what's that?'

'A man,' he pointed to his chest, 'who lives a charmed life of comfort and leisure.' He grinned widely.

'You and your six sofas.'

'Exactly.' Rhys pointed at Gordon. 'How many people do you know who have six sofas to choose from when they walk into a room?'

Jenna stood, kicking some stray straw pieces with her toe.

The agitation in Gordon's blood melted. 'Sorry,' he said to Rhys. 'I don't know why I'm entering into a stupid debate with you. I'm just really tired after today.'

'Nothing stupid about our debate,' Rhys said.

Gordon's heartbeat slowed as he looked at Jenna. 'Do you actually want me to leave tomorrow, Jenna?'

She looked up and shrugged.

He inhaled the frosty night air as a slow panic twisted around his heart. He didn't actually have to rush back to London at all this week. He could do job searches from his phone. As far as Edward Creaton was concerned, he would also need to touch base with him. The game might not be over yet. Perhaps Gordon could phone him tomorrow, pretend he was delighted about the Health & Safety order, yet warn him the Priddys weren't giving up. A glimmer of hope stirred within him. There might, with the tiniest bit of luck and careful strategic bluffing, still be a chance that directorship would be in the offering.

He exhaled. Staying here meant continuing to lie to Jenna about his role at The Remblents Group. Not being truly himself around her felt more and more deceitful. Although, his cover was only temporary. He looked again at her lowered eyes…lashes the colour of straw…

'Aren't I staying for Thanksgiving next week?' The words were out before he could stop them.

A smile tugged at her lips.

He tried to stop his grin. 'I've been looking forward to that New York Pecan pie.'

'Georgia,' she said. 'It's a southern recipe.'

'Even better.'

She nodded and turned toward her house.

'Uh huh,' Rhys said as they stood watching her walk away. 'People think I'm oblivious, but I notice everything.'

'What have you noticed then, Rhys?'

He nudged Gordon with his elbow. 'Lyle.'

The next morning, out in the field, Gordon pulled his mobile from his pocket and dialled Creaton's number.

'Ah, Gordon. To what do I owe the pleasure?'

'Nice work with that Health & Safety order,' Gordon said, his throat tightening from the pretence. 'Next steps, though. The Priddys want to overturn it, so I'll need to persuade them…'

'No next steps.'

'The Priddys will—'

'Have to accept the Right is worthless. Thanks for your help, Gordon, but it's no longer needed.' Creaton clicked off.

Panic rushed through Gordon. The bastard was so certain. He would have paid for top legal advice.

He scrolled through his phone and found his brother-in-law's number.

'Richard, it's me, Gordon.'

'Hey, how's it going?' Richard said. 'You at work?'

'Yeah, I've got a work question, actually.'

'You mean for you? I'm sorry Gordon, I don't do employment law—'

'No, no. It's not about employment law. It's a question, though, for the hotel group.'

'But they have their own lawyers. If I get involved—'

'Okay, I know, but Richard, listen for a minute. It's this unusual situation.'

'Go on.'

'I know someone who has a Right to run sheep through our flagship hotel. It's connected to an old covenant to allow the animals through the land to get to a London market.'

'Is this some sort of joke?' Richard chuckled. 'Wait, this sounds familiar… didn't you mention sheep when you came over for dinner recently?'

'I did, but look….' Gordon winced as the ewe nearest him baahed.

'Good lord,' Richard said. 'Are the sheep in the hotel right now?'

'No. I'm in Wales.'

'What on earth are you doing in Wales?'

'It's work related. Listen, I wanted to ask about what would happen if you ignored a Health & Safety order.'

'That's serious if your company has been doing that.'

'No, what if I… this friend of mine did. The one who had the Right to run sheep through the hotel.'

'A friend of yours? I'd tell them not to be so bloody stupid. Not complying with a Health & Safety order is a criminal offense. He or she would face criminal proceedings.'

'Prison?'

'More likely a serious fine, but let me tell you, destruction of property could result in a felony…'

'I don't think the sheep would do that, destroy any property.'

Richard laughed. 'Gordon, stop. Tell your friend to forget it. It's madness. Besides, if your company finds out you have a friend who's about to run sheep through their top hotel and you're encouraging it, you could lose your job.'

Gordon was quiet for a few moments. He watched as a ewe trotted towards the opposite fence. Several followed behind her. 'I already have. Lost my job.' His chest ached with finally admitting the truth to his successful brother-in-law.

'What? Gordon, what have you done?'

He shuffled towards the fence to see what the sheep were looking at. Jenna's tiny figure in the distance made its way up the path carrying what looked like a bag of feed.

'One more question, and I'll let you go.' Gordon said into the phone. 'Can a Health & Safety order be overturned?'

'For keeping sheep out of a hotel? I doubt it.'

Gordon let out a slow exhale.

'Hey, come home,' said Richard. 'Charlotte's been trying to get hold of you. She wants to have a birthday lunch for you. She's inviting your Mum and Dad, and also Mark and Eleanor for a week on Sunday.'

'Tell her thanks, that's really kind of her. I just need to see if I can tie up some loose ends here first and then I can let you know.'

There was silence. Then a sigh. 'Of course,' Richard said, his voice clipped. 'Let Charlotte know about your birthday.'

Gordon spent the next few days mucking out paddocks, moving hay bales and filling troughs. What he needed was for some bloody random good luck to fall into his lap, like it seemed to do for every other person on this planet. In the meantime, he kept busy, avoiding the others on the farm as much as possible until he figured out what to do next.

By Sunday morning, three days after the Health & Safety order shock, he was no further forward in figuring out his course of action. This after looking up property solicitors on the internet and shoving more expenses onto his credit card for advice that was woolly at best. He'd spent hours each day researching covenant laws. When finding information on one site, it appeared to contradict what he next read on another.

Trudging along the path towards the indoor paddock with his head down, it was time to face facts. He couldn't stay here. Yet there was nothing to go back to in London. Apart from a flat that was weeks away from an eviction notice if he didn't find a job soon. He kicked the paddock gate open and one slat fell loose to the ground. He grimaced. There was a toolbox around here somewhere. He'd seen Alan using it. He found it on a shelf and brought it down to the bench. Grabbing some tools, he set about repairing the gate.

Footsteps crunched up the path as Gordon pulled some loose nails from the box. Jenna sauntered towards him, carrying a thermos. She handed it to him. 'It's coffee,' she said, offering it to him.

'Rhys style with a bit of brandy?' He said, forcing a

grin. He laid the nails on the bench, then took the thermos and placed it next to the toolbox.

'Not at this time of morning,' she said. She nodded at the hammer lying on the bench. 'What are you doing?'

'Loose panel on this gate. I reckon my job for the next few days will be checking every single fence on this farm.' He looked at her, at the curve of her cheekbones as she glanced around the paddock. Tingling rushed through him before dissolving into sadness. He needed to figure out his life before anything else.

He picked up the piece of wood from the ground. 'I need a pen, need to mark where to make a second hole, make this panel more secure. Oh, wait….' He put the panel near his feet. Reaching into his jacket, he retrieved his grandfather's pen pouch from his shirt pocket.

'That's a pretty fancy pen to bring out here.'

'My grandfather's. Gave it to me when I was eighteen.' He pulled the sleek black pen from its case. 'Said it was what he used to sign the contract when he became CEO of his company.'

'Why do you carry it around with you everywhere?'

He shrugged. 'Silly, I guess. It's supposed to be for luck. He told me there was good fortune in it and that I'd need it one day to sign something important. The thing that told me I was where I was supposed to be in life.'

'And you're going to use it to mark an old piece of wood?'

He laughed. 'I might as well use it for something. I can't see myself ever signing anything like a CEO contract.'

'Don't be so hard on yourself,' she said.

He twiddled the smooth pen between his thumb and forefinger, then smiled.

'Save it,' she said. 'You just never know.'

He sighed. 'I guess so. But if I haven't used it by this time next year, I might as well sell it on eBay.' He put the pen back into its pouch, then shoved it in his pocket. 'I can fix the fence without needing to mark it, I reckon.' He picked up the piece of wood and ran his finger near the bottom. Then he turned to pick up a nail.

'You've been avoiding me,' she said.

His finger halted. 'Not deliberately.' He breathed in.

'Yes, deliberately. We need to talk about last Thursday. I thought when you agreed to stay for Thanksgiving that maybe we'd moved forward a little from that Costa moment.'

'I know. Sorry. I'm confused about my life just now.' He dropped the nail and ran his hand through his hair.

'Well,' she lifted her hands in the air and laughed. 'God knows what I should make of that. Forget it, okay?'

He gazed down at the nail by his feet. Then bent to pick it up. 'Don't want one of the sheep eating this.' He stood and sighed. 'Jenna. I don't want to forget it.'

She looked at him.

'I'm not sorry we kissed.'

'Then what exactly is going on?'

'I'm trying to come up with a plan. Something that will help Alan. And me, with my own future. Although the two aren't really connected. Not anymore, I suspect.'

'I don't know what you're talking about. What do you mean, not anymore? Just how much were you planning to get from this deal?'

He shrugged. 'A job.'

Realisation dawned in her eyes. 'Oh, I see. The insurance company. I bet I can guess. You lost your job when you failed to sell the policy for the Right and now you're trying to prove something to those brokers. And what? They offered you a job if you succeeded?'

He winced. 'Pretty much. But I think the thing you're most right about is that I'm trying to prove something to people.'

'Oh, come on, Gordon.' She stepped towards him and touched his bottom lip with her finger. 'What is it about yourself you need to prove?'

He parted his lips.

Her finger froze. She removed it and stepped back. 'Sorry.' She brushed the hair from her face. 'Apart from that near miss with a college lecturer, I haven't been with anyone since my husband died. I'm still a little unsure what I want to happen here exactly.'

'Should something happen?' Gordon asked. 'With me returning to London soon?'

'Hasn't something happened already?' said Jenna.

Hope flickered in his chest. He was perhaps putting in a barrier where one didn't need to exist. London and Wales were only six hours apart.

She bit her lip. 'Although I'm a little confused, maybe taken by surprise.'

'I get that,' Gordon said. 'I'm a little confused, too. I broke up with someone recently.'

She peered at the ground and nodded. 'Was it serious?'

'I proposed. Was turned down.'

She looked at him, surprise in her eyes. 'Oh. Okay. Right. Sorry.'

'Don't be.' He gazed down at some straw stuck to the tip of his muddy boots then said in a low voice, 'I like you. A lot.'

'I like you too,' she whispered.

He turned to take the thermos from the bench. A little orange bug crawled from around the side of the container and onto his hand. 'I don't believe it. A ladybird?' he said. 'In November?'

'They hibernate when it turns cold. Probably a little colony of them somewhere in here.'

The insect crawled along his fingers and Gordon smiled. 'That's so strange. We were just talking about my Granddad.' The insect crawled around his thumb and onto his palm. 'When I was five years old, my Granddad told me if I found a ladybird hidden beneath forest leaves, it meant good luck was about to fly into my life.'

'Ladybug.'

'What?'

'You Brits. Why do you call them ladybirds when they're bugs?'

'Why do you call trousers *pants*?

Jenna giggled. 'Do you still believe in it? That ladybugs bring luck?'

'No, of course I don't, but every once in a while, when I trudge down an autumn path, my foot kicks a leaf aside and I know I'm still searching for that little bit of hope.'

She reached up and put her finger to the side of his face, then stepped back. 'You loved your granddad, didn't you?'

'Of course.'

'Is that why you have a soft spot for Alan?'

His mouth gaped open. 'Wow, I never thought of that. But, no, they're very different.'

'It's nice.'

'What?'

She shrugged. 'You keep saying to us how you're this ruthless business man—'

'I never said ruthless.'

'Business athlete,' she teased as she poked his cheek again.

He grabbed her fingers before she could pull her hand away. 'If you keep touching me, I'm going to have to kiss you,' he said.

She stepped back, giggling. 'No…slow. We should take things slow, right?' She turned and sauntered towards the next field.

He watched her, his heart expanding at the bouncy gait, at the wild hair pulled into a ponytail.

I like her more than a lot.

Chapter Twenty-One

'What the hell is going on?' Mark's voice bellowed through Gordon's mobile on Monday afternoon while he went out to fill some troughs. 'Mum's phoned me. She said you asked Dad for money because you lost your job?'

Gordon dropped the bag of feed at his feet. Several sheep trotted over. He sighed. 'Look, Mark, this isn't any of your business. I don't need you going all older brother on me.'

'Oh, I am going to go older brother on you because after I spoke to Mum, I spoke with our sister.'

'About me? Why?' One ewe fought to push her head into the bag of pellets and the others crowded in near her. 'Hang on, Mark.'

'I won't hang on…'

Gordon put the phone in his pocket and filled the trough while the sheep pushed through his legs and around him to get at the feed. He pulled the phone from his pocket. 'You were saying?'

'You've lost your job, Gordon! And now you're in Wales! Something to do with some crazy scheme about selling sheep in London—'

'I'm not selling sheep.'

'Richard told Charlotte something about a sheep run and markets in London –'

'No, it's not selling sheep,' Gordon said.

'What then? What?'

Gordon pressed his lips tightly. Jesus, he couldn't tell him the truth. 'You're right. I'm selling sheep in London. But not to markets,' he said with a grin. 'To people in posh houses in Notting Hill and the like who are too lazy to mow their lawns.'

Silence.

'Still there?' said Gordon.

'That will never catch on.'

Gordon bit his lip to stop himself laughing.

'Gordon, Mum said you told Dad you're searching for a new job and that's why you wanted money from him. Get your arse back in London now before I tell him what you're really up to.'

'I'll be back the day after Thanksgiving.'

'Thanksgiving? What the fuck are you talking about now?'

Still holding the phone, he picked up the feed bag to bring to the next field. Several of the sheep followed him. 'Greedy buggers, you lot just ate,' he said.

'Who are you talking to?' said Mark.

'Got to go, my brother. Need to bathe and perfume some sheep for the Notting Hill house owners, and I have a shepherdess waiting with another list of chores.'

Mark gave a dark laugh. 'Now I get it. It's to do with a woman. I can see that you could probably get a naïve Welsh shepherdess to like you. You were punching way above your weight with Stacey.'

Gordon froze. The muscles in his body tensed. 'How dare you…' he pressed his lips together and ended the call before he unleashed years of frustration with Mark into a vile tirade. Anger pumping through him, he stomped along to the next field and filled a trough. Decades of ridicule from his older brother burned inside him. He grabbed the empty feedbag as the sheep pushed their way around him to get to the trough.

Reaching the front of the guesthouse, he threw the empty feed bag to the ground and strode inside, his suppressed anger threatening to rise.

Stacey had not been too good for him.

Jenna being a shepherdess in Wales did not make her naïve.

The house was in silence, which meant Rhys was out doing some work for a change. He went to the kitchen, then opened and slammed cupboard doors until he found it. The glass bottle with the amber liquid. He grabbed the bottle from the shelf. Rhys still owed him for the flowers, anyway. He untwisted the cap and took a swig.

The brandy burned comfortably down his throat. Screw it. He needed someone to talk and drink with.

He strode towards Jenna's cottage and knocked. The door opened. Jenna's flushed face appeared, and she smiled. 'Hey, I'm just doing some baking for Thursday. You know, Thanksgiving.' Her eyebrows pinched together as she looked at him and she stood back. 'You wanna come in?'

He stepped over the threshold and followed her into the kitchen. Sweet smells of vanilla and treacle wafted through the room. 'Your pecan pie?' Gordon asked.

'Uh huh. Just put it in the oven.' She narrowed her eyes. 'You okay?'

He forced a smile. 'Want to join me in a drink?' He held out the brandy bottle.

'That bad, huh?' Jenna said as she eyed the bottle, then turned to pull two mugs from a shelf. She placed the mugs on the table and sat, motioning for him to do the same.

Gordon sat, then poured a little of the brandy into each mug. 'Sorry, I know you're busy. I just needed…someone to talk with…'

'Just tell me what's up.'

He looked at her. Her natural strawberry blonde curls falling around her perfect make-up free cheekbones. She outranked Stacey on so many different levels, yet his family never accepted him as worthy.

His brother's words burned a sadness in his throat as began to speak. 'Remember that talk we had just outside London? Near the Costa Coffee place? Before we uh…..'

'About wanting to grasp at a power that keeps eluding you?' she said.

He took a gulp from his mug, then set it down on the table. Leaning forward, he said in a low voice, 'Jenna, sometimes I feel inside my chest there's this tight ball of anger, or pain.'

She gazed at him.

'If I try hard enough,' he said, 'I can imagine it's gone. But then what's left is emptiness. Like if I opened myself up, no one would be inside. I'm this empty oyster shell, with no pearl. You asked me once why material stuff, the big house, the director's status, why it was important to me? Having stuff I can see, touch, it at least proves I exist.'

She dipped her chin. Soft curls had escaped from her ponytail and framed her face. 'You exist.' She gazed up at him and smiled. 'I'm looking at you.'

'I mean, me existing on the inside.'

She leant forward and peered into his eyes. 'I see you, Gordon. Inside too.'

His heart thudded. 'Tell me,' he whispered. 'What do you see?'

'Someone who will win because the need to prove himself is so strong.'

'And what if I don't win?' he said. 'I just stay an empty oyster shell, don't I?'

She shook her head and smiled. 'An empty oyster shell? You? No.' She looked at him, cocking her head to the side. 'You like thinking in metaphors, don't you? As I said before, like a poet.'

He took another sip from his mug, then chuckled. 'I wrote a poem once. It was about a bat who was scared of the dark.'

'Cool,' she said.

'If you say so. Although it actually won third place in a school competition when I was ten years old.'

She leant forward again. 'Recite it for me.'

'It's stupid.' He smiled.

'Don't be like Rhys who hides his haikus. Recite it for me or no pecan pie for you on Thursday.'

'You drive a hard bargain, madam. Okay.' He cleared his throat.

'The time came to return to the cave
But Boris hid in the park
If he was lucky, they'd leave him

And the moonlight would save him
For he was a bat afraid of the dark.'

Jenna howled with laughter. 'Boris? Why was he named Boris?'

'I don't know,' he said, laughing with her. 'I told you it was bad.'

'For ten years old? I love it.' She clapped her hands. 'Is there more?'

'Of course there is. Several stupid stanzas worth. But I'm afraid you'll have to pay me with Pecan Pie before you're allowed to hear more.'

'Gordon Slee, you are adorable,' she said, her voice low and husky.

A tingle ran through his lower body.

'Third place, huh? So who won first prize?'

'Amelia O'Callaghan, ' he said. 'She wrote a poem about the donkey who carried the Virgin Mary into Bethlehem. The staff were judging the contest in the lead up to Christmas. I should have stuck Christmas lights in the park trees my bat hid in.'

Jenna giggled.

'Maybe added a line about how the bat led the shepherds to the manger.'

'Why not a shepherdess?' She smiled.

He leant forward, closer to her face. 'You want me to lead you to a manger?' He gave her a playful smile. 'I know a comfortable one. You'll have to ignore the Black Sabbath music coming through the walls.'

She stopped laughing and leant back. 'I can't.' She whispered. 'Not yet.'

His cheeks burned with embarrassment. 'I know. I'm sorry. I was joking. I didn't actually mean it.'

She looked at him.

'Well, I did sort of meant it,' he said. 'But like, another time.' He swallowed. 'Hopefully.'

She half stood, then leaned forward over the table and kissed him gently. 'We have plenty of time.' She sat back down.

The heat from his cheeks spread to the tips of his ears. 'Yeah,' he said breathlessly. 'For now, I better go before I change my mind about taking things slow.' He gulped the last of the brandy, then pushed his chair back. As he stood, he reached down to touch her cheek. 'If you ever need to talk…about anything… I'm here for you too.'

She smiled and nodded. 'I know you are. I like how you let me open up about me and Dylan. And that silly college lecturer.' She bit her bottom lip. 'And my fears of ending up dying alone, with sheep instead of Alsatians or cats finding my dead body.'

He smiled as he stroked her chin. 'That will never happen.'

'These are the things I can't talk about with Rhys and Alan.'

His heart squeezed. 'You can open up to me about anything, anytime you need to.'

She nodded. 'I can, only because I feel you do the same with me.'

Guilt stirred as he stepped back. It was okay. Business lies didn't count. And he'd come clean soon enough.

'Hey,' she said and smiled. 'Did you get a prize?'

'For what?'

'The school poem.'

'Ah, yeah.' He quietly pushed his chair under the table. 'I got a small trophy.'

'I bet your parents still have it on display somewhere, don't they?'

He gripped the back of the chair, then shook his head. 'No. Why would they? I didn't come first.'

Her eyes widened with sadness.

'But it's fine,' Gordon said and smiled. 'One of these days, my family will see what I'm really worth.'

Chapter Twenty-Two

Tuesday morning, Gordon woke to two text messages on his phone. Jesus, who's texting at six am?

The first one was from Charlotte. He groaned. Bleary-eyed, he opened the message.

Phone me today. I've been waiting to hear from you. I need to know if lunch next Sunday is going to be for your birthday or not. Mum and Dad are coming and they'll be put out if you're not there. Plus, what sort of cake do you want? C x

The second was from Tej:

I know it's early, but I wanted to touch base before starting work later. Big news. Big news for you! Call me when you get this.

He pressed call on Tej's text. It went to voicemail and Gordon left a brief message to say he was awake. Dropping the phone to the floor, he laid on his back with a sigh. He would phone Charlotte later, when he took a break for lunch.

Lunch. It actually would save time if he started bringing it out in the fields with him instead of trudging back here each day.

Twenty minutes later, dressed in his jeans and boots, he grabbed the rucksack from the floor and squished his waterproofs into the front pocket in case it rained. There was a thermos inside the back pocket of the rucksack, so he made himself an orange squash drink and shoved it into the bag. He opened the fridge to put together a chicken sandwich from a deli meat package he picked up in town, then opened the cupboard next to the sink to look for some cling film or tin foil to wrap it in. Several pots and different sized lids clanged to the floor.

'What are you making a racket over?' Rhys shouted down the stairs.

'I'm making lunch.'

'Bloody hell, it's breakfast time.'

Gordon bent down and gathered the saucepans and lids and pushed them back into the cupboard. He shoved the chicken meat package back into the fridge and, before closing the door, grabbed a half full container of strawberries. He pushed this into the top of the rucksack.

A little while later, he was outside, lifting a bag of feed from the barn. He trekked towards the first field. As he trudged up the path, his mobile rang. Gordon plonked the heavy bag onto the gravel and pulled his phone from his back pocket.

Tej.

He pressed to answer.

'Mate, hey, I thought that text would get your attention.' Tej chuckled. 'I meant to phone you last night, but I've been seeing this new lady and…' he laughed.

'Spare me the details,' Gordon said. 'What's the big news?'

'So, listen. I've told them all about you.'

'Who?'

Tej laughed. 'Who? The new company I'm working for. I'm telling you, they're interested. This department is growing fast, and they suggested taking someone on to joint manage with me. My guess is it means the same package and promotion prospects for you, like it does me.'

Gordon stepped back. Oh, my God. Was this it? His random good luck crashing through, the ladybird crawling on his hand? No more pressure to do the impossible in changing that Health & Safety order for Alan.

His chest tightened. How would this help Alan?

'Anyway,' Tej said, 'formal interviews are starting next Monday, but it would be good if you could meet me Friday after work and I can give you the lowdown on everything, prepare you for the interview. I can tell you now, they're keen.'

'Are they?'

'I bigged you up a bit. Told them about your scrupulous eye on the accounts records when we worked together before.'

The ewes baa-d. 'I wouldn't use the word scrupulous,' said Gordon.

'Mate, chill. Go with the flow.'

'Okay.'

'Oh, and send a CV over to me to give to them.'

'I haven't updated it yet.'

'Update it then. Email it to me. I'll text you my new work email now. Then we'll meet Friday?'

'I haven't got my laptop with me and I've got to be here until Thursday at least—'

'Where's here?'

'Wales. On the sheep farm.'

'Bloody hell. I thought I heard some animal making a noise. I figured maybe you had some mad woman in your bed.' Tej sniggered. 'Wales again, eh? Listen, you know you can't do the sheep run gig, as much as I'd love to see you piss off Creaton. If the new company gets wind you're shaking down your previous employer….'

'I'm not shaking anyone down, but I do need to try to close this still.'

'Why?'

'Something I've promised some friends here.'

'If they're friends, they won't let you ruin your career prospects.'

'I have to do it. These people need my help. And crazily enough, if I did end up brokering a deal where the Right no longer belonged to the Priddys, I might still be in line for a possible directorship at The Remblents. I know Creaton thinks he's won, but if it starts to look like he hasn't, he'll still want my help. Besides, deep down, I know he feels he owes it to my grandfather, despite all his game playing.'

There was silence. Finally, Tej said, 'Oh mate. That will never happen.'

'It could….'

'No, no, no. I had a drink with Bethany last Thursday night. Apparently, Creaton was full of himself in the office that day. Boasting how he outsmarted those Welsh farmers with some sort of legal thing.'

'Yes, but these farmers are determined. Whether Edward realises it or not, he still needs me to get rid of this Right.'

Tej sighed into the phone. 'It's not that.'

'What is it then?'

'When Creaton was mouthing off about his great coup, he also told people he was relieved to get you off his back, saying how you were after a role you'd never be suitable for. Sorry, to be the bearer of shit news, but you need to know.'

A coldness ran through Gordon's veins. 'Bastard.'

'I know. Bethany called him a prick. Not to his face, to me. Anyway, come back tomorrow and get your CV ready. The people I work for are much nicer.'

One of the sheep trotted over to sniff the feed bag at Gordon's feet. 'I can't come back yet. Thursday's Thanksgiving.'

'Where? America? You said you were in Wales.'

'Shepherdess is American.'

'Okay. Weird. Thanksgiving in Wales. If you say so. Will you be back Friday?'

'Yes. I'll come back Friday.'

'Great stuff. I have to go. I'm at the tube station, but mark my word, mate. With this company, you and me will be directors by Spring.'

Lunchtime, he sat on a bench outside a paddock, forcing down dry lumps of his sandwich. His stupid, grasping hope had kept him from acknowledging the truth. Creaton had never intended to give him that role. Not even through the early days when he happily let Gordon add hours of extra unpaid work to his duties. Heat flushed through Gordon's body. If Granddad could see this, he would not just be rolling in his grave, he'd be clawing his way out of his coffin to grab a hold of Creaton's neck.

The swallowed lumps of bread hardened in Gordon's stomach. All those years Granddad supported Creaton in his rise through the ranks. Gordon inhaled deeply. Don't worry, Granddad. Edward Creaton will get his comeuppance.

A light drizzle tapped his face as he slowed his breathing. He sat inhaling the calming scent of the damp air, then grabbed a strawberry from the container. Biting into it, he looked around the field. Along the fence, a sheep was butting her head against the wiring.

'Oh, Molly.' He strode towards her, then shoved the half-eaten strawberry in his jacket pocket, so he could pull her from behind with both hands as Jenna had. Molly scuttled and turned, then poked her nose into his jacket.

'What, you like strawberries?' He pulled it from his pocket and held it out to the ewe on a flat palm. She gulped it eagerly, her thick tongue tickling his hand. When she'd finished, she shoved her nose into his pocket again.

Gordon backed away, chuckling. 'Enough now. There are no more in there.' She followed him as he walked back to the bench. 'No,' he said, turning and waving his arms. 'Shoo. Go.'

She scuttled off, and he laughed. Typical. He'd finally discovered a trick in getting her away from the fence, yet by the end of the week he'd be gone.

Sitting on the bench again, he thought about his conversation with Tej, the enthusiasm in his friend's voice. Gordon could make this new role the answer. As for Jenna, he could come see her on weekends. Yet somehow, he'd still need to make some amends to Alan for getting his hopes up and failing with the Right plan.

He breathed in. If he thought about it pragmatically, was Alan any worse off than before Gordon came up to Wales a few weeks ago? No. He couldn't feel guilty for a problem that had started years before.

Yet, he did feel guilty.

Exhaling, he pulled the phone from his back pocket,

then scrolled to his sister's name.

'There you are,' she huffed through the phone. 'Nice of you to finally get back to me.'

'Sorry, I've had a lot on my mind. I'm away at the moment.' He sat shuffling his feet back and forth along the grass.

'In Wales!' she said in an accusing tone.

'Yes.'

'Look, I'm trying not to get angry with you. I actually do want you here on Sunday for Mum and Dad.'

'I know. I've just been trying to sort something to do with work.'

'Gordon, Mark told me about this new start-up of yours. A sheep grooming business in Notting Hill? Are you crazy?'

'I'm not doing it. Not doing anything with sheep.'

'You're not?' she said.

'No. I was winding Mark up.'

'Oh.' She laughed. 'Of course. I feel stupid now.'

'Look, I'm coming home Friday. For good. I'm about to be offered a new job. I hope.'

'That's good news. See you Sunday then. One O'clock. Don't be late.'

'I won't. And thank you.'

'Oh, and I didn't know if I should tell you this,' Charlotte said, her voice hesitant. 'Stacey called me. She wanted to ask about sending you a birthday card. She said she wasn't sure exactly where you were. Seemed you had mentioned Wales to her when you broke up. She just wanted to know if she should send the card to your flat in Brixton.'

He breathed in to loosen the sudden tightening in his chest.

'Look,' Charlotte said. 'Will it make you happy if I invite her for Sunday? Not that I think it's a great idea, but –'

'No. Do not invite her for Sunday.'

'Good. I'm pleased you feel that way. I'll just tell her you're back Friday if she wants to send you a card.'

'No, you don't need to tell her—'

'Yes, I do. I promised I'd phone her back. I keep to my word even with people I don't necessarily like.'

'Just leave it, Charlotte.'

'See you Sunday.'

Chapter Twenty-Three

'Are we supposed to exchange gifts?' Gordon said as he and Rhys strode from the guesthouse on Thursday morning to check on the sheep in Clover field.

Rhys stopped. 'You want to give me a gift?'

'Thanksgiving,' Gordon said. 'Do we give each other gifts later?'

'Nah. It's not Christmas.' Rhys continued walking.

'Well, I don't know how it works.'

'Hostess gift. Bring her some flowers.' Rhys shrugged as he made his way towards the gate. He turned as he pushed the lever open. 'In fact, I should get something too, shouldn't I? We'll go into town after. You go into the florist and I'll nip into the shop next door and get a box of chocolates.'

'You're not meeting your friend in the alleyway, are you?' Gordon said.

'Nah.' Rhys chuckled. 'Anyway, we'll go at midday.'

Gordon strode off, to rotate the fields. His heart squeezed. Less than twenty-four hours and he'd be leaving here. Before that, he'd need to explain everything to Jenna. How he couldn't do any more for Alan regarding the Right. Yet, that didn't mean there wasn't a future for him and Jenna.

He reached the side of the barn and grabbed a crook. Sunlit clouds crowned the lopsided hill behind the building. Strolling towards the next field, he worked out what to say to Jenna. She'd already said she wanted to go part-time with the shepherding in the future. She might agree to bring the future forward a little. He could still visit Bryn Nefyn on weekends. Months down the line, they might find a nice flat together in London. Maybe even Notting Hill. She could open a cheese shop there. Then, on weekends, they could both come to Wales. She could see the sheep, do a little shepherding if she fancied it. Or, if she didn't want to move to London that soon, he'd be patient. Weekends in Wales wouldn't be a bad thing until she was ready.

Guilt descended on him. There was still the issue with Alan. Having to tell him to give up on the Right. Gordon's throat thickened. He had done his best to help.

He had failed.

At eleven-forty-five Rhys shouted up the path towards him. 'Hurry up. Time to go!'

Ten minutes later, Gordon glanced at Rhys as he drove them both into town. 'Your car not fixed yet?'

'Don't need to be when I've got myself a chauffer,' Rhys said.

Gordon sighed. *Not for long.* As Gordon drove them down the gravel drive, Rhys pushed a CD into the dashboard player and turned the volume up. Creedence Clearwater Revival blasted from the car speakers.

'Can we turn that down?' Gordon shouted as he leant towards the volume control.

Rhys put his hand over the player buttons. 'No. My soul needs music.' He paused. 'So does yours.'

The music pounded through Gordon's head all the way to the village. Finally, he pulled into a parking space near the florist shop and switched off the ignition.

Silence. At last.

'You get the flowers,' Rhys said. 'I'm going next door for chocolates. Meet you back here.'

An ice-cream van pulled up behind them. Rhys smiled as he opened the passenger door. 'You want an ice-cream?' Rhys asked.

'No, I don't want an ice-cream in this weather. It's cold.'

'Cold? You ought to be here in January.'

Gordon got out and strode into the florist shop.

'Back again?' the shopkeeper said. 'Did Jenna like the flowers?'

'How did you know—'

'Who else would they be for? What are you getting her

today? I bet she liked those roses.'

Gordon pressed his lips together. He couldn't afford another seventy pounds on a ridiculously enormous bunch of flowers. Then again, now that he and Jenna were… something of an item, would he look like a cheapskate to go down a level? He turned around, studying the blooms on display, trying to decipher the less expensive ones. Carnations. No. That's what Rhys usually got her.

Some long stemmed sunflowers caught his eye. Tall, with towering amber heads. 'How much are these?'

'Fifteen pounds for six.'

'Okay. Give me a dozen.'

He got back to the car and placed the sunflowers tied with the raffia onto the back seat. Pulling his phone from his pocket, he scrolled to find his university pals' WhatsApp group.

New job, new relationship. It was time to rekindle an active social life, starting again with this group. He smiled to himself. They would like Jenna. He thumbed a quick message, suggesting they all meet for a post birthday pub crawl. 'Have to do the family thing on my actual birthday. But let's have a real celebration the following weekend.'

As Gordon pressed send, Rhys opened the passenger door and threw a box of chocolates towards the back. He plonked himself into the passenger seat while licking an ice cream cone.

Gordon snickered, then smiled. 'You're such a kid, Rhys. But, apart from the music, I think you're actually growing on me.' He turned the key in the ignition.

'Wait, not yet,' Rhys said. He opened the passenger door and turned his cone upside down. The ice cream plopped to the ground. Next, he pulled a plastic bag of something that resembled crushed oregano from inside the cone. He dropped the cone to the ground, then closed the door. 'Ready now,' he said, shoving the bag of weed into his jacket pocket.

Gordon exhaled heavily. 'The ice-cream van driver

deals pot? Does your friend Hari Heddwas know about this?'

'Hari *the* Heddwas and no, he doesn't bloody know. Are you suggesting I fraternise with bent cops?'

Gordon grimaced, then started the engine. 'Rhys. Music at a normal level or I tell Alan about the ice cream van.'

Rhys laughed. 'Have it your way, but do you know what your problem is? You haven't worked it out yet. We're put on this earth to enjoy ourselves.'

'In the gospel, according to Rhys?' Gordon said as he pulled away from the curb.

Rhys shrugged. 'I told you, I write haikus, not gospels.'

'Well either way,' Gordon said, 'you're not one to lecture me about my life.'

'Why not?'

'Have you ever actually had dreams or goals?'

Rhys laughed. 'I already live the dream. Why do I need goals?'

Gordon sighed. 'You don't understand.' He glanced at Rhys. 'Tell me, apart from the farm, what exactly have you done, where have you explored, besides living …' Gordon waved at the window. 'Here.'

'Turn left at these crossroads.'

'Where are we going?'

'Morfa Nefyn.'

'We'll be late for Jenna's.'

'We won't. This won't take long.'

Rhys directed him onto the main road into the little village. He got Gordon to pull up just in front of a bus stop on a street full of houses with a few small shops.

'Come on,' Rhys said as he bolted from the car. He strode ahead. Stone walls about six feet high with overgrown hedges hemmed them into the narrow lane. The bracken and brambles brushed Gordon's coat as they marched through the winding path.

To the right, a little white cottage appeared in the clearing. Rhys stopped and gazed at it, before turning to Gordon. 'There you go. The origin of why you're here right now.'

Gordon breathed in as he stared at the bright stone cottage. 'Mari's house?'

'Yep. The one Hen daid bought for her and her kids after the mining disaster.'

Twigs cracked beneath Gordon's shoes as he stepped closer to look past the hedges at the house. The cottage and its gardens appeared well tended. A kid's bike rested against the side wall. 'Who owns it now?' asked Gordon.

'Different owners over the years. That extension there, that's new. After Mari died, her kids, who by then were adults living in England, they kept this on as a holiday cottage. Would bring their own families in the summer. Taid spent a lot of time here visiting with them all. Then he would bring Alan, and later me, to visit with our cousins. I like seeing it. I like remembering when Taid brought me here. My cousins and I would run up this lane, racing each other to the top.' Rhys turned to walk up the path. 'Come. There's more I need to show you.'

Gordon followed him through the path to a wooden V-shaped gate, hinged in a way for only one person to squeeze through at a time.

'What's this sort of gate called?' Gordon asked.

'A kissing gate,'

An image of Jenna flashed through Gordon's mind.

'Trust you to have an interest in the name of this one,' Rhys said.

Gordon stomped after Rhys up the single path. Earthen banks of heather and brambles hugged into them. Beyond the bracken he glimpsed fields of sheep on either side.

They went through a second kissing gate as they hiked up the hill, the grassy path leading them towards the top of a cliff.

'There,' Rhys said as he gestured for Gordon to come forward towards the edge.

Several metres below, a sweeping crescent of bright wintry sea sparkled against sands brushing up towards the cliffs. Gordon gazed at the tiny boats bobbing near the edge of the crescent sands, then out towards the blue-grey mountains in the distance. Above, the sky seemed to stretch into infinity, with the odd fleece-like cloud set against the piercing blue.

'Over to the left,' Rhys said. He pointed to a far off white-sided building with a slate roof housed right on the beach. 'The Ty Coch Inn. You know it was once voted the second best beach pub in the world? And beyond that peninsula there are rocks where you can see the seals resting and bathing.'

Gordon gazed towards the roof of the Ty Coch. An image of him and Jenna drinking pints of lager on that cold sunny afternoon flashed through his mind.

He looked down. The edge of the water drew a turquoise band around the bay. Gordon's heart swayed with the beauty of the scene before him.

'Second best beach pub in the world,' Rhys said again, still gazing towards the pub. 'I can't even remember where number one was, but I don't need to know. You see, when you've got this, why would you ever want to be anywhere else?'

Chapter Twenty-Four

The aroma of roasting turkey, sausage, onion and traces of cinnamon and sherry filled Jenna's cottage. She rushed into the sitting room as Gordon and Rhys greeted Alan. Her face red, she brushed damp curls from her forehead.

'Oh my God,' she said, taking the wrapped sunflowers from Gordon. 'These….' She buried her face in the flowers, then beamed. 'I don't know why I just did that.' She giggled. 'Sunflowers don't really have a smell, but they're my favourite.' She looked at him, her eyes sparkling. 'How did you know?'

His heartbeat quickened. 'I don't know. I just… guessed.'

Alan cleared his throat. 'Is it time to sit at the table yet, Jenna?'

'Oh, sure. Pour yourselves some wine. I'll bring everything through.'

'Do you need some help?' Gordon said. Maybe they'd have a few minutes and he could tell her he needed to speak with her later. Alone. Nerves shout through the hunger in his stomach.

'No, you sit. You're my guest.'

Gordon bit his lip, then wandered towards the long table that had been set up at the side of the sitting room. Jenna had created decorations with pine cones and silk autumn leaves which stretched along the linen tablecloth. Alan took a seat at the head of the table and grabbed a bottle of wine.

'Jenna seems bubbly today,' Rhys said as he winked at Gordon. 'More so than usual.'

Alan filled his wineglass to the brim. 'Her daughter announced she's making the trip up from uni to have a post-Thanksgiving meal with her this Sunday. That means, don't eat all the sherried sweet potatoes, Rhys.'

Jenna shuffled in, wearing oven gloves and carrying two steaming casserole dishes. 'Don't be silly. Have all the sweet potatoes you want, Rhys. I can make more.' She looked at Gordon. 'Maybe you can help bring the turkey through?'

Gordon pushed his chair back.

'Jenna,' Rhys said. He looked from Jenna to Gordon. 'Isn't that my job?'

'Oh, sorry.' She waved her hand. 'Yes, of course, Rhys.'

They sat eating the turkey with cranberry sauce, sausage stuffing, the dollops of sweet potato and white mash. There was barely room on their plates to add the array of vegetables Jenna had passed around the table.

Rhys dropped his empty corn cob onto his plate and sat back. 'So our Emma is coming up from uni this weekend,' he said, then grinned at Gordon. 'Does she know, Jenna, that you have a cariad?'

Jenna blushed.

Gordon looked at Alan, who gave him a hard stare.

'What's a cariad?' Gordon said. His heart had inexplicably thumped as Alan continued to glare at him.

Rhys leant forward and said in a loud whisper, 'Sweetheart. Lover.'

Alan huffed. 'Enough, Rhys.'

'Enough yourself.' Rhys' palm hit the table as he glared at Alan.

'Enough of what?' Alan said.

'Our cousin's son, who's dead, has been dead for two years. It doesn't make us owners of Jenna's love life.'

Jenna sat upright, pink dots spreading across her cheeks. She leant forward and grabbed a bowl. 'Anyone want more mashed potatoes?'

Gordon peered at Alan, his pulse quickening. 'There's no love life…' He looked at Jenna; her face a mixture of surprise and anger. 'No, that's not what I meant,' he said.

'I don't need to hear any of this,' Alan's cutlery clanged to his plate.

Jenna jumped up and gathered casserole bowls from

the table. 'Gordon, would you help me bring some plates through?' she said.

'Are we going to do the thankful stuff?' asked Rhys.

Jenna looked at him.

'We always do it before dessert.' Rhys said to Gordon.

Jenna stood rigid, holding the bowls of sweet potato and mash.

'Jenna,' Alan said in a soft voice. 'I'm sorry. Rhys is right. What you choose to do is none of my business.' His eyes teared. 'I spent a good portion of my life secretly loving someone who other people, people I had cared for, told me I wasn't allowed to love.' He swallowed. 'Didn't stop me either.'

Gordon held his gaze and gently nodded.

Alan narrowed his eyes at Gordon. 'Just as long as you mean it. With Jenna.'

'Well, okay,' Jenna said in a high-pitched voice. She plonked the bowls back onto the table and rushed to sit. 'Let's do the thankful statements.' She rubbed the back of her neck and gave a strained smile. 'I'll start. I'm thankful Emma will be home tomorrow for the weekend and I get to create an extended Thanksgiving celebration to include her.' She looked to Alan.

Alan sat back and exhaled. 'I don't know. Let me think.' He looked at Gordon. 'I guess I'm grateful to you, Gordon. For giving me hope we can finally do right by my great grandfather and get what we deserve for that bit of London land he sold. I know you'll find a way.'

Gordon's heart thudded.

Rhys chuckled. 'You left something out.'

Alan raised his eyebrows.

'You're also thankful Gordon's going to show those villagers, right?'

'Show them what?' Gordon said.

'You've forgotten?' Rhys said. 'About nineteen-ninety-six?'

'Nineteen-ninety-six?' Gordon's eyebrows furrowed.

'Oh, that fete.'

'It wasn't a fete,' Rhys said. 'It was the local sheep trials and Alan's sheep were a disaster. They came fifth place.'

Gordon looked to Alan, who stared at his half empty wineglass. 'At least it wasn't last place,' Gordon said, his heart still thudding. He'd have to find a way to let Alan down gently about this Right. Maybe phone him from London next week, pretend he'd seen the solicitor and was told no way.

Rhys cackled as he smacked his hands together. 'Oh yes. That was last place.'

Alan looked at Gordon. 'Moving on. What are you thankful for?'

Gordon nervously bit his lip. His big news about this possible new job was for him to discuss with Jenna, not announce at the table.

Rhys sniggered and shook his head. 'Nineteen-ninety-six,' he said. 'They're all still talking about it.'

'You enjoy it, don't you, Rhys?' Alan said. 'Reminding me that everyone still talks about what happened with my sheep in nineteen-ninety-six.'

Rhys stared at Alan, and the air between them grew heavy.

'Tell me something,' Gordon said to Rhys, hoping to appease Alan. 'According to the gospel of Rhys, you can make sheep dance. Why couldn't you get those sheep to win the trial that day?'

'Didn't want to steal Alan's limelight,' Rhys said, then downed the rest of his wine. 'Anyway, you haven't answered the question. What are you thankful for?'

He'd be thankful to get back to London tomorrow, away from these two brothers and their quarrel, but he couldn't say that. Nor was he prepared to say at the table how he was thankful for his friend, Tej, lining him up with the new job. He cleared his throat. 'Friends. I'm thankful for friends.'

Alan nodded. 'Me too. Especially new ones.' He looked

at Gordon.

Gordon felt the heat rise to his cheeks.

'I'm thankful to have you as a friend too, Gordon,' Rhys said. 'Because what I'm really thankful for is The Grateful Dead have announced they're doing a concert in London next Spring.' He leant towards Gordon, wide-eyed. 'So, I'm coming to stay at your flat, okay?' He chuckled. 'Yes sir, I'm grateful for the Grateful Dead.'

Alan leant forward in his chair. 'You,' he pointed at Rhys. 'Are not going to London.'

'So what if I am, Alan?'

'Not to that Wembley stadium again.'

Rhys cackled. 'I love Wembley stadium.'

'You love running around it naked do you?' Alan said.

Rhys stood, 'This is where you exaggerate! I was not bloody naked.'

'I had to drive all the way down to London to get you out of that jail cell.'

Jenna looked at Gordon and rolled her eyes.

Rhys slumped down into his chair again. 'I was not bloody naked. I was in my underpants.'

'Running around Wembley stadium.' Alan said.

Rhys banged his fist on the table. 'How could I be running in a crowd? I was walking!'

'You ran past the security guards to get on the stage.'

'But when I got on the stage, I was skipping.' Rhys pursed his lips and nodded. 'It was ELO. Everyone gets in the spirit for Electric Light Orchestra.'

Alan shook his head, then looked at Gordon. 'You see? This is what that stuff he smokes does to him.'

Rhys huffed. 'I've got no mynadd for your misunderstandings of life, Alan.'

'Mynadd?' Gordon mouthed to Jenna.

'Means patience,' she whispered, then stifled a giggle. 'Come on you two,' she said to Alan and Rhys. 'That rock concert was years ago.'

'Tell him, Jenna,' Rhys said. 'Tell my brother that was

not normal weed that wanker outside Wembley stadium sold me.'

Jenna laughed as she and Gordon reached the kitchen. 'You don't need to put Rhys up in London, you know. He can get an Airbnb or whatever.' She grabbed some ice cream from the freezer and shoved it in the microwave. 'Thirty seconds on defrost should work.' She pushed her hands into oven mitts and pulled the pie from the oven. 'I'm sorry about Alan earlier. He'll be fine….'

'I know.'

She placed the pie on the counter, shook off the mitts and turned to him. 'But look, about Sunday. Emma will be here and, well, it's far too soon for you to meet my daughter. You and I are still getting to know each other and I know we like each other but…'

'Hey, it's okay. I won't be here this weekend, anyway.'

'Oh? Where are you going?'

'I'm going to London tomorrow. My birthday lunch with the family is on Sunday.'

She clapped her hands to her cheeks. 'Oh my God, I can't believe I forgot.'

'It's okay. Anyway, I'll be staying in London after tomorrow.'

'Staying? For how long?' The microwave pinged, and she turned to push open its door.

'Jenna, it's where I live.'

She stood, her hands about to reach for the ice cream tub, then she stopped, turning to face him. 'I know but, you're coming back to continue with the plan. The hotel and the sheep?'

He shook his head. 'It can't happen.'

'What do you mean?' She took a step back against the counter. 'What… you're giving up?'

'We have to.' He stepped towards her. 'Listen, I have news. I've got a job interview with a new company. The prospects are brilliant.'

'And this is why you're giving up on us here?' She

turned towards the counter and tugged at a drawer, the utensils within rattling.

'No. I'm not giving up on you.' He took a deep breath. 'I have a plan. It includes us. I wondered if we could talk later. After Rhys and Alan have left.'

'What's the job?' She turned to look at him. 'Another insurance company?'

'Insurance?' The blood pounded in his temples. He forced a smile. 'No, there's something else I've been wanting to tell you. I just didn't know how. But if we're going to be together, I want to wipe the slate clean of any secrets.'

'Secrets?' Her eyes widened.

'I'll tell you later. When we're alone.'

'Oh no, if you've got secrets, you better tell me right now.'

He breathed out. 'It's complicated.'

'Just tell me what this new job is.'

'It's a hotel group.'

Her brows pinched. 'You're not going to tell me it's The Remblents Group? The hotel we have the Right against?'

'No,' he forced a laugh. 'I used to work with them. But not anymore.'

'When?' Her eyes widened. 'When did you work for them?'

He swallowed. 'Recently. For just under two years. It ended a few weeks ago. Well not officially… yet… but the writing has been on the wall.'

She stood back. Then she turned, pulling a cake slicer from the drawer, before dropping it onto the counter. 'I've been so stupid,' she whispered.

'No, no you haven't. Let's talk about it all later.'

She wiped her face with the back of her hand. 'You were on their side all along.'

His heart thudded. 'Okay, I admit it. That's how it started out for me. But that was before I got to know Alan and Rhys…. before I got… closer to you. That's when things started to change for me.'

She turned abruptly, her eyes flashing with anger. 'You admit it? You were on their side?'

'Jenna…'

She turned away from him. 'You've been lying to me. All along. Even after we talked about how honesty was the most important thing to me.' She shook her head. 'It's okay. I've dealt with worse than this, you know, being a widow…'

'Jenna, please, if we can talk later—'

'What about Alan and Rhys? You've lied to them, too. You've taken their hopes and shoved them in the garbage can for your own gain.'

His heartbeat quickened. 'It's not like that. I wanted to help them.'

Jenna removed the ice cream from the microwave and slammed it on the counter. 'Alan warned me, you know. Told me not to trust you.' She pulled some bowls from the cupboard.

'I wanted to help. I just couldn't find a way. Believe me, I've been trying to think of one.'

She opened another drawer and banged some spoons on the counter.

'If I do figure something out for Alan, I promise I'll do what I can.' He watched as she grabbed an ice cream scoop and plonked it into a bowl. 'Come on, Jenna. I'm feeling scared.'

'Of what?' she turned towards him, eyes flashing with anger.

'Losing you?'

She laughed, but it was an outraged laugh. 'How dense are you?' She pressed her lips together. 'You've already lost me. The moment you told me you lied about working for the hotel.'

'Jenna please… from now on you'll get nothing but the truth from me. If you'll just give us another chance.'

She looked at him and held his gaze, then pointed to the closed kitchen door. 'Hell, I'm not someone who would be with a guy who deceives a friend, especially one who's in bad health.'

Alan. She must mean Alan. 'What's wrong with his health?'

'Like you care,' she muttered. 'Never mind,' she waved her hand. 'Been going on for years. None of your concern anyway,' she said. 'It never was.'

He breathed in, attempting to ease the aching in his heart. 'I'll find a way to help. Like Alan said to me in there.'

'I want you to leave. Right now. I don't ever wanna see or hear from you again.'

He exhaled heavily. 'Just let me…'

'Or do I have to go in there and get those two brothers to chase you off this farm with a shotgun?'

He gazed at the floor and shook his head. 'Okay. As you wish,' he whispered. He turned and ambled towards the utility room, out through the back door and into the night air. Without his coat, the November evening bit through his shirtsleeves. As he made his way to the guesthouse for one last time, the stiff wind stung his eyes.

The following morning, he rose early and dressed, then shoved his clothes into his bag. Tiptoeing down the stairs so as not to wake Rhys, he creaked open the front door to quietly slip through.

'Where are you sneaking off to?' Rhys said from the top of the stairs. 'You disappeared last night too, without saying goodbye.'

Gordon froze. His heart heavy, he turned. 'I'm going back to London.'

'When are you back?'

Gordon exhaled heavily. 'I'm not.' He looked up at Rhys, his sheep-headed hair more wild than usual. 'Do me a favour. Any problems with Molly? She likes strawberries.

I mean, if you need to lead her away from a fence, or if she's refusing to follow the others into another field.'

'Two weeks a shepherd and he's preaching.'

Gordon looked at the floor and nodded. 'Yeah. Sorry. Thanks for putting me up, Rhys.'

'Hey,' Rhys shouted. 'Seriously, when are you coming back?'

'I think you'll need to ask Jenna.' He stepped out into the crisp air, the grey morning light beginning to dawn as he closed the door behind him. Grabbing his keys from his pocket, he opened the car boot and threw in his bag. Before opening the driver's door, he stood, taking one last look at the lopsided hill beyond the guesthouse. Everything about his time in Bryn Nefyn had been askew to expectations, even the hill that, instead of peaking in the middle, decided a little too late to rise to the right of the landscape.

He allowed himself a glimpse towards Jenna's cottage. Smoke billowed from the stone chimney, signalling she was already up, perhaps making breakfast, or even baking again for her daughter's visit. His throat tightened, and he opened the car door to head towards the life he had always been destined for. A business role within a hotel group in London.

Chapter Twenty-Five

Gordon pushed his way through the throng of Friday night drinkers; the office workers congratulating themselves on getting through another week of closed deals, big results, or holding onto jobs they secretly feared losing.

Tej stood near the end of the bar. 'Hey!' he said as Gordon approached. 'What are you drinking? A lager, right? I'll get you a lager.' He gave the order to the barman. 'You never sent your CV to me,' he said, turning back to Gordon. 'Don't worry, I covered for you, said I could guarantee you had an outstanding track record.' He handed Gordon a dripping pint. 'Bring that updated CV with you on Monday, okay?'

Gordon nodded. 'Sorting it this weekend.'

They moved through the crowd, lager pints in hand.

'Look at that, two women taking up that table for four,' Tej said. 'Let's grab the seats at the end.'

They plonked their pint glasses on the table and sat. The two women glanced at them, then returned to their conversation.

'Hey, guess what?' said Tej. 'I met up with Bethany after work yesterday. This will disappoint you…'

Gordon took a sip of his lager. 'What will?'

'She knows how Creaton got that scar. He told her one day after he came in from a boozy lunch. She said the arsehole leant over her desk to whisper that her boobs were gorgeous, or something sleazy like that. So, to annoy him, she asked how he got his ugly scar.'

'Sleazeball. What did Creaton say?'

'He said he slipped down a ladder while painting a window frame at home. What an idiot. Apparently ripped his forehead on a tiny piece of metal sticking out from the side of the thing. Seems not only does he refuse to buy the right insurance at work, he won't even pay for a new ladder.'

Gordon grimaced.

Tej waved his hand. 'Sorry, forget him. Remblents is in our past.' He leaned forward. 'So, this job. Currently, I'm the manager in a department of sixteen. Not assistant manager, not senior clerk or any of that bullshit, but *manager*. But here's the beauty of it. It's for six months only. Ask me why it's only six months?'

'Why is it six months?'

Tej sat back and smiled. 'In six months' time, my title changes to director.'

'That seems… incredible,' Gordon said. He glanced at the cocktails the two women at their table had in front of them. The rim of each glass had a strawberry wedged along the top.

'Play your cards right and you could be up for the same deal,' Tej said. 'Huge pay rise, your own office. A personal assistant.'

The woman nearer to Tej picked up her cocktail and sipped. The strawberry slipped off the rim. She caught it with her fingers just in time.

Molly. He hoped Rhys would remember about the strawberries.

'Mate, pay attention,' Tej said. 'I know the ladies are pretty, but that's not why we're here.'

The woman glanced at Gordon and Tej, then shuffled her chair a few inches away from them. Her friend, nearer to Gordon, did the same.

Tej took a sip of lager. 'You okay, mate?'

Gordon shrugged. 'Yeah. Of course.'

'Great. Now, let me give you the lowdown on what these directors are looking for and then you can get the next round of drinks in.'

At just after eight, he arrived outside his old Brixton flat. The streetlight above flickered as he climbed the steps and fumbled in his pocket for his keys. From the other side of the street, a car door slammed. Heels clip-clopped towards

him.

'Oh, what a coincidence,' Stacey said with a wide smile. 'I was going to pop in and see Miriam.' She looked different. The nearby streetlamp illuminated new highlights in her hair.

'Miriam downstairs?' Gordon said. 'I don't remember you ever popping in on her.'

'I was passing'–

'Passing. Right, does *he* live near here?'

'Who's *he*?' She looked down and laughed. 'Oh, the guy I was seeing?' She shook her head. 'Adam wasn't right for me.' She smiled. 'So, the Wales thing. Is that finished?'

'Yes.'

'Have you still got your job at Remblents? Your sister mentioned something about you being up for redundancy.'

Gordon exhaled heavily. 'Did she? Look Stacey, why are you here?'

'To see how you are?'

'I thought you came to see Miriam.'

'Not just Miriam…' Her fingers twisted the strap of her shoulder bag. 'So, are you back now? Back at Remblents?'

'It's possible Tej has set me up with something better.'

'Oh,' her eyes widened. 'That's good news. Hey, why don't we grab dinner or something? Celebrate your possible new job?'

He looked at her, waiting to feel the longing that didn't appear. The long drive from Wales this morning and then the three pints of lager with Tej had perhaps made him weary. 'I'm tired tonight.'

'Oh. Of course.' The corners of her mouth twitched.

This was something new. Stacey insecure.

'Soon?' she said. She bit her lip again. 'I guess you're busy. It's your birthday on Sunday, isn't it?' She gave him a sad smile then lowered her chin and looked up at him beneath her lashes. 'You want to celebrate a little with me this weekend?'

He breathed in.

'Come on. It's your birthday.'

'Stacey, we're not—'

Her eyes widened. 'Unless you're seeing someone else?'

His heart thudded. Jenna. That was gone. 'No,' he whispered. 'I'm not seeing anyone.'

'Good. What are you doing tomorrow?' she asked.

He exhaled slowly. 'I suppose we could do something tomorrow night?'

She beamed, the familiar Stacey returning. 'Perfect. You choose where and text me the details.' She leant in and kissed his cheek, her warm lips lingering for an extra second, a whiff of her Chanel perfume greeting him. She leant back and grinned, then turned and trotted down the steps, her designer heels clacking across the dark pavement towards her car.

'Stacey?'

She turned with a wide smile. 'Yes?'

'Aren't you going to check on Miriam?'

'Oh,' her eyes widened. She waved her hand. 'I'll phone her in the morning.'

On Saturday morning, he sat in his kitchen, updating his CV. A niggling feeling stabbed at him. He picked up his mobile from the table, then scrolled his WhatsApp until he reached the university pals group. He'd sent that message days ago and not one response. A heaviness descended as he checked to see how many of the nineteen had even bothered to read the message.

Thirteen.

Thirteen people read it and not one of them had bothered to answer.

He needed to find new friends. It was a new era for him, after all. New job, perhaps eventually a new flat. He should give more time to Tej. Maybe Tej had a social circle.

He slid his mobile across the table and conjured the image of himself as Chancellor of the Exchequer walking into Downing Street. Christ, he could sort out the country with a few strokes of his computer keys, a tap on the calculator. Those uni pals would all want to be his friend if he was powerful, successful. He waited for the image to soothe him. Instead, it faded, leaving behind an emptiness.

It didn't work anymore. Even his fantasy world had rejected him and left.

Stacey. Maybe he still had Stacey.

Stacey sat at the restaurant table, at an angle to him, close enough for her leg with the sheeny tights to press against his calf. Her perfectly polished nails grabbed a napkin. She set it across her lap, then smiled, her thick coral lips glistening in the low light. She plucked the napkin in front of Gordon, then with both hands, smoothed it over Gordon's lap.

His thighs tingled and his face flushed with embarrassment. He pushed her hands away. 'Come on, Stacey, what are you doing?'

Her laugh tinkled as she said, 'Don't you like being looked after?' She handed him the wineglass their waiter had filled. 'It's your birthday tomorrow. Let's get smashed.' She smiled, revealing a coral fleck on her front tooth.

'You've uh, got lipstick on your teeth.'

She sat upright. 'Do I? Oh.' She rubbed her tooth with her finger. 'Better?'

'You know, you look great without makeup, too,' Gordon said.

She took a gulp from her wineglass. Setting it down, she gave him a tight-lipped smile. 'Any other complaints?'

'It wasn't a complaint—'

'Good, because I want us to have a nice evening.' She squeezed his thigh. 'A sort of reunion, if you like?'

The waiter brought them their starters.

'So,' Gordon said, tucking into fried calamari. 'It's all over with… what's his name?'

Stacey rolled her eyes. 'Oh. Adam. Yes.' She took a bite

of her smoked salmon.

'I hope you don't mind me asking,' Gordon said. 'I'm curious. You thought he was perfect for you, or did I get the wrong impression from that phone conversation we had? You said the two of you were alike.'

'I thought we were.'

'It hurt,' Gordon whispered, placing his fork down.

Stacey stopped eating. Her eyes widened. 'I'm sorry,' she said. She moved her hand towards his. 'Gordon, I made such a mistake. Adam…he….' She squeezed his fingers. 'You don't want to hear about him.'

'I do, actually. I want to understand why you thought he was better than me.' He slipped his fingers out from beneath her hand, then held them over his eye.

'The twitch starting?' she said.

He nodded.

'Oh Gordon,' she whispered. 'He wasn't better than you.' She sat back and took a sip of wine. 'I'll tell you the truth about him. He made me feel I existed only to make him look good when we were out. He'd do things, like get irritable if my dress was an inch too short, or a smidgen too tight, anything that suggested I wasn't his version of Queen of Elegance.' Her eyes misted.

Gordon moved his hand to cover hers. 'He sounds controlling.'

She nodded. 'Yes, that was exactly it.' She looked at him. 'You never did that to me. If anything, you put me on a pedestal. It used to annoy me, but now I realise it was kind of nice. How you appreciated me.' She held his gaze. 'I've missed that.'

His chest tightened as he waited to feel something apart from confusion.

'Hey,' she said. 'Enough about Adam. Tell me about this new job of yours.'

The waiter came to the table. 'Have you finished your starters?'

Gordon looked at his half-eaten calamari. 'Yes. Bring

the mains when you're ready.'

Stacey raised her eyebrows. 'In a hurry?' She smiled and pressed her leg into his.

As they tucked into their main courses, they ate mostly in silence. Struggling for a conversation that didn't involve what happened between them a few weeks ago, Gordon sat back when he finished and forced a smile.

'Did I ever tell you I wrote a poem once that won a prize?'

'Did you?' Stacey looked at him.

'It was about a bat who was afraid of the dark.'

Stacey put her cutlery down onto her empty plate and wrinkled her nose. 'That makes no sense.'

'Well, it's not supposed to. It's a poem, a story.'

'You don't write poetry.'

'I wrote it when I was ten.'

She scoffed. 'Why are we talking about something you did when you were ten? Tell me more about your job interview.'

'There's nothing to say about it until I've had it.' He took a sip of water. 'Let me tell you about these sheep in Wales. There's this one that likes to butt her head against the fence. But I figured out a way to get her to follow me.'

Stacey grimaced, then looked around.

'You're not interested in Wales, are you?' said Gordon.

'Should I be? You looking after smelly farm animals?'

'They're not that smelly. Well, maybe a bit, but it's funny how quickly you get used to it.'

'Eeuww. No, thank you. The smell of manure when I'm just driving near the countryside makes me sick. Oh look, here's our waiter. Shall we get some dessert? Or actually,' she said as the waiter took their plates, 'I might have some cheese.' She glanced at Gordon. 'Oh sorry, I forgot. You hate the smell of cheese.'

Cheese. An image of Jenna came to mind, and he pushed it away. 'I can change.'

'What?'

'Order the cheese.'

Stacey shrugged. 'Okay.' She turned to the waiter. 'A cheese plate for me.' She looked to Gordon. 'What are you having, darling?'

His skin tightened. *Darling.* 'No, I'm full. Nothing more for me.'

She pressed her lips into a hard line as she smiled. 'Something's up with you.'

'I'm probably just a little nervous about Monday.' He scrunched the napkin in his lap. *Don't think about Jenna when the cheese comes. Don't think of the farm anymore. Don't think about how they must all be saying you're a complete shit.*

'That's not good.' She frowned in concern.

'What's not?'

'You being nervous about Monday. You were so confident yesterday. I know a director's position is a big step up for you—'

'Manager's position. Not director yet. And I haven't got the job yet, it's an interview.'

She slumped back in her chair. 'Oh. Why did I think you already had this job? And that it was probably a director's position?'

'I don't know,' Gordon said. 'Why did you think that?'

She scowled and shook her head. 'You haven't changed, have you?'

He tensed. 'I thought you missed who I was?'

'I haven't missed this, Gordon. The fantasies, the dreams. What will you do if you don't get this job?'

He sat back. Forcing a laugh, he said. 'I don't know.' He slammed his palms on the table. 'Make sheep's ice cream?'

'Oh, Jesus Christ. I can't believe it. I'm sitting here with the same old Gordon.'

He leant closer to her. 'Were you expecting someone other than me?' He stood and pulled some notes from his wallet. Nearly the last of the cash that was available in his bank account. He didn't care. He'd change his fortune somehow, no matter what.

'I'll get this,' she said. 'It's your birthday weekend.'

He ignored her and banged the cash on the table. Some of the other diners turned and looked. 'You were right about what you said a few weeks back,' he said. 'You and Adam are alike in every way.'

Her eyes widened. 'How dare you….'

'But you're also wrong about something. I'm not the same Gordon. I no longer need yours or anyone else's approval of how I live my life.'

Chapter Twenty-Six

'You never told me what flavour cake you wanted,' Charlotte said, clearing the lunch plates. 'I made lemon drizzle.' She left the room to bring the dirty dishes to the kitchen.

Gordon glanced across at his parents. His father had been polite but subdued during lunch. No doubt Mark had passed on a wild story about Gordon opening a sheep business. He looked towards the end of the table where Richard, his brother Mark, and Mark's wife, Eleanor, were deep in conversation about a planned skiing trip for next February.

Gordon leant across the table and smiled towards his father. 'You know my interview tomorrow,' he said. 'This is it, Dad. I can feel it. This time next year, I'll be on six figures, bonuses. That money you gave me fifteen years ago? I'm going to give it back with triple interest.' As he widened his smile, he felt his mouth stiffen. Why was he bothering? Did he really think he'd get his father's approval this time? The suspicion that he would never be good enough squeezed around his chest.

He just wished he didn't care.

His father pursed his lips and shook his head. 'Forget about that money. I just want to see you getting your life in order.'

Gordon nodded.

'And you're certain you're going to get this job?' His father said. 'It's just the initial interview tomorrow, isn't it?'

Gordon blinked rapidly. 'I'm as certain as I can be.'

His mother looked at him as Charlotte came back into the room with some side plates for the cake.

'Why did Mark tell us you were doing something with sheep?' his mother asked. 'Is that why Stacey left you? You were planning on something silly?'

Charlotte's eyes flashed at Gordon. She plonked the plates on the table. 'Mum, that's none of our business,' she said.

Gordon gave her a small smile. *Thank you.* His cheeks flushed as he remembered the Health & Safety order he'd shoved into his back pocket. Just in case he had a moment with Richard, an opportunity to keep his promise that he'd at least had a solicitor read it over before dismissing it.

'By the way, where are my grandsons? They've left the table already.' Gordon's mother asked Charlotte.

'All three of them upstairs. My guess is Oliver is teaching the twins computer games.'

His mother raised her eyebrows. 'Shame none of you had a daughter. A girl would stay at the table and chat with her grandparents.'

Gordon laughed. 'What sort of sexist thing is that to say?'

His mother glared at him.

He reached for his wineglass.

'Me? Sexist?' She huffed. 'You obviously don't remember I was a career woman before it became commonplace.'

'I remember,' he whispered into his wine, before taking a sip.

'That doesn't mean I don't know the difference in how children can behave. I did raise three. Unlike you.'

He looked at her and she held his gaze.

'I thought with Stacey,' his mother said. 'With how she was getting on in age, that she'd at least want to settle down and have a baby with you.'

'Okaaay.' Charlotte drawled as she sat down. 'Changing the subject. You know what's amusing?' She said to Gordon. 'I was thinking about this the other day.' She giggled. 'You up in Wales playing around with some sheep?'

'I wasn't playing.'

Charlotte leant forward over the table and passed the side plates around. 'When we were kids and I would sing *Gordon had a little plan*, like the Mary had a Little Lamb song.' She shook her head and laughed. 'Earlier this week, I blamed myself for your moment of madness, running off to a sheep farm. I thought I'd ingrained something into your subconscious.'

His parents exchanged a stern glance. 'You weren't serious about that sheep parlour, were you?' His father said.

Richard, Mark and Eleanor stopped talking and looked at Gordon.

He plonked his glass onto the table. Red wine sloshed over the rim, then dribbled down the glass towards Charlotte's embroidered tablecloth. 'There was never going to be a sheep parlour. It was a joke.'

Mark stared at him. 'Really? Why were you in Wales?'

Gordon breathed in.

'Oh, come on, it's Gordon's birthday,' Charlotte said. 'Let's get the cake. Richard, come help me light the candles?'

Gordon watched them disappear into the kitchen. His father cleared his throat.

'Forty-three years old.'

'Yes, Dad. That's right.' Gordon grabbed a napkin and dabbed at the red stain beneath the glass.

His father looked at him.

'And I am getting my life in order.' Gordon said.

'Yes. Yes, you will.'

Gordon scrunched the napkin into his lap. 'It's true. This time I am getting it right. It's a job with genuine prospects. I'll probably get a bigger flat, eventually. Then perhaps with an end-of-year bonus, I'll have a deposit to get on the housing ladder at last.' He sat back, rubbing a hand over his face. The plan of threatening a sheep run through his former employer's hotel was, as Charlotte said, a moment of madness. Jenna's smile came to mind. The soft complexion, the lashes so light, the colour of straw.

He swallowed back the guilt. Jenna hated him and he couldn't blame her. She'd be telling herself that what had happened between the two of them meant nothing at all to Gordon. Then she would tell herself how none of it mattered anyway, because he was a man who couldn't keep promises. Not even get his brother-in-law, the solicitor, to pore through the Health & Safety order before confirming it was a stupid, hopeless plan and had been all along. He shuffled in his seat and the folded Health and Safety order crinkled in his back pocket.

His father's glare burned into him.

'Excuse me,' Gordon said. He pushed his chair back and strode into the kitchen.

Charlotte and Richard were lighting candles on the cake.

'Gordon,' Charlotte said. 'You'll spoil the surprise.'

'I know what a cake with candles looks like,' Gordon said. He turned to Richard. 'I wanted to give you something. To look at for me, please.' He removed the folded letter from his back pocket. 'It's that Health & Safety Order. About stopping the sheep in London.'

Richard put the lighter he'd been using for the candles onto the counter. 'Not the hotel thing again? Gordon, I thought you'd told your friend—'

'I did. But I also promised them you'd look at this.' Gordon winced. 'It would help me out. Just so I can keep my word. Tell them you looked at it and there's nothing in there that can continue their Right to run the sheep.'

'Guys,' Charlotte said. 'I've got half a cake lit here.'

'Okay, okay.' Richard exhaled slowly, then leant against the counter to read the order.

Gordon watched him as he studied it. A sudden panic hit him. What if there was a loophole? He'd have to ditch the interview and head back to Wales, and it could all fail again… He swallowed. 'Just look at it and tell me it's impossible.'

'Darling,' Charlotte said, lighting the rest of the candles. 'Not now. The cake.'

'Hmmm… yeah,' Richard said, still reading the order.

'Go ahead with the cake,' he said to Charlotte. 'I'll be through in a minute.'

Gordon stared at Richard. He'd found something. He could see it on his brother-in-law's face. His heart pounded. The job interview tomorrow. No, no, no. He had to take this job.

Charlotte held up the cake with the burning candles. 'Come on, you two.'

Gordon followed Charlotte into the dining room, his pulse racing as Richard stayed behind in the kitchen.

Charlotte took the lead in singing *Happy Birthday*, and the rest of the family, apart from Richard, still in the kitchen, joined in.

'Make a wish.' Charlotte said, holding the cake in front of him.

Jesus, which wish? He rubbed a hand over his face. *One, there's a loophole and he can help the Priddys.* He looked at his parents, watching him expectantly. *Two, he's completely free from the Right madness and can rebuild his London life.*

His father stared at him. *Two. That was the sensible wish.*

'Hurry, before the wax drips into the cake,' Charlotte said.

He blew out the candles.

Richard came into the room and took his place at the end of the table.

Gordon raised his brows at him.

Something in Richard's eyes held a wariness. Then he frowned and shook his head. 'Nothing,' he said.

Charlotte glanced at her husband, then leant over the table and pushed a knife into the cake. Gordon winced as if the blade had pierced his own heart.

The first time fate granted him a wish, yet in doing so he suddenly felt stuck.

Like a sheep with his head lodged in a fence.

Chapter Twenty-Seven

Monday morning, Gordon sat in front of three of the directors at Tej's new place of employment, The Cardman Group.

He crossed his polished shoes below his ankles. Ankles which wore perfectly matching dark socks. An unusual confidence pumped through him. This morning he employed no fantasy persona. At long last, it seemed embodying Gordon Slee was surprisingly enough.

'You've not been a finance manager before. What makes you think you can do this role?' the woman who introduced herself as head of human resources asked. She wore thick glasses which slid down her nose. She had a warm smile.

Gordon sat forward. 'Well, when I was with my previous employer, I was in effect the manager. I know my title was officially Assistant Manager, but I reported to the financial director.'

A young woman, Cardman's answer to Bethany with the big hair and a fake tan, walked in carrying a tray with coffee and biscuits. She set it on the side table next to Gordon, then placed a steaming mug in front of each of the directors. She looked at Gordon. 'I didn't know how you took yours. Milk and sugar there next to your mug.'

'Oohh, biscuits!' the older man seated next to the HR lady said. 'Thank you, Mimi.'

'You've now left the Remblents Group?' The third director sat forward, a slickly groomed man about ten years younger than Gordon. He smiled at the young woman as she excused herself from the room.

Gordon took a gulp of his coffee and burned his tongue. He bit his lip to stop himself from wincing, then set the mug down. 'There have been redundancies. I'm assured it was nothing to do with the quality of my work.'

The older man, with grey hair so sparse, Gordon wondered why he bothered to attempt a comb-over, shuffled the paperwork in front of him, then sat back. He'd introduced himself at the beginning of the meeting as the company's financial director. 'So I can contact your former FD, ask for a reference?' he asked.

Tingling grew in Gordon's chest. Stalling, he picked up the coffee again and took another gulp, his throat burning as the liquid travelled down.

'We can't do that,' the HR woman said. 'We can only apply for a reference from the previous employer's HR department confirming employment dates.'

The Cardman FD frowned. 'Bloody rules. What's to stop me from picking up the phone?'

The HR woman raised her eyebrows and gave the FD a small shake of the head.

Gordon breathed in, cooling the burning in his throat. He was right to feel confident today. Good luck did appear to be on his side for once. Things were finally going his way.

The FD looked at him. 'What have you been doing since leaving the Remblents Group?'

Gordon shrugged nervously. 'It was only a few weeks ago. I've been spending time in Wales. Doing work on a farm. Voluntarily. You know, sort of giving back to the community while looking for my next career move.'

The FD leant forward. 'Really? What sort of work?'

Gordon's eye twitched. 'Sheep herding.'

The FD sat back with a wide grin. 'I've got a place out in Surrey, plenty of land. Recently got myself four sheep. My wife wasn't thrilled at first, but they're rather fine animals, aren't they?'

'Yes, sir.' Gordon said. He chuckled. Relaxing, he poured some milk into his coffee and took a leisurely sip. 'They are fine animals. A bit naughty too sometimes.' A sudden image of Jenna came to mind, her pulling Molly back from the shrubbery. *Jenna.* Next, an image of himself, with his hands gently guiding a ewe's face through the torn wire in the fence.

His heart panged.

'Yes, they are a bit naughty,' the FD said. 'Always getting caught in the brambles at my place.' He shook his head and smiled.

Gordon raised his eyebrows. 'I can give you some tips. How to lead them out of the brambles.'

The HR woman cleared her throat. 'Getting back to our questions….'

The FD tapped his pen on his notepad. 'I like that,' he said. 'Someone who fills his time with worthwhile activity. Gordon, would you say you're someone who has a desire to keep extremely busy during your working day?'

'Absolutely,' Gordon said. 'As long as I'm doing the job well.' The sheep. He had done the job well with the animals. Even Molly had responded to him lately.

'The responsibilities as finance manager here are huge,' the FD continued. 'The workload might be heavier than what you were used to in your previous job. But it sounds like you're not shy of hard work.'

'No, sir. Not at all. Especially if it's me working with Tej as a co-manager. We were a great team at Remblents.'

The three directors exchanged glances. The young director leant forward. 'I think you've misunderstood. This is a role for one person. One manager.'

Gordon blinked. 'I'm confused. You already have a finance manager, my friend Tej. What's my role going to be?'

The directors looked at each other again. The FD cleared his throat. 'Gordon, the role you're being interviewed for is for the finance manager.'

Gordon's throat tightened. 'Wait, what's happening with Tej?' He glanced at each of the directors. All three looked down at their individual piles of paperwork.

Gordon swallowed 'You're firing Tej?'

'We can't discuss our other employees with you,' the HR woman said.

'He's only been with you for a few weeks.'

The three directors continued staring at their paperwork.

'Oh,' Gordon said. 'He's on probation and you haven't even told him he's not staying.' He looked at each one of them again. 'Can you even do this?'

The HR woman sat up straight and shuffled the papers in front of her. 'Yes.'

'Let's get back to why we've got you here,' the Finance Director said. 'If we were to offer you the job —'

'I'd say no.'

'Excuse me?'

Gordon sat rigid, a sudden coldness washing over him. He hadn't meant to say that. Not out loud. He looked at the FD, whose eyes held something akin to shock.

'What did you just say?' The FD asked slowly.

Gordon stood, his mind dizzy, but his legs strong. 'I'm sorry. I need to go.'

'What the hell are you doing?' the FD said.

'The job. This company, I don't think it's for me. You're asking me to stab a friend in the back.'

The young male director leant forward and smirked. 'This is business, not playdates with pals on a sheep farm.'

Gordon pressed his lips together, then shrugged. 'Yeah, well.' he said. 'I guess I'll take the sheep farm, then.' He turned and left the boardroom, striding out through reception, then back down the elevator and out onto the street.

Fuck. What had he just done? He panted as he made his way towards the tube station to rush home to his flat.

He couldn't do this. Not to Tej, who for fuck's sake, had got him the interview.

He walked back to the flat from Brixton station, his legs hollow, stomach twisting with anxiety. His parents would no doubt phone this afternoon to ask how the interview went. His mother would immediately phone Charlotte, who would tell Mark and Richard. He remembered their faces yesterday at lunch. The mixture of pity and hope for Gormless Gordon.

Apart from Richard. His face held something different. Gordon forced himself to breathe steadily as he attempted to work it out. The anxiety in his stomach hardened.

Caution.

Richard's eyes held caution.

Desperate to understand, he stood outside his block of flats, then took out his mobile to find Richard's office number. He raked a hand through his hair. It was a stupid, empty attempt to find some shred of hope.

But it was all he had. He pressed Richard's number, then told the assistant it was important.

Seconds later, a heavy sigh came through the phone. 'Gordon. What is it?'

Gordon stood staring at the front door of his building, rubbing the back of his neck. 'Information. What it was you actually saw in the Health and Safety order.'

'Gordon, I'm busy, I've got a meeting. I can't…'

'You saw something, didn't you?' Gordon said. 'When you read that Health & Safety order?'

'Do you want me to say yes or no?'

'I want to know exactly what you found.'

'You know you can read through it yourself.'

'I have, but I couldn't make heads nor tales of the legalese.'

'I'm not doing this,' Richard said. 'I'm not going out of my way to give you some far-fetched loophole.'

'Far-fetched?' Gordon said. 'So there is one? A loophole?'

Richard sighed. 'No. If you end up with a criminal conviction and I helped in any way, your sister would divorce me.'

'It would be my decision,' Gordon said. 'Please.'

'No. I'm sorry,' Richard said.

The line clicked off.

Chapter Twenty-Eight

Charlotte arrived at Gordon's flat that evening. He opened the door to her, then shoved the cold take away containers to the side of the coffee table, near his laptop, as she sat down on the sofa.

'Good lord, Gordie. Don't you clear up? You're usually such a neat freak.'

'It's only from this evening. I've been busy.' He moved the laptop away from the take away containers. 'Research.'

Charlotte wrinkled her nose, then pulled a parcel wrapped in silver foil from her bag. 'Some cake left over.' She placed it on the coffee table next to the smeared sweet and sour sauce puddle. She pulled an envelope from her bag. 'And you forgot the card from your nephews.'

'Sorry.' Although he wasn't sure what he was sorry for. Her demeanour seemed rigid. Richard must have said something about Gordon pulling him out of a meeting today.

'Mum said you didn't get the job,' said Charlotte.

'Dad phoned me, so I told him the truth. I was offered the job and I didn't take it.'

She stared at the congealing sweet and sour sauce on the glass topped coffee table.

Gordon stood and strode into the kitchen. He came back with a sponge and paper towel, then began to clear the mess.

'You turned them down.' Charlotte shook her head. 'You have no job, no money to pay your rent.' She sighed. 'No relationship. No prospects for anything.'

Gordon finished wiping the table, then stood tall. 'The thing is, Charlotte. I did have a relationship. It was just the start of it, but it felt…' he scrunched the paper towel in his hand, before bending to place it carefully on the table with the sponge. 'It felt like it could have been the real thing.' He stood again and exhaled heavily.

Charlotte gasped. 'Oh Gordon. What happened?'

'Gordon Slee happened. I blew it. As usual.'

'Well unblow it. Fix it.'

He pressed his lips together. 'I'm not sure it's the sort of thing that gets fixed with a bouquet of flowers or a box of chocolates.'

'You could try at least. Not red roses though, that's too bold. Yellow. Yellow roses mean *I'm sorry.*'

He pictured the yellow sunflowers he'd already given her for Thanksgiving. She probably threw them in the bin the night he left.

'I don't know what it is about my brothers,' Charlotte said. 'Between you with your break-ups and Mark and Eleanor having counselling.'

'What?'

'Oh. Maybe I wasn't supposed to tell you that.' She breathed in slowly, before exhaling in a huff. 'Eleanor said she was tired of living with a man who snapped at the slightest thing. Like if his favourite golf towel was still in the wash basket because he'd forgotten to put it in the machine. Or if the Mercedes that had just come back from the garage suddenly needed a new brake light. He'd fume for ages over the silliest things. She said he needed to do something about this repressed anger inside of him.'

Gordon's mouth gaped open.

'I've told you before. We all felt it, Gordon. The pressure of perfection from Mum and Dad when we were growing up. I've worked through my issues… I think.' She gazed up at him. 'And I have a feeling you might be working through yours?' She gave him a small smile, before she shrugged. 'But Mark? He keeps it all tightly bound and buried beneath his heart.'

Empathy floated through Gordon as he sat. 'It's probably time for Mark and I to stop butting heads, and maybe start opening up to each other.'

Charlotte nodded. 'True. But, you need to fix a few things for yourself first. Perhaps, see if you can win your new lady back?'

Longing tugged at Gordon's heart. He could phone that florist in Bryn Nefyn. Flowers weren't a cure, but they would at least be a start. His credit card limit would surely stretch to another "award winning" bouquet.

Charlotte sat forward. 'Anyway, I didn't come here to talk about Mark. There's another reason I'm here.'

Gordon waited.

'Richard told me you phoned him at the office today. I told him if you were that desperate, he should help you.'

'Really?'

'Oh, for God's sake, Gordon, you're my brother. And for the life of me, I don't understand really what you're up to but …. well, if this stupid Health & Safety order is so important to you….' She reached into her bag and pulled out a small white envelope. 'From Richard.'

Gordon reached for the envelope. 'Thank you,' he whispered.

'Please don't get yourself into any trouble.' She stood.

He stood and hugged her. 'Don't worry. As a friend of mine in Wales might say, I'll soon be in a position of impenetrable power.'

She shook her head and laughed. 'Oh my God, if you say so, and on that note, I'm leaving.'

Gordon sat rigid on his sofa, late into the evening, with the television on mute and the unfolded paper from Richard in his lap. His brother-in-law had highlighted in green one sentence.

'This order is granted on the basis that allowing the Right to proceed as intended by Mr Priddy could interfere with The Remblents Group compliance of food hygiene standards, of which the hotel has a legal duty when preparing food for the safety of its guests.'

Richard had stuck over it a handwritten post-it. 'Gordon, the smallest of loopholes, but if you want my advice, don't do this.'

Frustration hardened in his stomach. He couldn't see it. The loophole was where? He read the highlighted sentence again and again, and still, he couldn't see the answer. Letting out a hard sigh, he dropped the paper to the floor. He must be an idiot.

A moment later, he sat up straight. No, he would not be beaten. He could call Richard first thing in the morning. Once Gordon understood, he'd do whatever it took.

He woke in the early hours; the sheets damp from his sweat. He'd had a dream, bordering on a nightmare. Alan had about fifty sheep with him at a national trial and he shook with nerves as he lead the sheep onto the field. Rhys appeared and cackled as he ran through the field, his sheep-headed hair blowing in the wind, his arms knocking over the sheep barriers.

Gordon sat bolt upright in bed.

Barriers.

That's it.

They could advise the hotel they were using sheep barriers. No chance of the sheep getting into food preparation areas. That's what Richard meant. Find an action to ensure the sheep don't get into the kitchen.

His heart pounded with excitement. He looked at the clock on his bedside table. Four-thirty am. He could get up and get to Wales by mid-morning to tell them the news.

Chapter Twenty-Nine

On the way up to Wales, his heart beat faster with excitement as he spied the rising hills dotted with white specks of sheep.

Soon after, pulling up the gravel and dirt path, giddy nerves filled him as he reached the guesthouse. Despite his apprehension about Jenna's reaction to him returning, the heaviness in his heart told him how much he longed to see her. Flowers. He hadn't sent the flowers. It was okay. He was about to give her something better.

He smiled at Rhys' cracked wooden sign. *The Gwesty.*

He would make this right for all of them. Not just Jenna.

Jumping out of the car, he sprinted up to the front door, knocked, then remembered Rhys always left it unlocked.

Opening the door, he called out. 'Hello? Rhys?'

The house was still. Silent. Of course, Rhys was out in a field, doing the job Gordon had abandoned. A twinge of guilt shivered through him as he strode towards the first field. It would be okay. This time, he really would help them.

Several ewes stood grazing in the field. No sign of Rhys. Or Alan. He trod up the next hill.

The roof of Jenna's cottage peaked through the shrubbery near the top of the hill. His heart filled with yearning. *Be brave. See her. Apologise. Explain how you'll make it up to them all.* He turned to take the path towards her cottage.

Standing at her back door, he knocked, then waited, wishing he had a huge bouquet of yellow roses.

In a nearby pen, a teenage boy in overalls and boots laid straw bedding.

Gordon turned the knob on Jenna's back door. He wouldn't go in, he'd just call through.

Locked.

The teenage boy stood and looked at Gordon. 'They've gone out.'

'All of them?' Gordon said.

The boy nodded.

Gordon's mouth went dry. 'Who are you?' he asked the boy.

'I'm from the local college. Work experience.' He trudged over toward Gordon. 'Old man's in hospital. Rhys and Jenna went with him.'

'Oh, God,' he whispered. He looked at the boy, wisps of hay stuck to his overalls. Gordon's heart thumped. 'Alan? Is he okay?'

The boy shrugged. 'I don't know. He's old, right?' The boy turned and trudged back towards the pen.

Gordon shoved his shaking hands into his pockets. Guilt twisted and tightened around his heart. Alan had mentioned from the beginning his health wasn't good. Gordon swallowed. Alan hadn't looked well recently. Perhaps Gordon contributed to … he breathed in, then held his breath to halt the tightening guilt. Gordon had caused him stress and upset. The farm might not have been any worse off when Gordon left but that doesn't mean he hadn't had a negative impact.

Gordon arrived at the low two-storey hospital. He stood at reception, his hands fidgeting in his pockets, while an old lady with a blood-stained paper towel wrapped around her hand talked slowly with the man behind reception.

'She'd never done this to me before. It's just that she's getting nasty with her advancing age,' the old woman said.

Gordon huffed as he leant forward. 'I need to find a friend of mine. It's an emergency.'

The old woman turned around. 'How rude. Wait your turn.' She looked Gordon up and down. 'You're not even bleeding.' She tsked. 'You probably don't even have a cat. My Betsan is getting on in age and she can't help it—'

'Excuse me,' Gordon said, leaning towards the

receptionist. 'My friend's name is—'

'Gordon,' said a familiar voice.

He turned to see Jenna, her eyes puffy, her face paler than usual. 'Oh God.' He rushed towards her. 'Is he…'

She stepped back. 'He's okay. For now.' Her eyes flashed at him. 'What are you doing here?'

Gordon stepped forward, and she moved back again.

'Sorry,' he whispered. 'I came back to put things right. But that's not important just now. What happened to Alan?'

She looked at the floor for several long seconds. 'His heart,' she whispered. 'He's had problems with it the past few years. But he's stable.'

'Can I see him?' he asked gently. 'Unless you feel he won't want to see me?'

She sighed. 'I didn't tell him. About you. I said you left early because you had to get back to London for this interview.'

'Thank you,' he whispered.

'Just because they don't know about you and the Remblents Group, doesn't mean they weren't pissed off with you for rushing off after this new job.'

Gordon swallowed. 'Is it best if I go?'

Jenna breathed out. 'I think Alan's got more to worry about than if he's angry with you. If you really want to see him, I guess it's okay.'

He followed her down the corridor to a room near the end.

'Two visitors at a time,' she said as they walked. 'But Rhys has just gone to the cafeteria for a break. We've been here since five this morning.'

'Do you think… is it because of the stress with this whole Right plan?'

She shook her head. 'Alan's never been the same since he had to sell off some of his grandfather's land.' She sighed. 'Then when the community club eventually closed, the one Evan had set up… the guilt's been destroying him.'

She stopped and pushed the hair from her face. 'Honestly, this isn't to make you feel bad, but I think he was really looking forward to buying that land back. He'd allowed himself to get hopeful with the hotel pay-off. He even said he might get enough to help the former club members he believes he let down. Let them open a new place.'

'I'm sorry,' Gordon said. 'But look, the reason I came back… I think I've found a way to really help this time. To force the hotel to buy the Right.'

Jenna groaned. 'No. Not again. Don't you go in there and tell him that, getting his hopes up all over again. The excitement wouldn't be good for him. The let-down later will be even worse.'

'I won't let him down this time.'

'Yeah? What's suddenly changed with you?'

He gazed at her, at her angry eyes. 'Everything. If you let me, I'll explain it to you.'

'Later.' She turned, then stepped towards the next doorway.

Gordon followed her into the narrow room with four beds. Alan was in the first bed. His body seemed smaller, vulnerable, underneath the wires and probes attached to his chest. The machines bleeped out the recording of his damaged heart.

'Alan. I'm sorry,' Gordon said.

'For what?'

'To see you here, like this.' He looked at Alan's pale face, then at the blue hospital gown dwarfing Alan's thin body. 'And I'm sorry for leaving the farm before I sorted things for you.'

Alan gave a weak chuckle. 'I always suspected you would. Told Jenna, didn't I?' His eyes moved towards Jenna. 'Didn't trust him.'

The shame burned in Gordon's stomach. 'I know. You were right, but I may have found a way to prove myself trustworthy.'

Alan's weak laugh turned to a cough.

Jenna stood and placed her hand on Alan's shoulder.

His cough settled, Alan looked at Gordon. 'I always wondered what was really in it for you,' said Alan. 'You were blackmailing them for money, right? More than just a commission?'

'No. Not exactly. It was to do with a job I thought I'd get.'

'In insurance?'

Gordon looked at Jenna and she nodded.

Gordon swallowed. 'But at the same time, sir, I did want to achieve something for you.'

'I know you did, son. In your own strange way. So, what are you doing back here? Didn't you have some big London interview?'

Jenna stepped forward. 'Alan, have they given you anything to eat?' She shot a warning glance at Gordon. 'Not now,' she whispered to him.

'I heard that,' Alan said. 'Come on, what are you doing here?'

Jenna gave a tiny shake of her head.

Gordon breathed in. 'If I'm allowed…' His heart thudded as he glanced at Jenna. 'I want to help out on the farm.'

'Really?' Alan said. 'Is that because you didn't get the London job?'

'They wanted to offer me the job. I said no.' He looked again at Jenna.

She flicked him a surprised glance.

'Why didn't you want the job in London?' asked Alan.

'They were bastards. Besides,' he added with a forced smile, 'they didn't have any sheep for me to look after.'

'Ha,' Alan said. 'A lot of them are bastards. Unfortunately, son, I haven't got the money to pay a farmhand. It's why we have the work experience students. So what are you doing here?'

Gordon peered at the floor. 'I'm just following my heart.'

'And it led you back here, did it?' Alan said.

Gordon peered at Jenna. 'I guess it did.'

Chapter Thirty

That afternoon at the guesthouse, Credence Clearwater Revival was back on the Rhys playlist. Gordon knocked on Rhys' door.

'What is it?' Rhys shouted.

Gordon opened the door. A pale-faced Rhys sat on the bed. His eyes rimmed in pink, as if he'd been crying.

Gordon backed out of the doorway, embarrassed. 'I'm sorry.'

'It's okay,' Rhys said.

Gordon exhaled. 'Alan's going to be okay, though. He seemed fine.'

Rhys shrugged. 'I think there's only so much that heart of his is going to take. I'm going back to see him later this afternoon.' He looked at Gordon. 'Give me a lift?'

'Sure. What about Jenna?'

'She's got too much to catch up on she said. Already promised Alan she'd rotate some sheep.'

Gordon strode out towards the fields. He hadn't taken his boots out from the back of the car and soon regretted the mud slopping up the side of his shoes and onto his socks. He found Jenna in a field, arm outstretched, crook in hand, guiding the sheep onto newer grass. Walking towards her, his mud-caked socks squelched in his shoes.

She closed the gate on the sheep and turned.

He stepped in front of her, then put his hands in his pockets, bowing his head.

'You going to tell me now why you're here? After I told you I didn't want to see you again?' Jenna said.

'You want the real reason I'm here or the secondary reason?'

'I'm not sure I want either. Why don't you start with the secondary one?'

'I think I've found a loophole in the Health & Safety order.'

'For real? Are you being serious with me?' She dropped

the crook to the ground and folded her arms.

'I'm done with the lies, the stories, Jenna.'

A sheep baahed and Jenna nodded. 'And this loophole you found? Will it work?'

'Honestly? I don't know. But I definitely think it's worth trying.'

'And what happens if you get another phone call about some great job in London?'

'I'll ignore it.'

'You will, huh? Just like that. And I'm supposed to believe you after you deceived us about working for The Remblents?'

'I was wrong,' Gordon said. 'And I said to you, I'm not ever going to lie again.'

She bent to pick up the crook.

'Look, I don't expect you to understand, or forgive me for what I did,' Gordon said.

'Explain it to me then. Why was it so important to come up here and lie to us and then leave to run after that shiny new job?'

He looked towards the grazing ewes again and shrugged. 'Something I've been wrestling with my whole life.'

'Oh yeah? And what's that?'

He turned his gaze towards Jenna. 'This feeling that I don't belong anywhere. And I've let it drive me to make stupid decisions. To trust the wrong people. I'm sorry you got caught up in it.'

'Where is it you don't belong?'

'Anywhere.' He grimaced. 'We talked about it a bit, outside that coffee shop, in your kitchen. I'd never told anyone about it before. This fear that I have to prove myself. I mean, have something to show materially to confirm I exist. I don't want any of that anymore.' Some sheep in the next field baa-d. Gordon's heart momentarily lifted at their innocent call. 'Look, it doesn't matter.'

'You are about two words away from me telling you to

go home. Prove to me you can talk honestly with me.'

He grimaced. 'Okay, when I was a little boy…' he looked down at his mud-covered shoes and shrugged again from embarrassment.

'Yeah, a bit stupid wearing your shoes out here,' Jenna said. 'Anyway, what happened when you were a little boy?'

'I heard my mother say that I wasn't planned. My parents considered their family complete after they had my brother and sister.'

'Gordon,' she said. 'It doesn't matter. I remember reading somewhere that about half of pregnancies are unplanned. Hell, Emma was unplanned. I was only twenty-years-old. I spent that whole pregnancy ambivalent, questioning if Dylan and I were ready. But once she was born, I knew it was meant to be exactly as it happened.'

He pressed his lips together.

'Come on,' she said. 'You were meant to happen, Gordon.'

'I know. I just wished my parents believed it.' He looked away.

'Talk to me about it,' she said softly. 'You know, like when you talked to me about the cows.'

He shrugged. 'Okay. Not that it really matters, it's just when I think about my parents, there are things… like when I was a little boy at school, I'd open my lunch box and again, I'd have the sandwich made with the heel of the bread loaf. My brother and sister never got that. Or Sunday lunch when Mum put the plates around the table, it was always me who got the end piece of burnt roast beef. Like these constant reminders I was the one they didn't want. Not that I think they did it consciously…'

'Gordon.'

'I know, it's stupid. And I've drawn a line under it, but sometimes when I'm around them, my parents, the memories fight back. Like not coming to the school nativity play because I didn't have a line.'

Jenna's eyes glistened. 'Okay, you're sure that's why

they didn't come? Maybe they were busy?'

'Never busy when Mark or Charlotte had a performance or a recital or… whatever. Although, I've since realised Charlotte had some wounds she'd been nursing too. And Mark…' He stood tall and breathed in. 'It doesn't matter anymore. I need to stop focusing on the past. Nobody had it perfect, did they?'

Jenna lowered her eyes. 'They weren't always very nice to you. Your parents. I'm surprised you're as strong as you are.'

He forced a laugh. 'Me, strong?' He looked towards the grey hills in the distance. 'Maybe. I guess so.'

'Any good family memories?' she asked.

He squinted at the white mountain tops. Memories rushed in. Birthday parties as a kid. The vision of the chopper bicycle he never dared ask for, yet it magically appeared beside the Christmas tree when he was eleven. His parents' beaming faces when he took it for its first ride. He swallowed back the tightness in his throat and smiled. 'Yes. Definitely. There are some happy times mixed in there.'

Jenna stepped closer to him. 'What were you in the play?'

'The play? Oh, you mean the nativity. A camel.'

'A camel?' She grinned.

He chuckled. 'I was a bloody good camel, too.'

'And I thought you were going to tell me you were a sheep.'

He gazed at her, watching her eyes, searching for a hint of absolution. 'Would you be my shepherdess if I was?' he whispered.

She shook her head. 'Don't do this. You know you're not forgiven.'

'I know. I accept that. But in time?'

She gave him a watery smile, then turned away. 'Come on, you should get back to the guest house and get Rhys back to see Alan.' She chuckled. 'And change out of those stupid goddamn shoes.'

Gordon turned and made his way down the path.

'Hey,' Jenna called out. 'What was the first reason? The main one why you came back?'

He swung around, his shoes slipping in the mud. Hands to the ground, he caught himself, then stood and gave a shy grin. 'Do you really have to ask the main reason I came back?'

She stared at him, a smile tugging at her lips until she bit down on the lower one.

Gordon dropped Rhys near the hospital entrance.

'Aren't you coming in?' asked Rhys.

The engine running, Gordon shook his head. 'I should give you time alone with your brother.'

'What did I ever do to deserve that?' Rhys smirked.

Gordon laughed. 'Let me find a parking space, then. I'll say hello again for a few minutes and then maybe get something from the canteen.'

Fifteen minutes later, Gordon sat in a stiff hospital chair at the side of Alan's bed. Alan had some colour to his face again, the sight of which eased the tension in Gordon's shoulders.

Rhys sat about a foot away, nearer the end of the bed, his elbows on his knees, face resting in his palms. Like a kid, Gordon thought, wishing he was home playing his music and probably getting high.

'You sorted things with Jenna yet?' Alan asked Gordon.

Gordon pressed his lips together, then nodded. 'Getting there.'

Alan stared at him. 'Good, because if you care about her, you need to make it right. When I was your age, I wasn't allowed to love the person I wanted. Not if I wished to keep my parents and other people happy, and if I wished to run a successful farm without most of the locals and suppliers shunning me.'

'It must have been hard for you,' said Gordon.

'Yes, it was hard for someone like me when I was nearing your age. 1980s, times were changing, but not quick enough. The whole AIDS thing started, which stoked the prejudices of the ones who wanted to keep their ugly views. There were times I thought, why am I here if I can't love who I want to love?'

Gordon nodded.

'But I chose to be with him anyway,' Alan said. 'And we were married just as much as anyone else who'd signed a piece of paper. I made the right decision. It's the reason we're all here, after all. To find and share love. To hold on to it when it's real.'

Gordon sighed. 'I'm glad you had that. That real sort of relationship has kind of eluded me so far.'

'Bollocks,' Alan said. 'You've got it easy. It's right in front of you. Don't screw it up.'

'Easy?' Gordon grinned. 'We are talking about the feisty New Yorker, aren't we?'

Alan chuckled, then coughed. Gordon stood and left Rhys to have time alone with his brother.

Sometime later, Rhys sauntered into the cafeteria while Gordon drank murky tea from a plastic cup.

'Looks like water from the sheep's trough,' Rhys said.

'Tastes like it too.'

Rhys raised an eyebrow. 'You drink that stuff? Anyway, we should go. You've got a busy day tomorrow.'

'Have I?' Gordon asked.

'Those hay bales haven't been moving themselves while you've been away.'

Despite the saggy mattress and the familiar musty smell in Gordon's guesthouse bedroom, later that night, he settled himself in for a heavy sleep. The four-thirty am rise this morning, followed by the six-hour drive to Wales, then the shock of Alan in hospital. It had all exhausted his nerves. He breathed steadily. It was all calming down. Even Jenna had perhaps softened a little more than he'd expected.

He'd work on that.

Pulling the scratchy duvet over himself, he closed his eyes, allowing himself to drift off and fall into a deep slumber.

A fierce pounding on the door woke him. Gordon sat up, blinking in the darkness as the door creaked open.

'What time is it?' Gordon said.

'Three-thirty,' Rhys replied.

Gordon rubbed his eyes. 'What the fuck, Rhys? Why are you waking me up in the middle—'

'Alan's died.'

Chapter Thirty-One

Jenna set about making the funeral arrangements. Rhys spent the next two days roaming the fields in a daze.

'He's not taking this well,' Jenna said three days after Alan's death. 'We knew, Rhys and I, that this would come. But you're still never prepared for it, are you?' She wiped the tears that had escaped down her cheeks.

They were ambling through the tupping field. Nearly all the ewes had a coloured marking on their hindquarters. Gordon breathed in, attempting to ease the ache in his chest. He'd only known Alan a few weeks. He couldn't imagine the heartbreak Jenna and Rhys must be feeling. He strode a little closer to Jenna, then reached out and squeezed her shoulder. 'Is there anything I can do?' He asked soothingly. 'Help with the arrangements?'

She stopped and shook her head. Looking around the field, she said, 'Blue ram's caught up a bit with old Red, I see.' She wiped another tear from the side of her face. 'One of Alan's favourites.'

They carried on walking. He wasn't sure if this was the time to ask. But he had to know. The thought of Rhys possibly losing his home on top of losing his brother was too much.

'Jenna, can I ask a practical question? What's going to happen now? I mean to the farm. I'm guessing Alan's left it to Rhys, right? And you'll work with Rhys to sort out the debts?'

Jenna looked away.

'What?' Gordon said. 'You're going to tell me Alan hasn't left the farm to Rhys?'

'No, he has but… it's complicated,' Jenna whispered. 'The farm has to be sold.'

His heart thudded. 'Sold? Where will Rhys live?' He stepped towards Jenna. 'Where will *you* live?'

She shook her head. 'I don't know yet. I don't really care right now.'

'Of course,' he said, his voice lowered. 'I understand.'

They walked on until she suddenly stopped again.

She looked at him, her chin trembling. 'I've only just found out. About the farm. After making some phone calls yesterday. Needed to let people know Alan passed. I'm the will's executor.' Her eyes flicked towards the ground. 'Accountant told me everything.'

'Do you want to share it with me?' Gordon said.

She looked up at him. 'Seems the reason Alan wanted that money from the hotel wasn't just to buy back the land he'd sold a few years ago and pay off a few more debts. There are just too many debts, Gordon. The farm has to be sold.'

'I'm so sorry…' Gordon stood, a sudden coldness washing over him. 'But the sheep?'

Jenna turned and strolled through the grazing ewes. 'Let's hope we sell it to someone who wants a sheep farm. They might even want me to stay on as I know the animals.'

'And Rhys?' Gordon said, following her.

Jenna shrugged. 'Maybe we'll get enough money for the farm to pay off the debts and get Rhys a little flat in the village.'

'No…'

'He likes being in the village,' Jenna said. 'He knows everyone there. There's the pub—'

'Oh Christ, Jenna, but this is his home.'

She turned and looked at him. 'This is life, Gordon.'

He plodded down the path towards the guesthouse, his heart heavy with the weight of the awful fate that lay ahead for Rhys. He'd just lost his brother. How could he now lose the only home he'd ever had? Gordon's own problems, his lack of job, the rental flat he was about to lose, it all seemed so small in comparison.

He remembered the day Rhys took him to see the old family cottage, explaining how lucky he was to have this life. Gordon pulled his mobile from his pocket to phone his brother-in-law. Maybe Richard would know someone who did probate law. Gordon stopped. What was he thinking? A lawyer wasn't going to fix this. Debts didn't go to the grave with the deceased. Like expectant vultures, they pounced on what remained. He glanced at his phone before putting it back in his pocket. There was a missed call message on the screen.

Tej.

A new dread piled on top of the weight of his worry for Rhys. Had The Cardman Group already given Tej the shove?

He pressed call.

'Hey,' Tej's voice was low. 'Let me take this out into the corridor.'

'You still at work?'

'What? Yeah.' Tej laughed. 'It's only one pm. You think I'm part time or something?'

A trickle of relief ran through the ache in Gordon's chest. 'I guess you were calling earlier about my interview. You probably know I said no.' He swallowed and added, 'Sorry.'

'Hey mate,' Tej said. 'I don't blame you. I'm not sure what's going on, but I've been getting a strange vibe from the FD this past week. You free to meet up for a drink again tonight? A swift Friday night pint?'

Gordon swallowed. 'I'm in Wales.'

'What?'

'I'm back in Wales.'

Laughter came through the phone. 'Oh man, you just love those sheep—'

'Tej, please. Not now. The farmer, my friend, he's died.'

'Oh… Sorry, mate. That's too bad. You gone up for the funeral? Give me a call when you're back next week.'

'Yeah, I'm not sure when the funeral's going to be, but Tej…'

'Yeah, mate?'

Gordon rubbed the back of his neck. 'Maybe if you're not happy with the Cardman Group, keep an eye out for something else?'

Tej sighed. 'Normally, you'd say something like, "Stick it out, you've got a great opportunity going on for yourself." I just got this weird feeling from you right now.'

Gordon's throat tightened. He'd promised Jenna from now on he would always be honest. Tej was a mate. He deserved the truth. 'They were interviewing me for your role.'

'What?' Tej went silent for several seconds. 'Oh, man,' he finally said.

Gordon rubbed a hand over his face. 'Sorry.'

'Jesus bloody Christ. The Bastards. They're all bastards, Gordon. I had lunch with Bethany the other day. Anyway, she only told me this a few days ago. That guy from the farm, your friend. Oh hell, I hope it's not the one who just croaked it. He came to the office to see Creaton a few years ago.'

'Yes, it was Alan. The friend who just passed. Alan told me he'd gone to the hotel group.'

'Yeah well, Bethany was in that meeting taking notes. Before Alan arrived, the board already agreed they would pay him off for the Right. Like big money. The solicitors had alerted them to the covenant, like a year before that, and Creaton was shitting himself because he didn't pay the premium for the farmer making a claim.'

'But Alan wasn't offered any money,' Gordon said.

'I know. That's what Bethany told me. What happened is, just before the meeting, Creaton decided to bluff your friend. Creaton knew the hotel were about to lose out because of him so instead of offering this money the board had agreed, he decided to play hardball.' Tej sighed. 'Bethany said she felt bad for the guy, because he seemed really nice and just wanted what his family deserved. The farmer guy stood up looking really sad and when he left the room, Creaton laughed. Turned to the others and said

"He backs down easily!"'

Anger burned in Gordon's chest.

'He's always been a bastard,' Tej said. 'Wouldn't even give me time off to go to India when my grandmother died. Said that only applied to immediate family. Like grandparents aren't close family.'

'I didn't know that,' Gordon said. 'I'm sorry.' He gazed towards the guesthouse, then beyond it at the hill with the lopsided peak.

'Gordon?'

'What?'

'You still planning on screwing him with those sheep?'

'Thinking about it.'

'Mate…'

'What?' Gordon said.

'Get the bastard.'

Chapter Thirty-Two

Mourners packed the church. Gordon recognized some faces. Hari the Heddwas, the florist woman, the teenage boy on work experience who told Gordon that Alan was in hospital that day. The boy sat with half a dozen other kids his age, no doubt also apprentices who had been working on the farm. The locals from the village crammed the pews full. It warmed Gordon to know that despite the earlier prejudices Alan may have faced decades back, these villagers loved him.

Gordon sat between Rhys and Jenna in the front pew. Jenna's daughter, Emma, sat on the other side of her, having taken compassionate leave from university.

'I feel like a bit of an imposter,' Gordon whispered to Jenna. 'Everyone here has known Alan for years.'

Her fingers crept along the bench and met Gordon's. His hand tingled from her touch.

'I want you here with us,' she whispered back. 'And you need to make sure Rhys gets up to do the eulogy.'

'Rhys?' Gordon said a little too loudly.

'Yes?' Rhys turned towards Gordon.

'Of course, who else?' Jenna whispered.

The vicar nodded and Rhys stood, then strode up towards the pulpit. There was a purpose in his walk that Gordon hadn't witnessed before. He wore a jacket and tie over a pair of faded jeans with trainers. His Ron Man T-Shirt had been replaced by a wrinkled button-down for today.

'I thought about giving this eulogy in haikus,' Rhys said into the microphone, then grinned.

A few people tittered.

'Only because Alan never believed I wrote them.' He gave a sad smile. 'For the philistines amongst us,' Rhys said. 'A haiku is only seventeen syllables. A line of five syllables, then seven, then five again. This one was a challenge for me. I can write haikus for magpies, for summer rain, but, for a man like like Alan? Could anyone here actually describe him in seventeen syllables?'

A few people murmured, 'No.'

'Well, I did have a go.' Rhys pulled a scrap of paper from his jacket pocket. 'I'm hoping if he's up there listening it will suitably annoy him.'

Emma, next to Jenna, giggled, along with some of the teenage boys behind her.

Rhys cleared his throat, then leaned into the microphone. Feedback screeched through the church. Rhys took a step back. 'Sorry about that. Anyway, I'll try again. Seventeen syllables. Here we go:

'Know it all, Alan
I will turn my music low
When your sheep win a show.'

More laughter from behind, this time louder.

'That's it. Seventeen syllables folks.' He folded the paper and stuffed it back into his pocket.

'Well done,' one of the college boys softly called out.

'Nah, I cheated. That last line was six syllables, not five.' He smiled again at the college apprentices and they laughed.

Then he pressed his lips together before taking a slow breath in. 'The truth is, I tried to write him a real haiku, until I realised for Alan, it would be impossible to describe him in only seventeen syllables.' Rhys looked slowly around the congregation. He clasped his hands in front of him, then moved his gaze to the coffin in front of the pews. 'No, a haiku doesn't cut it. If I'm going to talk about my brother,' he said in a hushed voice, 'I'm going to have to use words that I'm not restricted on.

'Alan, all of us here. We'll remember your warmth. The way you cared for the farm and your animals.' Rhys looked up to gaze around the congregation. 'You were proud of your sheep and knew they were capable of much more than people round here gave them credit for.'

Some people lowered their heads.

'But most of all,' Rhys said. 'You looked after the people around you. Even me, when I know I drove you crazy. But what are younger brothers for?'

A light ripple of tittering from one of the pews.

Rhys grimaced. 'You cared so much for people, your family, me, Mam and Tad, our cousins,' He glimpsed towards Jenna and her daughter, his eyes glistening.

Jenna took a tissue from her bag, then buried her face in it.

'Not forgetting your loyal partner, Evan.' Rhy said. 'That's what I'll remember most. How even back in the dark old days when you thought the world was against you and for what you were, you still put the most important thing in life first. Love.'

Rhys peered towards Gordon and nodded. 'Alan said that on the day he died. That the reason we were all here on this earth is to find love. To share it. To hold on to it.' He looked at the coffin, and his eyes teared. His chin trembled as he murmured, 'I never said this to you when you were alive. I love you, brother.' He pressed his lips together to stop the trembling. 'And I promise to hold on to that love.'

'You did well, Rhys,' Gordon said to him outside the church.

Rhys pushed his shoulders back. 'Course, I did.' His eyes glistened with tears, and he forced a smile.

The villagers offered their condolences to Rhys and Jenna. They eyed Gordon curiously as he stood there.

Jenna's daughter stood chatting with the group of college students. Gordon watched as a young girl stepped forward to give Emma a hug.

'She knows them, of course,' Jenna said. 'Went to school with some of their older brothers and sisters.'

'Listen, Jenna,' Gordon said. 'There was something Rhys said in the eulogy that's got me thinking.'

'What's that?'

Another villager, an older woman, stepped forward and clasped Jenna's hands. 'We loved him so much. I'm so sorry for your loss.'

When the woman walked away, Jenna turned to look at Gordon.

'It's okay,' Gordon whispered. 'We can talk later.'

'No,' Jenna said. 'Whatever you're thinking, tell me now. What about Rhys' eulogy?'

He sighed. 'It's about the sheep run. I think we need to do it. Except the sheep have to go through the hotel. For real.'

Jenna stepped back. 'Why? I thought you said the hotel would cave into the threat this time?'

'I know, but…' He bit his lip. 'There was another promise I made to Alan when I first came here. Not just about the money.'

'Did you?'

'Yes. One about restoring the village's pride in his sheep. I think it was important to Alan. That's why I think we need to do it.'

She shook her head. 'Gordon, it's over. The accountant phoned me yesterday. We have a buyer for the farm.'

His heart pounded. 'What about Rhys? And you?'

'There'll be enough money to get something for Rhys in the village.'

'And you?'

Another villager walked up to her. The man grasped her hand, told her to get in touch if she needed anything.

She thanked him as he walked away, then turned back to Gordon. 'You don't need to worry about me. Alan left me a proportion of the farm, too. I'll probably get myself somewhere with a small bit of land, maybe keep about twenty or thirty sheep.'

'And what?'

She gave him a sad smile. 'Maybe finally open up that cheese making business.'

'And what about the rest of the sheep?'

'The new buyer is a property developer. They're building houses. It won't be a sheep farm anymore.'

Gordon's legs went weak as Jenna turned to walk towards the group of college students.

'Jenna, wait. Remember what you said to me that day we were in London with the sheep? When we were parked outside the coffee shop.'

She turned back and grimaced. 'I won't forget that day.'

'You said you wanted to help me grasp success?'

She raised her eyes to the sky. 'This is just….'

'Have you changed your mind?'

She sighed. 'Come over later. After..' she waved a hand towards another group of villagers mingling outside the church '…. this has all finished.'

'And discuss the sheep plan?'

She nodded.

'It's not for the money. Because you're right, we might not get any.'

'So, what's the point?'

'It's for Alan.'

Chapter Thirty-Three

Gordon and Rhys sat on the sofa in Jenna's front room. She poured them each a brandy.

'Go on,' she said to Gordon. 'What's the plan? Before I change my mind and tell you how you need to forget the whole thing.'

'Are you sure you're okay to discuss it all now? After today?'

'You said it was for Alan,' she said.

'It is.'

'So, go on then. Tell us.'

'We show that we're supporting the hotel's compliance in keeping the food preparation areas clean. It's simple.'

'Is it?' she raised her eyebrows.

'We send ahead to the hotel some of those metal barriers that you use to get the sheep into the pens. Instruct them to put them along the entranceways to the kitchen, to the restaurant. Have them along either side of the foyer. We'd have to send instructions on how to fit them together.'

'Who's going to deliver those?' Jenna asked, taking a sip from her brandy glass.

Rhys sat forward, 'I have a mate down at the betting shop who has a cousin who supplies those barriers and the cousin's friend owes me a favour….'

'There you go,' said Gordon. 'Rhys has a contact who'll sort it.' He turned to Jenna. 'You never know, we could just possibly get enough money to save the farm.'

'I'm not getting the point here,' Jenna said. 'What exactly are we hoping to accomplish from this exercise? You said it was for the sake of running the sheep for Alan, but now you think they'll still pay up for the Right? I can't see how that would happen. If the sheep are behaving, they could make this like a tourist feature for the hotel.'

'Not with the Remblents. The clientele they have is not for tourists. It's for top class business people, celebrities sometimes. As a one-off, they might make use of it for marketing, but not if we said we were going to do it week after week.'

'Week after week?' Jenna's eyes widened. 'I told you, the farm will be sold soon and there will be no Right descendent.'

Gordon exhaled slowly. 'It's a bluff. We can't let them know about the farm sale. The game will be up then.'

Jenna shook her head. 'We can't lose these buyers.'

Rhys sat forward. 'I say we listen to the business athlete.'

'No, Rhys. We have to move forward with the sale,' Jenna said.

'We? Are you forgetting that I'm the Right descendent here?' He smiled at Gordon. 'I'd like to see them defaid get their little trip to London, enjoy a bit of afternoon tea.'

Jenna shook her head. 'It seems pointless.'

Gordon leant forward. 'I want us to do this. Really want us to do this. I don't see a downside.'

Jenna laughed. 'Oh my God. Don't make me laugh, today of all days.'

'Look,' Gordon said. 'Scenario One. They pay us the money and the farm debts are cleared, meaning Rhys gets to stay here. Then hopefully the portion Alan bequeathed to you could still be used to start your cheese-making business.'

'Hmmm. I'd stay on the farm too.' Jenna peered into her brandy glass with a wistful stare. 'Rhys and the work experience kids would still need a shepherdess. Until I trained one of them up. Then I might look into my cheese shop.' She looked at Gordon, her eyes hopeful. 'And if they don't offer to buy the Right?'

'At least I've kept my other promise to Alan. His sheep will have been the first ever to be paraded through a top London hotel.'

'Sounds good to me,' Rhys said. 'Shut them villagers up once and for all.'

Gordon nodded at Rhys. 'I'm sure it will. I might need you to sign a letter giving permission for us to run the sheep. As you're the new descendent. In case they try to use that as a loophole this time.'

'I've given you my permission.'

'I need a letter to show to the hotel.'

'No letter needed. I'm coming with you.'

Gordon rubbed the back of his neck. 'I'm not sure if the three of us can fit in the front of the trailer.'

'I'll ride with the sheep.'

'You can't do that,' Gordon said. 'It's not legal.'

'Ahh,' Rhys waved his hand. 'It's all about doing things legally with you.' He knocked back his brandy. 'Okay, we'll do it your way. My mate down at the pub has a neighbour who has a brother who's got a bigger vehicle. Three people can sit in the front of the truck's cab. Back of it holds more sheep too. About fifty or sixty, I reckon.' Rhys stood, smiling. 'I'll have another brandy, Jenna. Celebrate getting Alan's sheep in a show at last.'

'Although,' Gordon said. 'Be prepared the hotel still might give us the money beforehand. Which means the sheep won't run through the hotel. But at least we could get enough to let you keep the farm.'

Rhys nodded, then looked at Jenna. 'Well then, see? Just like the man said. It's a win, win.' He raised his empty glass to the ceiling. 'We're in a position of impenetrable power, brother.'

Jenna sighed. 'I'll get us another brandy.' She strode towards the kitchen.

Rhys turned to Gordon. 'But no letter. I'm coming with you. That's your proof of my permission.'

Gordon nodded.

'And I'm not just sitting in the truck.'

'Why? What are you planning to do?'

Rhys settled back into the sofa again and smiled his wild grin. 'I'm going to watch those crazy defaid run amok through that lovely big hotel.'

Gordon exhaled. 'You know, the more I think of it, if we end up bringing around fifty sheep, I'm expecting them to do a deal when we reach the steps.'

Rhys smirked at him. 'You thought those animals were stupid. Now you think they're smart enough to do deals. Make up your mind.'

Gordon chuckled.

Jenna came back into the room and topped up their glasses.

'If these directors do a deal,' Rhys said. 'Jenna and I will give you something out of it.'

'Oh God, no. Rhys,' said Gordon. 'I was never after that.'

'Not even a broker fee? A business athlete fee?'

'No need.'

'Stop,' Rhys said, his voice unusually stern.

'Stop what?'

'Treating me like some kid. If Jenna and I end up with some good fortune thanks to you, then I want to give you a gift. Don't insult me by refusing it.'

The next morning, Gordon and Jenna strode towards the tupping field.

'I still can't believe he's gone,' Jenna said. 'I still expect to see him over there, sneaking Blue Ram a few grapes.'

'Did Rhys tell you that Molly likes strawberries?' Gordon asked.

'I bet she does.' Jenna stopped walking. 'Can I ask you something?'

'Of course.'

'What happens after London? I mean, after the sheep have either run through the hotel and you've kept your promise to Alan about shutting the villagers up finally, or the hotel has given us enough money to keep the farm.' She bit her bottom lip, then looked at him. 'What happens with you? The next day. And the day after that? What will you do?'

Gordon stepped closer to her. 'I thought I'd made that clear. I'd like to stay here. In Wales.'

'You have no family here. No friends.'

'No friends?' Gordon's heart squeezed.

She turned and looked out towards the hilltops. 'I meant, I thought you had that big crowd of university friends you liked hanging around with.'

'No. That's sort of … gone. It just took me a while to see it.'

'What will you do work wise?'

'I'll help you out in the cheese shop.'

She laughed. 'You hate cheese.'

He joined in the laughter, then stopped and said, 'Wait. But why not? You'll need someone to do the books for you. I'm very good with that.'

She shrugged, then smiled.

Grinning, he stepped a little closer, then said, 'As long as you promise we'll make sheep's ice cream too. With lots of strawberries.'

She giggled. Her eyes creasing, the straw-coloured lashes lowering. He moved forward.

She stepped back.

'Sorry,' he said. 'You've not forgiven me yet.'

'It's not that.'

'What is it, then?'

She sighed and shook her head. 'Let's walk.'

They moved through the tupping field until they reached the gate. Gordon grabbed the lever and stopped. He raised the heel of his hand and this time pulled the lever slowly as he opened the gate, then stood waiting for Jenna to walk through before following her up the hill.

When he caught up with her, they walked in silence for several minutes. The sound of his breathing and a distant baahing punctuated the early winter air.

'Sitting in that church yesterday,' she said. 'The last time I sat in a pew looking at a coffin was two years ago.'

Gordon continued to walk with her in silence.

'He loved me so purely, you know,' Jenna said. 'Dylan.'

Gordon nodded.

'Sometimes when I think about it, I'm not so sure if anyone could ever love me like that again. Which is okay. Love can be different in every relationship, I'm sure.' They moved towards the next gate. 'But yesterday it struck me that maybe I want to keep that lasting memory of having been loved so fully.'

Gordon stopped. 'Why are you saying this? What makes you think you can't ever have that love again with someone?' He looked down at the mud on the toes of his boots. 'Listen to me. I know what I want, Jenna. I mean, I thought I wanted the big job in London, the status, the mega salary.'

She looked at him.

'But since I started spending time in Wales, I've felt something different. A sort of peace, an acceptance of myself.' He looked around the field. 'And it's okay. I understand it might not be what you want or what you're ready for. But I like being with you. It feels, I don't know. Natural with you. It's like you see me.'

He reached out and brushed a strand of hair from her face.

She didn't back away this time.

'I want to spend my life here with you,' he said. 'Scanning pregnant ewes in January, birthing baby lambs with you in the Spring; walking along Welsh clifftops with your hand in mine, I want to sit on a rocky beach eating ice cream with you–'

'Cheese.'

'What?'

She grinned. 'You'll eat cheese with me.'

He threw his hands up into the air. 'Okay. If that's what it takes. I'll eat cheese with you. The biggest, smelliest, foulest piece of cheese you can find.'

She laughed.

He grabbed her shoulders. 'Jenna, I just want to be

with you.'

'Definitely not London?'

'I'll have to go back and visit my family.' He rolled his eyes, and she laughed again.

'I used to think being successful meant I had to have possessions and things to prove I earned my place in this world.' He puts his hand over his heart. 'It's not about any of that, is it? It's what you feel in here.'

She stared at him. 'You never needed to earn your place.' She shook her head, smiling. 'You're already here.'

'I know.'

She turned to walk away, then looked back and smiled. 'And I'm kind of happy you're here.'

He stumbled after her. 'Only kind of?'

She gave him a shy smile and shrugged. 'A little more than kind of.'

'Does that mean you've forgiven me?'

She stopped and turned towards him. 'I've been thinking about something. Alan believed we were given this life to share and hold on to love. He's right. But, until I heard that, I've never given much thought as to there being a reason for each of us being here.'

She reached out and touched the side of his face. 'I've been thinking what I believe my reason might be. It's we're in this world to learn how to forgive each other.' She stepped back and looked at the ground, the moss-covered gravel crunched into the path. 'I had to learn to forgive Dylan for getting cancer and leaving us, even though it wasn't his fault.' She looked away as she blinked back tears. 'Then I realised I also had to forgive myself.'

'For what?'

'For years, I carried around this guilt for running off and leaving my New York family to be with Dylan in Wales. I hadn't even realised I was carrying it. The fear that I'd broken my parents' hearts, gave birth to their first grandchild over three thousand miles away.' She shrugged. 'But it worked out okay in the end. They came and spent a lot of time with Emma here in Wales.'

He nodded. 'You forgave yourself by focusing on the good times with Emma and your parents.'

She looked at him and smiled. 'I did. And that's what I do with Dylan now. So yeah, I think we're here on this earth so we can figure out how to forgive.' The dimples in her cheeks deepened. 'I guess I forgive you then.'

He took a step forward and gazed at her lips, then hesitated.

'Come on,' she said, turning away. 'Let's get to the next field. Check on your favourite.'

'My favourite?'

'See if Molly's banging her head against a fence.' She stopped then and reached out her hand.

He grasped her fingers. The warmth from her forgiveness shot through to his heart. Holding hands, they strode towards the next gate. Gordon reached out for the lever. 'I think I've actually got the hang of these gates now. After you.'

He followed her through the gate, then froze.

She walked ahead, then turned and stopped. 'What is it?' She turned back to look across the field. 'Oh, the cows…'

He breathed in and allowed his heartbeat to slow. 'It's okay. I think I can be with them now.' He looked around the field at the brown and white animals, tails swishing, peacefully chomping the grass. 'I can get used to this. I don't think I'm scared anymore.' He gave her a slow smile, then stepped forward and brushed another curl from her face. 'Not of cows, anyway. Although with you…' placing his hand over his heart, 'I might be very scared… of losing this.'

She looked down and chuckled. 'Let's go over to Rhys' house,' she said. 'I'd like to read through that Health & Safety order, if that's okay? I'm still a bit nervous about it all.'

Rhys walked past the bedroom and stopped, did a double take. 'Eh, no women in the house. Next thing you know, she'll be leaving makeup in the bathroom cabinet.'

'I'm just looking at the health and safety order,' Jenna said as she sat on the single bed, paper in hand. Gordon sat next to her, reading over her shoulder.

'Why?' asked Rhys.

'Wanted to read this myself. I guess I'm nervous if this really is a loophole.'

Rhys stepped into the room and snatched the paper from her hands. He rubbed his stubbly chin as he read through it. 'Ah, we're alright,' he said, handing the paper back to her. 'Them defaid know how to respect barriers.'

'Is that what happened in nineteen-ninety-six?' Gordon grinned. 'They respected the barriers?'

'The hell they did. That was way before Alan got ill, when he was the one spending most of the time with them defaid. But in the last few years, since they've got used to me, they've turned into high performing sheep. No problems with them respecting barriers.' He looked at Jenna. 'You know that. You're their shepherdess.'

Gordon took his phone from his back pocket and turned to Jenna. 'In that case, if you two give me a few minutes on my own to compose a message, I'll re-start the plan.'

Dear Edward,

I'm back in Wales with two members of the Priddy family. Having taken legal advice, it appears they are only in danger of forcing the hotel group to breach Health & Safety if the sheep enter the area where food is being prepared or served. You now have their assurance this will not be the case. A skilled shepherdess and two shepherds will be guiding the sheep. Plus, for the hotel's added protection, the animals will be run within an area surrounded by sheep barriers. The barriers will be delivered to you on Wednesday afternoon. It is up to you to take responsibility to have your staff place these barriers in the foyer to create a run from the hotel entrance to the back fire exit, protecting the table areas and any passageways leading into the kitchen or towards the restaurant. The barriers will be delivered with instructions on how to secure them correctly.

The shepherds and sheep will arrive early afternoon the following day with a truck carrying a dozen sheep.

He read over the email, then deleted the last line.

The shepherds and sheep will arrive early afternoon the following day, with a truck carrying fifty sheep.

Regards,

Gordon Slee

Chapter Thirty-Four

Gordon drove down the motorway with a truckload carrying forty-nine sheep.

Jenna huffed. 'I can't believe they've ignored your emails again.'

Gordon sighed. 'They've taken delivery of the barriers, though. Part of the bluff, maybe.' His hands gripped the wheel as he shrugged. 'We won't know until we get there. Just remember the plan if they call our bluff.'

'You sure you're okay leading the sheep, Gordon?' Jenna asked.

'He's right,' Rhys said. 'Better to have me at the back controlling them up those steps.'

'You're just at the back for the first half of the sheep, Rhys. Then we need Jenna to get the others out and follow you while she brings up them into the hotel.'

'Easy enough,' said Rhys.

Gordon choked on a laugh. 'If you say so, Rhys. And you remember what you've got to do once we're inside the hotel?'

'When Jenna gets into the hotel with the last of the sheep,' he sing-songed, 'I'll go out through the front and drive this thing around the back for when you and the sheep come out through the fire exit door. Is that okay?' Rhys leant forward to put the radio on, then pressed some buttons. Static crackled through the cab speakers. 'Ah no. That bloody Barry's given us a truck with a rubbish aerial. I'll have to sing instead.'

'Please don't,' Gordon said, eyes on the stretch of traffic in front

'Baa baa black sheep running through ho-tel,' Rhys crooned.

'Rhys, we don't know that yet.' Gordon switched lanes to overtake a slow-moving car.

'Yes sir, yes sir, yes they will,' he sang, then turned to smile at Gordon. 'You can drive a little faster. Them defaid will be loving the ride. I reckon they're all excited about their afternoon tea.'

An hour later, Gordon pulled the livestock truck into the loading area outside of the front of the hotel. Two security guards rushed down the steps. Gordon's mouth went dry as he pulled the parking brake. 'What will it be this time?' he whispered. 'Another order? An offer to escort us in with the sheep?'

'Think positive,' Jenna said. 'Maybe an offer to buy the Right.'

'That's not positive,' Rhys said. 'It would mean the defaid made their journey for nothing. They want to dance down that corridor.'

A security guard reached up to tap on the driver's window. Gordon opened the door and stepped down.

'You can't park here. You need to go around to the side street.'

'I'm not leading the sheep out from there, getting them around a busy street corner.'

'No, you're not. You're taking them into the basement entrance around the back.'

'No,' Gordon said. 'That's not the deal.'

'We're allowing your sheep access to the hotel grounds. We set the barriers up in the basement. They can have a run through there.'

'The plan is to go from the front of the building to the back, as if it were a shortcut to market. That's how we've interpreted the Right.'

The security guard grimaced. 'We both know there's no market anymore. I suggest you get this vehicle around to the basement entrance before things get ugly.'

Behind the two security guards, a familiar figure in a dark suit swaggered towards the truck.

He stopped when he saw Gordon, mouth gaping open. He breathed in, then raised his chin as he strode towards him.

'Well, what do we have here? Gordon Slee,' Edward

Creaton said. 'Are you one of the shepherds?' he joked.

'Yes, I am.'

Creaton stared at him, then looked him up and down and laughed. 'You've really come down in the world, haven't you?'

Gordon exhaled, 'Not quite,' he said. He turned and stepped back up through the driver's door.

'Are we doing it?' Rhys asked as Gordon climbed into the driver's seat, slamming the door shut.

'They've found another legal hurdle to stop us?' asked Jenna.

Gordon pressed his lips together, then breathed out. 'Yes. They want us to go around to the side street and run the sheep through the basement.' Heat rose beneath his collar.

'Not good enough,' Rhys said. He pursed his lips. 'I promised y defaid afternoon tea.'

Gordon slumped against the seatback. 'We need to think. It won't affect them one bit having the run in the basement.'

'Hey. Business athlete,' Rhys said. 'Come on, use your super power. Haven't you got a line of bullshit that gets around this?'

Gordon shook his head. He turned to check his wing mirror and spied Creaton from his driver's window, laughing with the security guards, before giving Gordon a smirk.

His heart pounded with anger. The face Creaton probably wore when he laughed Alan out of the boardroom four years ago.

'You know, Rhys,' Gordon said. 'Maybe I can use your super power.'

Rhys grinned.

'What the hell is Rhys' super power?' Jenna asked.

Rhys cackled. 'Not giving a shit.'

'But,' Jenna said. 'We're breaking the Health & Safety order if we go on the main floor with no barriers.'

Creaton and the security guards made their way back up the hotel steps.

Gordon looked at Jenna. 'I'm going to say we're not. They are. We were clear. My emails said we were running the sheep through the main foyer. We provided the barriers for their protection. It was up to them to put them in the right place.'

'Woohoo!' Rhys shouted as he opened the passenger door and jumped out of the truck.

'Wait here for a moment,' Gordon said to Jenna. 'We'll bring out the first half, then once we've got them up the steps and into the hotel, bring the rest up and through the entrance.' He gave her a quick kiss, then jumped out of the truck to help Rhys.

They opened the back of the truck, dozens of sheep faces stared back. Apart from one who stood side on, butting her head against the trailer wall.

'Oh Jesus, Rhys. You brought Molly?'

'I thought she was your favourite.'

Gordon reached in and tugged at the fleece near her neck. Molly turned her head, then twitched her ears. As if by miracle, she turned towards Gordon completely, and then stepped down the ramp towards him. 'Maybe she thinks I have strawberries,' he said to Rhys.

'Later,' Gordon said to Molly. 'I'll bring you a whole bowl of them.' A small crowd gathered as Gordon ambled cautiously towards the bottom of the hotel steps, with Rhys and his crook behind, encouraging twenty sheep to follow between them.

Slowly, they led the sheep up the steps, Gordon in front, Rhys bringing up the rear. The onlookers began to laugh and clap.

A security guard stepped from behind Creaton, blocking Gordon's way. 'We said the basement.'

'That wasn't the information I gave to you.' Gordon said.

Creaton stepped forward. 'The agreement was to use

barriers. You're breaking the order if you don't use the basement.'

'No,' Gordon said. 'It's not my fault you've put our barriers in the wrong place.' He held Creaton's glare. 'Like it or not, we're coming in.'

For a split second, a flash of fear flickered in Creaton's eyes. He turned towards the security guards. 'Get some staff to run into the basement and bring those barriers into the foyer right now.'

'You're a bit late for that,' Gordon said.

'I swear, Slee, if you don't wait for those barriers to be put up, I'll have you arrested. As well as being a criminal, you'll be a laughingstock when this gets plastered over social media.' He nodded towards some onlookers who were recording the sheep on their phones. 'The entire country will be laughing at you.'

Gordon shrugged. 'I think they'll be laughing at you.' He turned and looked over his shoulder at the sheep crowding up behind him on the steps. Rhys stood waiting at the bottom, mouthing something Gordon couldn't make out.

'I think Mr Priddy's telling me we can't keep the sheep here on the steps much longer,' said Gordon. 'You'll need to step aside, Edward.'

'I say you wait.'

'The sheep won't wait. They might get restless. Or spooked by something.'

'Mr. Creaton,' a flushed faced security guard rushed towards him from inside the hotel. 'It's okay, we're ready.'

Creaton raised his eyebrows at the security guard, who nodded.

The onlookers clapped and cheered as Gordon pushed open the glass door, then shoved it back hard enough so it remained open. He turned to shout at Rhys. 'Tell Jenna to get the rest of the sheep.'

'You'll regret this, Slee.' Creaton hissed as Gordon pushed past.

Gordon steadied his breath as he ambled into the foyer. Ahead, the staff had set the sheep barriers along either side of the long corridor, between the gleaming grey and white pillars with floral displays boasting bright poinsettia and evergreen.

Right, easy now. Keep walking. His breathing intensified as he strode across the white marble flooring towards the corridor. A hushed silence fell across the foyer as he passed the mahogany reception area. Two people behind the desk stared wide-eyed. Four customers in front of the desk stood and turned open-mouthed.

The soft tinkling of Christmas music drifted through from the tea area, punctuated by the gentle sound of hoofs shuffling and scraping behind Gordon.

He glanced over his shoulder. About thirty sheep now. His heart pounded at the sound of skidding hooves. They just needed one sheep to fall over and it could all descend into chaos. He slowed his steps.

The smell of wool and lanolin intensified in the corridor. Rhys was quite a way behind. Jenna, hopefully, was at the back. A young couple walked towards them. The woman covered her mouth and laughed while her companion pulled her aside so Gordon could walk past with the sheep.

'Good lord,' a man's voice bellowed. 'Crikey, Jonathan. Come look at this.' Two men from the tea area leant out over a barrier. A third joined them. 'I didn't believe the waiter when he said it was for sheep.'

Ahead, in the distance, still a good hundred feet away, the sign for the fire exit illuminated. Just before then, the sweeping staircase. With a sigh of relief, Gordon noted the staircase had the barriers secured in front.

The sheep continued to shuffle and skid behind Gordon. The smell of dung joined the wool and lanolin.

Light chattering and cutlery clinking against tea cups grew more audible as he approached the tea area. Several tables of men and women, in business suits and smart casual wear, sat eating sandwiches, sipping beverages. Table by table, conversations halted. Heads turned and fingers on cups froze. The fire exit sign drew closer.

A woman at a table laughed. A ripple of titters from other diners. Sweat soaked the back of Gordon's collar and then….

No.

At a table just to the left of the last barrier, four men in business suits and one of them, the Chancellor of the Exchequer.

Gordon counted his breaths to calm himself. Nearly there. The exit door was nearing. He sneaked another look at the Chancellor, at the man he'd been in all his fantasies, and then he saw it. Gripped in the still fingers of the Chancellor of the Exchequer was a slice of cake and on its top, a huge strawberry.

A head butted the back of his knee.

'No Molly,' Gordon turned and whispered.

'Baaaaaaa.' Molly shuffled and skidded towards the barrier.

'Molly,' Gordon hissed.

With one strong head butt, Molly crashed through the metal gate, knocking it to the floor. A woman shrieked. The Chancellor and his guests jumped up from their table. Molly bolted towards the Chancellor, pushing her head into his legs, knocking him to the floor. The chancellor cried out as she plonked her front hooves on top of him, her nose fighting to reach the cake squashed between his fingers and held above his head.

'Just give her the cake!' Gordon shouted, his heart hammering against his ribcage. He rushed to stand over the Chancellor and Molly. 'Oh Jesus. I'm sorry, sir, just give her the cake with the strawberry.'

'My God,' a woman screeched. 'They're attacking people.' She rushed to grip the back of a chair while others crowded behind her.

The Chancellor stretched out his arm and unfurled his

fingers. Molly stepped off him and moved towards the cake-filled hand. The Chancellor whimpered as her thick tongue lapped up the strawberry.

Another sheep pushed down a second barrier. Then a third sheep and a fourth. All around guests shouted, while others hooted with hysteria as more sheep rushed into the tea area, knocking the gates down one by one.

'Are you okay, sir?' Gordon asked the Chancellor, his heart pounding while his eyes searched for Rhys and Jenna.

'Run, defaid, run!' Rhys cried out.

'Let me help you up, sir.' Gordon said, reaching out his hand.

The Chancellor groaned as Gordon pulled him to his feet. One of the Chancellor's companions handed him a linen napkin.

Gordon stood paralyzed as the Chancellor brushed down his suit covered in whipped cream and dried mud.

'I apologise…' Gordon said, 'The sheep weren't meant to get through… I brought them in to protest against the actions of the hotel directors…'

'No harm done,' The Chancellor stood tall, a streak of dried whipped cream on his lapel. 'I was always one for direct action in my heyday. Good luck, son.' He stepped over the fallen barrier and strode away with his peers.

Gordon bent to grab a sheep, then watched helplessly as several more crowded into the tea area. He covered his face with shaking hands as Rhys stepped towards him.

'Rhys,' Gordon said between closed fingers. 'What the hell's going on?' The sound of crashing plates and shouting reverberated around him.

'Not our fault. They were supposed to hinge those barriers together. We sent them the instructions. Lazy hotel workers, eh?'

Jenna rushed up behind them. 'Gordon, oh my God, look.'

'I can't look,' he said, hands covering his face as he

turned to Jenna.

'Oh, good God,' she whispered.

Gordon removed his hands and turned. In the room's corner stood a twelve foot Christmas tree. A sheep ran towards it, with several more following.

'Get out! Get OUT!' A waiter cried. 'Everyone out of this area!'

Customers bolted from behind chairs, some screamed. A woman tripped over a barrier lying on the floor. A waitress ran to pull her up. The giant Christmas tree trembled, then tilted forward, before smashing onto tables laden with crockery, sandwiches and cakes.

'The police are here,' Jenna said.

'I don't care.' Gordon's heart pounded as he surveyed sheep knocking over chairs, their hoofs dragging table cloths, tea cups crashing to the floor. 'I don't care anymore.'

'I'll handle it.' Jenna said as she marched towards the two officers.

'We'll never get them back in that truck.' Gordon said, surveying the annihilation of the tea area. Two sheep were now on tables, pulling apart cucumber sandwiches.

Rhys placed his hand on Gordon's shoulder. 'Who cares.' He smiled. 'Look at them all. Having such a good time. Best day of their lives, I reckon. And mine.'

Jenna rushed over to them. 'I've shown the police the Health & Safety order. Copies of correspondence. Told them it's a civil matter. They won't arrest us if we get them all back into the truck asap.'

Creaton stomped down the foyer, skidding on a piece of sheep dung. His nostrils flaring, he steadied himself before striding towards them. 'Get those bloody sheep out of here!'

Anger rose in Gordon's chest. 'I'll deal with him.' He marched towards his ex-boss then swallowed. 'Next week,' Gordon said in a steady voice, 'You ensure you have the barriers set up in good time so you can secure them.' He jabbed his finger towards the filthy floor. 'Here. In the lobby area. Like we informed you. We told you it would be the lobby area.'

'What do you mean next week?' Creaton sneered.

'Next week and every week after that. That's the permission the Right grants.'

Creaton's jaw hardened. He turned and surveyed the detritus of the foyer's tea area. Sheep stood on chairs, tables, stepped along the branches of the fallen Christmas tree, baubles crunching under their hooves. 'Get these fucking smelly animals out of my hotel.' He turned on his heel and stomped off, criss-crossing around the piles of dung.

Gordon turned and breathed in.

'Ah, these defaid aren't going nowhere,' Rhys said.

'Yes, they are. Jenna, if you can grab the crook and go to the left corner of the room. Rhys, you go to the right corner.'

'That's not the way to do it,' Rhys said.

'Just do it, Rhys. Please.'

'You have to get them into a corner,' Rhys said.

'I need to get them through the tables here in the middle.' Gordon strode through the broken crockery towards a waiter crouched on the floor, sweeping broken glass into a dustpan. 'You'll need more than a dustpan, mate,' Gordon said. 'But if you help me get these sheep out of here, it might make things easier for you.'

The waiter stood. 'How?'

'Bring me a plate of fruit.'

'What kind?'

'Anything. Apples, bananas, oranges. Just quickly please.'

A sheep climbed the table next to Gordon to pull lettuce from a sandwich as the waiter rushed off.

'I wouldn't mind a sandwich,' Rhys called out. 'Seeing as we're standing here.'

The waiter returned with a large fruit bowl stacked with

apples, bananas, and grapes.

Gordon took the bowl and moved to the middle of the room. 'Start edging the sheep towards me,' he called out.

Jenna and Rhys moved in unison, arms wide, huddling the sheep slowly towards Gordon.

Gordon grabbed a few grapes and threw them at the sheep in front. They shuffled forward. Carrying the fruit bowl, he turned and strode towards the front entrance, throwing another grape over his shoulder. The clip-clopping of hooves on marble sped up behind him.

'I thought we were going through the fire exit,' Rhys called out.

'And where do you think we left the truck?' Gordon said.

Rhys shrugged before turning towards a table to grab a plate of sandwiches.

'We don't need those,' Gordon said.

Gordon, Rhys and Jenna loaded the last of the animals onto the back of the livestock truck. Gordon's hands shook as he handed Jenna the fruit bowl, then helped Rhys pull the ramp up.

Jenna's eyes flitted nervously. 'Are you serious that we have to do this every week? It's not possible—'

'Stop your worrying,' Rhys said. 'I reckon we'll have the hang of it all next time.' He pulled an egg and cress sandwich quarter from his pocket, then shoved it into his mouth.

'Gordon, we can't do this again,' Jenna said. 'Today was a disaster. One of the sheep could have gotten hurt. It's a miracle they're all okay. Plus, apart from the sheep, it's not like I can delay the farm sale indefinitely.'

Footsteps approached, and Gordon turned. The Remblents Group's managing director, John Walker, stood in front of him, his face a mixture of shock and fury. 'Did I hear right that this is happening every week?'

'Yes. It is,' Gordon said, ignoring Jenna's gasp behind

him.

John Walker huffed.

'You know, John,' Gordon said. 'It never needed to come to this. Some weeks back, I tried to negotiate something. A deal that would protect the hotel and give the Priddys at least a little something for this covenant. You can check Creaton's emails.'

The muscles around Walker's mouth tightened. 'What's the best way to contact you? The email address Creaton has?'

'Yes.' Gordon held his breath.

The MD pressed his lips together, his face flushed with a quiet rage. He turned and strode back towards the hotel.

Gordon let out an exhale.

'What do you think that means?' Jenna said.

'Who cares,' Rhys said. 'Let's get back to Bryn Nefyn. There's a celebration roll-up calling my name.'

'We don't know yet if there's anything to celebrate,' said Gordon.

'I didn't see you as a glass half empty man,' Rhys said. 'Doesn't sound like the great attribute of a business athlete. I'm celebrating the fact these defaid have completed a public sheep run for the first time since nineteen-ninety-six.' He grinned. 'And it was mind-blowing.'

Chapter Thirty-Five

Gordon travelled to London by train on Monday morning. The email had arrived Friday afternoon with the invitation to meet with the directors. He entered the boardroom of the Remblents Group where four of them sat waiting.

Creaton wasn't there. The Managing director gestured for Gordon to sit opposite them.

Gordon pulled out a chair and sat, then scraped a hand through his hair, before sitting up tall. *You're in a position of impenetrable power.*

'We've put a proposal together. It's all here,' John Walker said, pushing some papers across.

Gordon skimmed the first few paragraphs. An offer to purchase the Right.

'I think the Priddys will accept we're being generous. If so, we can get that money sent over to Rhys Priddy's trustee by the end of the week.' Walker looked across to Bethany, Creaton's assistant. 'You'll arranged that transfer to Jenna Priddy once this is all signed?'

Bethany nodded. She stole a glance at Gordon and gave him a wink.

'We added interest to the sum we intended to pay four years ago,' John Walker said. 'The sum we had agreed to pay your friend when he came in here back then.'

Gordon nodded, biting his lip to keep from smiling. There was enough to pay off the debts, enough to employ farm workers, enough for Jenna to start her cheese-making business.

'I'm sorry, Gordon. About your friend,' John said. 'There's a rumour going around these offices that the company added to his health problems, which, of course, we can't accept.'

Gordon peered at Bethany, who smirked.

'This letter is for you.' Walker pushed another paper in front of Gordon. 'If you're happy to sign this nondisclosure letter about that meeting four years ago and ask Rhys and Jenna Priddy if they wouldn't mind signing it, too?'

Gordon looked up, and the managing director sighed.

'We've had journalists sniffing around since the sheep run. Especially with that photo of the Chancellor of the Exchequer leaving the hotel with cake smeared down the front of his suit.'

Bethany snorted. Walker turned to glare at her.

'Sorry.' She said. 'I guess it wasn't funny.' She raised her eyebrows to Gordon as her boss looked away.

Walker exhaled heavily. 'These journalists were told gossip about the hotel group speeding up your friend's poor health. Claimed one of our directors deliberately cheated him. Now, you understand we refute that. Alan Priddy wasn't cheated because we hadn't formally struck a deal. But out of good will and compassion for Alan Priddy's family, we've been generous with our offer to purchase the Right in the hope we can all draw this matter to a close.'

Gordon pressed his lips together and nodded. 'I'll take this back to Rhys and Jenna.'

'And you'll advise them to take it?'

Gordon skimmed through the pages. 'There was that other thing I mentioned in my email. The sponsorship.'

'For the new community club in Bryn Nefyn. The LGBTQ+?'

Gordon nodded.

'There's a separate confirmation coming for that.' John Walker said. 'We don't want it linked to this deal. We're doing the sponsorship because we believe in a worthy cause.' He turned to the other directors. 'That's another thing that will help put to bed this nonsense that we attempted to cheat Alan Priddy.'

Gordon nodded. 'Okay, I will recommend to the Priddys they agree to all this.' He shuffled the pages into a pile, then pushed his chair back and stood. As an afterthought, he held out his hand to John Walker.

The directors glanced at each other with smiles of relief. John Walker stood. He looked at Creaton's assistant again. 'Bethany, can you give us a moment alone with Gordon?'

Bethany picked up her notebook and gave Gordon a secret grin as she walked past.

The MD put his hands in his pockets. He looked down at the table, smiling. 'In case you're wondering why Edward Creaton isn't here, he's retiring. Probably more a case of jumping before he was pushed.'

'I see.' Gordon said.

'I read those emails. It was clear you were trying to protect us.' Walker said as he stared down at the table.

'Actually, I was at first. But then I thought the Priddys deserved more than what Creaton had been prepared to pay.'

'I have to say I do agree with you on that.' John shook his head. 'Last Thursday was a disaster. I arrived just as they evacuated the guests from the tea area. It was like a bomb had hit the place.'

'Your insurance,' Gordon said, 'they'll cover that?'

John waved his hand. 'Looked worse than it was. Some crockery. A Christmas tree. No, what I wanted to say was I watched you.' He raised his eyes to Gordon. 'The calm way you took control of the animals. How you coordinated and worked with the Priddys to strategically get the sheep into a huddle—'

'A herd,' Gordon said.

John continued. 'You led them out onto the street with confidence. Quite impressive after all the hysteria and chaos from the staff and customers.'

Gordon's lungs expanded with pride. 'Thank you.'

'Edward told us that you were after a sweetener from the board. For brokering a deal over the Right.'

Gordon stood tall. 'We had conversations about a promotion.'

John's smile was awkward, nervous. 'I'm aware he'd told you something to that effect.' He cleared his throat. 'We wondered if it helps to draw a line under things, you know, with the office gossip… these bloody journalists…' He peered at Gordon. 'We can offer you a director position here.'

A rush of adrenaline tingled through Gordon's veins. 'What? You're not serious…'

'And please don't think it's only because we're trying to buy your silence.' He waved his hand. 'After all, press stories these days last two minutes and then there's something else for people to whine about.' He looked at the other three directors. 'No, we've been talking. We think this company could use someone with your imagination, and mostly, with your courage to see things through, no matter what the obstacles are.'

Light-headedness overtook him as an overwhelming pride surged through his body. He placed a hand on the back of the chair in front of him, steadying himself.

John Walker beamed at him. 'Not to mention your ability to work calmly to lead a team during a crisis.'

Gordon's skin tingled with surprise.

'And most importantly, the aptitude to decipher what's fair. We prefer noble actions to cheating people out of what they deserve.' John smiled at him. 'What do you say?'

'I'm flattered.' Gordon's heartbeat raced. His grandfather? What would he say if he could see this? Gordon finally made a director at a top London hotel. Granddad had told him one day his purpose would find him. A sudden dizziness washed over him. Gordon held his breath until his mind cleared.

'Is that a yes?' asked John. He stepped over to where Gordon stood, then glanced at Gordon's shoes. 'Great shine to those.'

'Yes. I used lanolin. Pure lanolin.' His cheeks warmed as an image of those stupid beloved sheep invaded his mind. An image with Jenna, his beautiful Jenna, holding a ewe.

'When would you like to start?' John said. 'Assuming you've just said yes.'

Gordon gazed at his shoes. Jenna. Rhys. Molly and all the other crazy, woolly creatures. Walking the muddy fields, filling the troughs and then in March, new lambs coming into the world.

Lambing season. The best time of year.

He couldn't miss that. With Jenna…

Gordon shook his head. 'I'm afraid the answer's a no. But thank you.'

John's brows pinched. He turned to look at his colleagues. The female director shrugged.

'You've got something else, Gordon?' asked John.

Warmth expanded around his heart. 'Yes.' His lips stretched into a huge smile. 'Yes, I've got something better.'

Chapter Thirty-Six

Seven months later….

Gordon and Jenna stood outside the high street store.

'It will be perfect,' Jenna said. 'This is the one I've had my eye on. What do you think?'

Gordon stepped into the shop, surveyed the windows at the front that stretched from the ceiling down to a metre from the floor. He turned and observed the shell of the room, then looking towards the shop window again, in his mind's eye, he could see the counter. With a window above it where he could serve ice cream cones to the passersby on the street.

To the side of the shop, along the wall, a longer counter already stretched which could house the various cheeses Jenna wanted to sell.

'There's a back room where we can store the cheese,' Jenna said. 'And room to hold more freezers for the ice cream.'

'Will you be making the cheese here?'

'I spoke with Rhys. There's lots more space in our farm workshop. He's letting us keep that rent free for now.' She nudged him and giggled. 'Maybe you can eventually pay him with your special strawberry vanilla ice cream.'

'Without the hidden surprise inside the cone?' Gordon said.

'What? What's inside the cone?'

'Never mind.'

Jenna's footsteps echoed along the wood flooring as she surveyed the space. She swung around with a beaming smile. 'But opening a shop here means getting up earlier than five thirty am to see the sheep. You okay with that?'

He stepped towards her and grinned. 'Not easy getting out of bed early these days.' He brushed aside a curl from her face.

She looked at him, raising an eyebrow, the affectation

that she had somehow transformed into an endearing one. Stepping back, she turned and asked, 'I'm being serious. What do you think?'

He gazed at her as she turned back to him; her questioning eyes twinkling, her cheeks glowing. 'Perfect,' he said.

'Really?'

'Really.'

The following morning, he sat on the saggy mattress in Rhys' musty spare bedroom. After months of sharing the cosy firm bed of Jenna's cottage, he'd almost forgotten the barren neglect of this room. He stood and picked up the white carnation from the windowsill and pinned it to his lapel.

Rhys opened the door wearing a wrinkled linen blazer over a T-shirt, jeans, and trainers. He looked at Gordon. 'Ah, forgot my flower. I'll just get it.'

The pews were filled with the familiar faces from Alan's funeral. Except the black suits and dark veils were replaced with pastel shirts, flowery dresses and over wide hats. Gordon's parents sat in the first pew on the right, along with Charlotte, Mark, their spouses and their kids.

Gordon stood facing Jenna. She beamed at him; her dimples deepening. The silk flowers threading through her soft curls matched the ivory lace of her dress.

'I declare you husband and wife,' the vicar said, then motioned for them to follow him. Jenna and Gordon took a seat next to each other at a table beside the altar, decorated with lavender sprigs and honeysuckle. Rhys and Charlotte left their pews to stand behind them as witnesses.

'You'll need to sign the register just here,' the vicar said, leaning over Gordon and picking up the pen next to the certificate. He held it towards Gordon.

Gordon's fingers touched the pen, then he waved it

away. 'It's okay.' He reached instead inside his suit pocket and drew out the leather pen pouch.

'Aren't you saving that to sign the lease on our shop?' Jenna said. 'The big business moment your grandfather said would happen for you?'

'This first. This is my major life moment.'

'Our life moment.' Jenna smiled.

Gordon scribbled his name. Nothing appeared apart from a scratchy indentation. 'Oh,' Gordon whispered. 'I should have checked the ink still worked.'

Jenna giggled.

'Have you got some paper for me to scribble this on?' Gordon whispered. 'I don't want to rip the marriage certificate.'

Rhys leant over and placed a vintage book of matches on the table. 'Open the cover and use that,' he said.

Gordon opened it. 'There's a phone number in here.'

Rhys shrugged. 'You can scribble over it. Haven't worn this jacket since nineteen-ninety-eight. I reckon that woman's given up waiting by the phone.'

At the outdoor reception, Gordon's sister, Charlotte, gave Jenna a tight hug. She stepped back and looked around the field set up with mismatched garden tables all borrowed from Rhys's various friends. Charlotte wrinkled her nose.

Gordon grinned. 'Not the same as having seventeenth century walnut tables, eh?' His smile grew as he observed the scene before them. Jenna's charming style ensured the tables came together in a magically eclectic theme, decorated with the honeysuckle, lavender and sunflowers that matched her bouquet. Beyond the tables, half a dozen sheep grazed peacefully.

'I wasn't thinking about antique tables,' Charlotte said, nudging her brother in mock annoyance. 'This is all wonderfully delightful. No, I was thinking more how you two were brave planning an outdoor celebration on a farm. I heard it rains in Wales more than it does in England.'

'We wouldn't have cared,' Jenna said. 'I would have just had Rhys' friends cram it all into an indoor sheep paddock.' She took Gordon's hand and squeezed it. 'It's about the rest of our lives, not the party.'

Charlotte smiled at Gordon. 'Hmmm, you finally took my advice.'

'What's that?' Gordon said.

She leaned in and whispered to him, 'About not looking for someone all showy on the outside?' She stepped back and looked at Jenna. 'Sorry, I didn't mean to be rude. I just want to say I had a feeling, a premonition you could say, that you were the woman for him from the very first time we spoke…'

'You mean at your birthday party on New Year's Eve?' Gordon asked. 'I thought you were too drunk that night.'

'Stop it,' Charlotte said. 'Anyway, I meant before then. When you two were driving to London together and she answered your phone. And she's since divulged to me that was actually the first time you brought sheep to London. You hadn't confessed you'd tried it twice.'

'Ah yes. The first time when they didn't get out of the trailer,' Gordon said. He looked at Jenna and she smiled. He wondered if they were both remembering the same scene. That first frenzied kiss outside the coffee drive-through after their failed sheep run attempt.

'Oh God,' Charlotte said, peering past Jenna. 'I've got to stop my sons. I think they're feeding your sheep grapes they grabbed from the cheese board.'

Jenna laughed, 'It won't hurt them,' she said, but Charlotte was off.

Gordon's mother strode up to them both, her stiletto heels sinking in the grass. She huffed as she reached Gordon and reached out for a hasty hug.

Gordon gave her a polite squeeze, then stepped back. 'Isn't this perfect?' he said, gesturing towards the nearby trestle table, decorated with sunflowers and raffia ribbon, laden with cheese and desserts. 'And your grandsons seem to love that we've allowed a few of the sheep to mingle nearby.' He pointed to the grazing ewes just beyond the smaller tables. 'The well behaved ones anyway,' he added.

'It's different,' Gordon's mother said, gazing around and then turning back towards her son. 'But then again, so are you. I mean, you've always been unlike Mark and Charlotte in so many ways.'

'Because I was the accident?'

His mother's face froze. 'Gordon…'

He smiled. 'Mum, we can talk about it. That was so many years ago. I'm over it.'

Gordon's mother's eyes misted as she looked at her son. 'There are no accidents,' she whispered. She lowered her eyes, then turned to look towards the fields, breathing in, and pushing her shoulders back, regaining control of her sudden weakness of emotion. With a loud exhale, she turned towards him again with a practised smile. 'I'm so happy for you, darling. I can see this life really suits you. Not to mention, of course, this lovely wife of yours.'

She turned to her new daughter-in-law. 'And Jenna, you've given me what I always hoped for. A lovely granddaughter.' She gestured towards Emma, standing with her American grandparents and Gordon's brother.

Eleanor stood next to Mark. Gordon watched as his sister-in-law reached her fingers to take Mark's hand.

'She's a bright girl,' Gordon's mother said, referring to Emma. 'Told me she's studying zoology. I've told her I'll travel to Bristol and have lunch with her on a Saturday when she's back at university.'

'That's a bit of a long drive,' Gordon said.

'Nonsense. It would be good for me to visit Bristol again. It's where I studied law.'

'Yes, I know.' Gordon said.

Jenna elbowed him. Then she leant towards Gordon's mother. 'That would be wonderful of you.'

His mother nodded, then she turned to Gordon and smiled. 'You know, now that I'm here, seeing you both so happy, I understand this life you've chosen for yourself. You have a sparkle about you I haven't seen before. Your grandfather would have approved.'

'Really?' Gordon said.

'Of course. His philosophy was to follow the work path that sparks dedication.' She pursed her lips. 'His passion was hotels. Mine was law.'

'And mine is sheep…' Gordon nodded and laughed. 'Not that I needed anyone's approval to choose this path.'

'No,' his mother said. 'But he still would have been proud.' Her smile stiffened as she forced herself to whisper, 'I am too.'

Tej strode over towards them. He grabbed Gordon's shoulders, then slapped him on the back.

Bethany stood behind Tej, before stepping forward to elbow him away. 'It's my turn to hug the happy couple,' she said. She gave both Gordon and Jenna a quick hug and peck on the cheek, then stood back and grasped Tej's hand.

'You two have been keeping this a secret,' Gordon said.

Bethany shrugged. 'No secret. We were friends first and it grew from there.'

Gordon smiled as he turned towards Jenna, 'The best way to a romance in my experience.'

The soft music that had been playing from Rhys' Wi-Fi speaker stopped. Familiar opening guitar chords blasted through the system.

'Oh Jesus.' Gordon groaned. 'Creedence Clearwater Revival. That's not a song I put on the playlist.'

Rhys pranced towards the small herd of grazing sheep.

Gordon sighed and turned back to Jenna. 'I guess we'll let the best man have his moment.'

'Oh my God,' Jenna said. 'Turn around again. Look at the sheep.'

Gordon turned. Rhys tread forward then back in time with the music while the sheep followed, nose to tail, stepping forward and back in a line behind Rhys.

'No, this isn't happening.' Gordon stared open-mouthed at the sheep as Rhys lead them, conga-style into a circular dance.

Hari the Heddwas appeared and put his hand on Gordon's shoulder. 'Didn't you believe my friend Rhys when he told you he could get sheep to dance?'

'I…' Gordon couldn't find the words. 'I thought it was a joke.'

'Really?' Hari said. 'Even after the way the three of you got them to perform those acrobatic feats at that big posh hotel?'

The shopkeeper from the florist joined them. 'I don't think I ever told you my name.' She held out her hand to Gordon. 'It's Bronwen. My sister's stopping by later to thank you for getting that sponsorship for the community club. She and her wife are up here advising the new committee on the setup.'

Bronwen's eyes twinkled as she nodded towards the dancing sheep. 'I can't tell you how proud the whole village is of the three of you. I heard how you trained those sheep to single out the politician who was about to raise taxes on small businesses like mine. I can't believe you knew that would happen months before the budget, but then you're from London, aren't you?'

Jenna pressed her nose into her bouquet to hide her giggles.

'You're happy with them flowers, I see.' She beamed at Jenna. 'Suits you more than the plain cream roses your uncle Rhys once bought you.'

Jenna raised her eyebrows to Gordon, and he smiled.

'Ah, look at the way you're looking at each other,' Bronwen said. 'If Alan could see you both… and what you did showing off his sheep…' She sighed, then reached into her purse. 'I was going to put this inside your wedding card, but then I thought it would be nice to hand it to you personally.' She pulled out a bright blue ribbon, with a rounded card stapled to its bow.

Gordon read the handwritten inscription. *Bryn Nefyn's Best Performing Sheep*

'We're all so grateful,' Hari said. 'For everything the three of you have done. But especially for making Alan's sheep the stars of our village.'

Gordon nodded, his throat tightening at the words on the ribbon card.

Hari peered over Gordon's shoulder. 'Oh look, are those slices of your pecan pie I see on that table over there, Jenna? I better get there before the sheep find it.' Hari led Bronwen to the trestle table. 'Then we need more champagne to toast that London Sheep Run.'

Gordon leant into Jenna's shoulder and laughed. 'That was seven months ago, that London sheep run,' he said.

'And they'll be talking about it for seventy more years.' She squeezed her bouquet.

He looked down at the ribbon in his hand. 'This is lovely, though. Alan would have been thrilled.'

'I know,' she whispered. She lifted her bouquet towards Gordon. 'I was thinking, would you mind if later, after everyone's gone, we drive to Alan's grave and give him these flowers?'

'I think that would be perfect,' he said. He rubbed the blue satin between his fingers, then reached over and tied the ribbon with its card around the stems of Jenna's bouquet.

Her eyes filled with tears. 'Even more perfect now.'

'Like you,' he whispered.

'No… like us.' She lifted her face to his and kissed him.

The love in his heart swelled. It spiralled until it felt like every cell in his body tingled with emotion and joy. He stepped back from her before the dizzying effects of happiness and the wonder of finding one's destiny overwhelmed him. Then he surveyed the familiar view beyond the farm of phantom-grey mountains rising behind clover topped hills.

He wasn't Chancellor of the Exchequer.

He wasn't a rock star.

He wasn't the captain of Tottenham Hotspur.

He was what he was always meant him to be, the hero of his own small, but magnificent life. And like the lopsided hill of Bryn Nefyn, he'd simply been destined to peak a little late.

THE END

Acknowledgements

When an author sets out to write a novel, the unexpected gift is the wonderful group of people who step forward to offer their help. I have been touched by the encouragement of some genuinely lovely souls who have supported me on this writing journey.

First of all, I want to thank Richard Mayers of Burton Mayers Books for choosing this story and bringing it to publication. Around the time we first spoke, I did have interest from other publishers, yet when Richard told me he owned a sheep and goat holding in Scotland, I knew my story had found its perfect home. His vision and incredible attention to detail to the text has been genius.

A big thank you to Robbie Guillory of Underline Literary for his guidance and suggestions during the early drafts of this book. Robbie, you always believed in this story and it was your enthusiasm that encouraged me to carry on writing it.

I knew very little about sheep and sheep farming when this idea for a story came to me. Therefore, I'd like to give huge shout out to Becky Bowles of Farmcraft Experiences. Becky is an amazing shepherdess who generously gave her time while showing me the basics of herding sheep. Becky, your patience and detailed answers to my many questions on sheep and running a sheep farm was invaluable.

Julia Taylor, a friend of one of my author buddies, is another lovely sheep owner who took the time to speak to me and answer many of my questions on the care of sheep. Many thanks for your readiness to help.

I would also like to thank the Facebook Group, Sheep Farming UK, for allowing me to lurk and also for enthusiastically answering a silly question of mine when I wanted to know if sheep had muzzles or noses. There was much replacing of the word 'muzzle' in my text when I was emphatically told it didn't apply to sheep.

A huge thank you goes to my two Welsh Beta Readers

who also happen to be wonderfully supportive and talented writing friends, Helga Jensen and Claire Evans.

I also need to thank my Welsh dialect checkers: Firstly, Viv and Pauline Pritchard who I met on a Nile Cruise. When they heard I was writing a book set in North Wales, they agreed to help me with dialect. A special thanks goes to Viv's brother, Eryl Pritchard, who once lived near Morfa Nefyn. I also need to thank Darren and Carol Grantham, who I met on the same cruise, for entertaining me with the ice cream cone story that I used in the scene with Rhys.

I am truly grateful to my writing mentors: Sophie Hannah, Stephanie Butland, Mark Stay and Mark Desvaux for their incredible guidance, support and continued encouragement. In particular, Sophie and Stephanie who each provided such intuitive editorial insights. This book would not be the shinier version it is without you.

In addition to mentors, every author needs writing buddies. I am lucky to have some of the best, including:

Katie Carr, whose notes on an early draft of this novel were priceless.

Jason Mann and Phillip Cogger, who along with Claire Evans and myself, form part of our inspiring monthly critique sessions.

Kate Baker, Zoe Richards, Linda Corbett, Sarah Whitton, Gloria Thomas, Suzie Hull, Kirstie Pelling, Deborah Rayner, Lizzie Lamb, plus all the lovely authors at the Bellmont Belles and Beaux. Thank you for your friendship, advice, support and laughter.

These are just a few of the many wonderful friends I've made during my journey, and if I've forgotten anyone, my sincere apologies. I promise to buy you a very large glass of wine for my penance!

There are also non-writing world people who have brought smiles, friendship and joy during the writing and editing of this book. My heartfelt thanks to my friends Talia Price, Marina Caldarone, Kirsten Host, and Helen

Wynyard-Wright whose loyalty and support have been second to none.

A promised shout out to Jan from Harwarden Post Office for her cheerful smile and making me a coffee while I was working on edits for this novel at Gladstone Library.

A very special mention to the Sing it Loud Community choir, many who didn't know when I turned up for rehearsals each week that I had spent my days writing and editing this book. You allowed me to forget about the intensive process by inviting me to joyfully sing in the soprano section on Wednesday evenings. This choir, along with our cherished late choir master, Seb Farrall, hold a forever place in my heart.

Next, come the people dearest to my heart. My beautiful daughter, Sophie Rockcliffe, and her amazing wife Kerry, who spent hours reading not only parts of this book, but my many short stories, giving their honest feedback, along with cheerfulness and laughter. I couldn't imagine a world without you both.

And finally, my husband Richard, whose surname was also the perfect wedding gift. You never stopped believing in me for a moment, even when I doubted myself. Your love and support has meant more than you can possibly imagine.

ABOUT THE AUTHOR

Karen Storey is an award winning fiction writer and has been featured on the acclaimed book podcast *The Bestseller Experiment.* As well as a novelist, she is a prolific short story writer. Her short stories have been published in various anthologies and placed in several international competitions. Her memoir pieces have also been published within the New York Times bestselling book series, *Chicken Soup for the Soul.*

Originally from New York City, Karen lives in Warwickshire, England and has written articles for *American in Britain* magazine. She lives with her husband, whose surname Storey was the perfect wedding gift. They share their home with a snarky cat who writes Karen's monthly author newsletters and a crazy little Bichon Frise dog who barks at his own reflection. You can visit her website and subscribe to her newsletter at www.karenstoreyauthor.com

The Approval of Sheep is Karen's first novel.

Thank you so much for reading The Approval of Sheep. If you've enjoyed this book, would you kindly consider leaving a review on Amazon? (You don't need to have purchased it from Amazon to do so). Reviews are tremendously helpful to a debut author and even a few words can make a big difference.

With much gratitude and love, Karen x

OTHER TITLES FROM BURTON MAYERS BOOKS:

www.ingramcontent.com/pod-product-compliance
Lightning Source LLC
La Vergne TN
LVHW091114080826
845145LV00008B/1906

9781917224130